D1463194

SOMEWHERE BETWEEN THE
SAND AND THE SURF

SOMEWHERE BETWEEN THE SAND AND THE SURF

THOMAS E. MONTANYE

This is a work of fiction. Names, characters, places, and incidents either are the products of the author's imagination or are used fictitiously. Any resemblance to actual persons, living or dead, events, or locales is entirely coincidental.

Copyright © 2021 by Thomas E. Montanye

All rights reserved. No part of this book may be reproduced or used in any manner without written permission of the copyright owner except for the use of quotations in a book review.

First paperback edition April 2021

Cover design by Emily Montanye

Printed in the United States of America

For Kay and Everett
And for my mother

SOMEWHERE BETWEEN THE SAND AND THE SURF

Prologue

Her breaths were measured. Her mind was free. And the water was cold.

But it was always cold. For years, her coach had been saying she would get used to it, and yet every time she jumped in the pool, the familiar chill rushed through her like lightning, jolting her forward like a thoroughbred released from the gate. Her father said that was why she was so fast, because she couldn't wait to get out of the pool. He wasn't wrong.

Over time, she had learned to embrace the discomfort. Now she liked it. Now she *used* it.

Today Sophie was a full body length ahead, the other six swimmers struggling to keep up with her fluttering toes. She couldn't see them, but she felt them. The sensation of understanding exactly where the other swimmers were, without seeing them, was difficult to explain. She just knew. Her mother once compared it to knowing you were being watched while sleeping. Her mother always knew just what to say.

Only twenty feet separated Sophie from another state championship. Her arms tore through the water and raced through the air like windmills. She took a breath and glanced at her parents cheering her on. They leaned forward on the edges of their seats, fists clenched and eyes wide, as though it was going to be a photo finish. Not today. Today she was too strong, and too fast.

Ten feet. Five feet. She slid her last stroke inches under the surface and glided to the wall. The whistle blew and the judge raised his hand. Three seconds later, the runner-up touched the wall, followed shortly by the rest of the competitors. Sophie tore off her goggles and released her hair from the constraint of her yellow swimmer's cap.

She was the freestyle champion for the twelve and under-age group. She was ten.

Her father pulled her tight to his chest immediately after she exited the pool. "I'm so proud of you, Sweetheart," her father beamed. He was ecstatic, maybe happier than her. He scanned the immediate area to make sure everyone knew she was his little girl.

"Thanks, Daddy."

Her mother knelt and kissed both of her cheeks. "Did you have fun, Sophia?" she asked, holding Sophie's still wet cheek in her soft hand. Sophie nodded. "You were a mermaid out there," she said. Sophie smiled. Her mother always knew just what to say.

Her parents knelt while she stood tall. Together they formed a triangle. She allowed every feeling to swim through her in that moment, consciously storing the images of her parent's smiling faces in the vault of her mind. Although she didn't know it then, it was these moments that would help her through the storms ahead, when the shine of the trophies had faded, and the feeling of triumph had been lost in the deep end of the pool.

Part One

1

The radio hummed a familiar tune, reminding him of a time when a song could ignite his imagination, allowing him to create a world in which he was the rock star, or hero. But that was a long time ago, the pages of those memories stuck together, hidden in the book of his life. Now it was just noise, no different from the hum of a fan, or the sound of the surf on a vacant beach. It was a memory snuffed out as quickly as a once-in-a-lifetime lightning strike. His world was now cast in shadow, alit only by the faint glow of a half-smoked cigarette.

A burst of lightning stretched out across the sky in the distance, temporarily lending a clear view of the flat, corn-covered landscape. A light rain collided with the windshield, and the headlights of his 95 Jeep Cherokee struggled to penetrate the darkness as they chased the faded yellow lines. The temporary illumination had allowed him to discern what appeared to be a wooded area up ahead, but he couldn't be sure.

He looked down at the watch around his wrist—the clock on the dash had been stuck on 4:30 for months. If he didn't find a hotel soon, he would be forced to settle for a parking lot. Although even that was beginning to seem like a long shot; he had seen nothing but farmland for hours.

Ryan pulled a long drag off the cigarette fixed loosely between his fingers. The small ember breathed to life, basking his features in a cold, orange glow. Ash, illuminated by the weak green light of the dash, floated like dead leaves into the dark void at his feet. Smoke curled up into his eyes, blurring his vision. The sting forced him to squint. After a satisfyingly painful moment, he released the smoke from his lungs. It moved through the gloomy interior like a moonlit river cutting through a dark canyon. After lingering a moment in stillness, it finally made its escape out the narrow crack in the window and into the night.

Reaching into the passenger seat, he fumbled blindly for the vague directions to a local hotel he had hastily scribbled down at the gas station's cashier's counter. The lady had told him to take the first right after two miles. Couldn't miss it. Two miles? He had been driving for at least a half-hour since stopping and hadn't noticed a single street sign.

She was a nice woman, who'd politely informed him that he was in Delaware, not Maryland, as he'd so wrongfully assumed. She had seemed genuinely concerned for him, and when she'd asked him how he had managed to get so lost, he'd replied, "I guess I took a wrong turn." She had said he must have made more than one wrong turn. "You have no idea," he'd answered.

As he searched through old receipts and empty cigarette boxes, his fingers fell upon the familiar texture of cool, strong glass, the kind that needed to be thrown rather than dropped to break it. He hesitated, thoughtful as his right arm straddled the center console. After a moment, he abandoned the search for directions and picked up the half-empty bottle of whiskey. With his left hand, cigarette held tightly between the index and middle finger, Ryan unscrewed the top and took a short sip. He twisted the cap back on and tossed the bottle into the passenger seat. Distracted, he failed to notice the yellow sign indicating a sharp bend in the road up ahead.

It happened in an instant.

Before colliding with a wall of pine trees, Ryan jerked the wheel to the left and slammed on the brakes. The vehicle began to slide sideways, as if it was on ice. It slid off the pavement, onto the wet grass, and slammed into the trunk of a mature pine tree, the passenger side door taking most of the impact. His body was rocked back and forth, as if he were on a rollercoaster that had taken a quick turn to the right, then left. Then he was motionless.

He didn't hear, think or feel anything for a few moments. The world was quiet. As he slowly regained control of his senses, he felt a stinging sensation on his thigh, as if he were being pinched. The cigarette had fallen into his lap and was burning through his jeans. "Shit," he said, and brushed it off. He stomped the butt out by his feet.

He unbuckled the seatbelt, turned on an overhead light, and squinted into the rearview mirror. A small scratch was under his eye. Nothing to worry about. He took a deep breath and exhaled as he considered stepping on the gas and peeling out of there. But after a moment, he decided to get out and inspect the damage.

The rain was mildly sobering, just enough to make him a little more alert. And the temperature was warm, even for early June.

As he rounded the front of the car, the damage revealed itself to be extensive. The passenger door was destroyed beyond repair, and the window had been blown out. The tree seemed to be just fine, as though it had simply shrugged the car off in annoyance.

Other than the door, the car seemed to be okay, though. Drivable, at least. He walked back around to the front.

He stood in the rain for a while, looking up into the darkness, focusing on each individual drop of water as it splashed onto his face. He opened his mouth and breathed in the saturated night. For a second, he allowed himself to consider how in the hell he had ended up there, in the middle of nowhere Delaware, on a deserted road on a rainy night. A spasm shot through him and he slammed his fists onto the hood. He lifted his head and screamed into the night, his voice echoing among the trees. But as quickly as it came on, the anger dissipated. He let his breathing return to normal.

As he made a move toward the driver's side door, a car screamed around the corner, music blasting and high beams blinding as it sped toward him. He narrowed his eyes against the light and turned away, making it clear he required no assistance. It appeared the car was going to ignore him. But his relief was crushed when the sound of screeching tires exploded in the dark behind him. The car reversed and headed straight back toward Ryan. He was still standing in front of the Jeep.

"Damn it," he said under his breath.

He turned and watched with indifference as the taillights came to a stop a few feet from where he stood. A young man exited the driver's side. Two others exited from the passenger side. All three wore loose-fitting jeans, even looser t-shirts, and boots that looked so heavy, they might sink through the ground.

The driver spoke first.

"Hey buddy," he said as he closed the distance between himself and Ryan, quicker than necessary. Ryan was able to make out a clean-shaven jaw, hair so short it could break skin, and the fakest smile he'd ever seen. The man stopped a foot away from Ryan. "You okay?" he continued.

"Took a pretty nasty spill, huh?" another voice said. The second guy had walked around the side of the Jeep, inspecting the damage. The third held back a bit, leaning against the trunk of the car, arms crossed.

"I'm fine," Ryan said, deciding to answer the first question. "Just a little slick. I can manage from here."

"A little slick out here, huh?" the man asked as he peered over Ryan's shoulder.

Ryan tried to focus his vision and tune his ears.

"Uh, yeah," said Ryan. "Close call, I guess. Thanks for stopping, but I can handle it from here." He turned and walked toward the driver's side door.

"Anything we can do to help?" the voice said from behind him.

"No, thanks," Ryan answered over his shoulder. He made it to the door and pulled on the handle.

"Woah," said the stranger, and he pushed the door shut before Ryan had a chance to slide into the front seat.

Ryan froze. Eyes low. Thoughtful.

He wasn't afraid. A part of him welcomed what he had a strong feeling was coming. But this wasn't a bar fight, and the only witnesses were the pine trees, which seemed to have become even quieter, as if holding their breath in anticipation.

"Noticed those Maine tags," the stranger said. "Long way from home."

Ryan turned to face the man. "Is there anything I can help *you* with?" he asked.

The fake smile widened. "As a matter of fact, there is," he said. "You can give me that watch." His head tilted with his eyes.

Ryan looked down at the watch around his wrist. It held no sentimental value, and although money wasn't exactly a concern, yet, the watch was worth more than his car. The potential cash he could get for it could make life much less uncomfortable down the road. He glanced over the man's shoulder at the two supporting characters, standing side by side now, waiting for their friend to make a move. Ryan drew in a deep breath and exhaled, wishing he had a cigarette. He could probably talk his way out of a broken nose if he chose his next words carefully.

Instead, he looked into the man's eyes and said, "Fuck off."

Almost before the words left his mouth, he felt a sharp pain in his stomach as the man's fist connected with Ryan's gut. Bent over, gasping for air, he felt another even sharper pain in his right eye. Everything went dark as he fell to the ground. Begging his lungs for a single breath, his vision blurred, and his mind went blank.

After what might have been a few seconds, the faint light of the headlights reappeared in his vision. A hand fished through his back pocket for a wallet that wasn't there. His face was on fire.

Feet were shuffling around his motionless body. He heard one of them say, "Should we just take the car? It's running."

"What the hell are we gonna do with this piece of shit?" the familiar voice of the driver said. "Come on, see if there's anything else worth taking."

"There's nothing in here," said a voice Ryan hadn't heard yet. "Just trash, and a bottle of whiskey. It reeks like a brewery."

"No phone, no wallet, but a Rolex?" one of them said. "He must have stolen it. Or it's fake."

"It doesn't look fake."

"What the hell do you know about Rolex's?" the leader of the trio snapped.

Ryan tried to get to his feet. He had made it onto all fours before a boot connected with his stomach. "Stay down," said the stranger. Ryan doubled over and curled up, clutching at his abdomen.

Under his cheek, Ryan felt a rumble through the pavement, as if something were stirring underground. A moment later a new set of headlights appeared from around the corner.

"Shit, someone's coming."

"We're outta here."

He heard feet shuffling and doors slamming. In no time, the sedan peeled away and into the night.

Ryan rolled over and pulled his legs to his chest, attempting to curb the pain in his ribcage. The rumble of an engine cut off and a door opened and closed. A hand touched his shoulder. Instinctively, he flinched.

"Take it easy," a deep voice said from above. "Nice and slow."

Ryan made it to his feet with the stranger's aid. Favoring his right side, he turned to face the man. The headlights of the truck were burning into his eyes while the figure in front of him cast a towering silhouette.

"You alright?" the shadow asked. It was bigger than Ryan, taller and wider.

"I think so," Ryan answered. It hurt to talk. "Thanks."

The man guided Ryan away from the light.

"You sure? Here, take a seat," he suggested. Ryan sat down against the back bumper of the Jeep. "You want me to call an ambulance or something? That cut looks pretty nasty."

Ryan touched his right temple with a light finger. He winced at the pain. A drop of blood rolled down his cheek. He looked up at the man. "I'm fine, really" Ryan said. "It's just a scratch."

"What happened?"

Ryan quickly recounted the events. When he had finished, the man asked if they had taken anything.

"Just my watch," Ryan answered.

"I'll call the police. I know someone in—"

"No, please," Ryan interrupted. He managed to stand upright. "It's no big deal. I should get going."

The man frowned. "Is there anyone you want to call?"

"No," Ryan answered. "Anyway, I don't have a phone."

"Where are you headed?" he asked, concern creeping into the man's tone.

Ryan looked down the road, into the darkness. "I don't know, actually. I was looking for the Quality Inn. But I think I missed a turn."

"The Quality Inn's about forty-five minutes that way," the man said, pointing in the direction Ryan had come from.

Ryan let out a dejected breath. He had been driving for hours, and the last thing he needed was to get lost all over again.

"But you aren't far from the coast," the man said, sensing Ryan's dilemma. "Maybe ten minutes. I'm heading there now. I know a guy who owns a small motel. He's a little expensive. Probably why he always has rooms available." He let out a short laugh.

Ryan could almost feel the hot water from the shower. "You don't have to do that," he said.

"It's nothing."

Without a better option, Ryan agreed to follow the man.

He limped around to the driver's side of the Jeep.

"You sure you're okay to drive?" the man asked.

Ryan gave him a thumbs-up as he eased into the front seat and turned the key.

Ryan had no way to tell the time as he followed the truck out of the woods, but if he had to guess, he'd say it took ten minutes exactly to get to the Seabreeze Motel. It was late, and the town they'd crept into was quiet. The rain had turned into a fine mist.

When Ryan limped out of the car, the friendly stranger was waiting patiently under the second-floor balcony of the motel, his frame spotlighted by a fluorescent overhead light.

The Seabreeze had two floors and twenty rooms. Light blue paint weathered by decades of wind and water faced the street. White doors evenly spaced throughout. A simple establishment. To Ryan, it might as well have been the Four Seasons.

He attempted to hide his limp as he moved toward the older man.

"I'm Ted, by the way," the man said when Ryan reached him. "Ted Galloway."

"Ryan," he replied. "Monroe."

"Nice to meet you, Ryan," he said. "Wish it were under better circumstances. But hey, could have been worse, right?"

"No kidding," said Ryan.

Ryan allowed himself a more thorough look at Ted. The man had gone well beyond what anyone would consider polite, and Ryan attempted to discern why. But he couldn't penetrate Ted's façade.

It was a brick wall of kindness.

"Well, let's get you a room," Ted said. He turned toward the front office.

"Why are you helping me?" Ryan asked.

Ted turned around and stared at Ryan. "Why not?" he said with a shrug of his shoulders, then turned back and continued.

After catching up and exchanging pleasantries with the elderly proprietor, Ted led Ryan to a door at the end of the first floor, farthest from the office.

"How much is the room?" Ryan asked as they walked.

"Don't worry about it," Ted said.

"I'll pay you back when I get some cash," Ryan told him.

"No problem," Ted replied. When they reached the door to the room, Ted turned to Ryan and said, "So, what brings you to Delaware?"

Ryan slipped his bag off his shoulder and dropped it by his feet. "I don't know, really," he answered. "I got lost."

"You got lost?" Ted asked. "Where were you headed?"

Ryan didn't have the energy to lie, so he answered honestly. "I don't know," he said.

Ted turned his head and squinted at Ryan, as if the younger man had suddenly become more interesting. Ryan avoided his gaze and glanced out into the night.

"So, is Maine home?" Ted asked. Obviously, he hadn't failed to notice Ryan's license plates. They must have stuck out like a black eye.

Ryan leaned his shoulder against the railing of the staircase. "Not for a long time," he answered.

"Any idea where you're heading next?" Ted asked. The

familiar scent of pity began to emanate from the older man like a sour smell.

"Haven't really thought it through," Ryan answered. "Maybe I'll try to find some work around here. Stick around for a while. We'll see." He was struggling to stay on his feet.

"Well, I won't keep you any longer," said Ted, picking up on Ryan's impatient movements. "I'm sure you're exhausted." He turned to go, then stopped. "Oh," he said, turning back. "Here's my number." Ted had reached into his pocket and pulled out a piece of paper that looked as though it had been torn off the corner of a notebook page. He handed it to Ryan. "If you stick around, give me a call. I might be able to help you find some work."

"What do you do?" Ryan asked. He slipped the paper into his pocket.

"I'm retired."

Retired? The guy couldn't have been more than fifty years old. "Hey, thanks a lot for your help," Ryan called after him.

"You got it. Ice that eye." And with that, the man disappeared into the lamp-lit mist.

The room was small. A queen-sized bed took up most of the space, leaving little room for much else. A circular table had been squeezed into the corner with two chairs pushed in so tightly, they were leaning back slightly, threatening to fall. A small flat-screen television was mounted to the wall opposite the bed. The walls were painted sky blue, and the sheets were white.

Ryan set his backpack down on the table. He pulled the bottle of whiskey out and set it on the nightstand. With some effort, he pulled off his shirt and slid out of his jeans. He made his way into the bathroom and turned on the shower, twisting the knob as far to the right as possible. Leaning his shoulder against the cool, tiled wall, he dropped his head in defeat. The water burned his skin red, and he watched with indifference as blood swirled around the drain and disappeared through the small holes. He stayed like that for a while, eyes closed and legs heavy as the water covered every inch of his body. He could have stayed like that for hours, but after about twenty minutes, he felt as though his legs would give out. He turned the water off, stepped out of the tub, and wrapped a towel around his waist. Finally, he looked at himself in the square mirror, which sat perched atop the sink that sprouted out of the floor like a white flower.

The swelling beside his right eye dominated his features. His wet, black hair hung down past his ears, tickling his shoulders. He watched his hand touch the beads around his neck, his fingers brushing over each individual letter. It was all he had left, the only evidence of another life lived.

He stared through the mirror, through the stranger on the other side, and remembered what he used to have. His face would heal, his ribs would mend, and the memory of tonight's events would fade. It was what he couldn't see that never would. The urge to throw his fist through the glass swelled inside him as his grip tightened around the sink. But it was quickly extinguished. As much as he hated that person, he knew he couldn't hurt him. Not anymore.

Using the walls for support, Ryan walked to the edge of the bed and climbed over top of the comforter. He sat himself up against the headboard and stuffed two pillows behind his back. His right elbow hugging his side, Ryan reached across his torso and grabbed the bottle of whiskey that had survived the crash with no apparent blemishes. He took a long sip, let out a long breath, and returned the bottle to the nightstand. Staring straight ahead, his gaze fell on a large painting of a lone seagull flying high over an angry ocean.

The curtains came down over his eyes and his body finally shut down.

A gray sky hung low over the water, like morning fog over a lake. But he wasn't in a lake. He was in an ocean, and monstrous waves crashed down upon him, one after another as he struggled to stay afloat. He searched around, head swinging as if on a swivel as his arms beat like a bird's wings under the surface. The clouds surrounded him like smoke, his eyes failing to see more than a couple feet in any direction.

"Ryan!" a voice called through the fog. "Ryan! Help, please," it called again. Ryan spun frantically, searching for its source. "Ryan, please. I can't hold on much longer," the voice said. He knew that voice.

"Sarah!" he called. "Sarah! Where are you?" He willed his vision to cut through the walls of gray. "Sarah!" he screamed as loud as his lungs would allow. But there was no response. Panic swelled inside him as another wave shoved him under. When he resurfaced, anger and hysteria took over. He began thrashing his arms, attempting to swim his way out of the circle of haze. But as he doubled his efforts, so did the ocean, as if it were consciously trying to keep him away from her. It felt like he was dragging his limbs through sand.

"Ryan," Sarah said again. This time her voice was a whisper.

She was close, but she was losing strength.

"Sarah, I'm coming. Hold on."

A break in the fog allowed Ryan a brief glimpse of her. He could only see the back of her head. But it was her. It was his Sarah. She was enveloped by the fog again a moment later.

He took off in the direction he had seen her floating, pushing every inch of his weighed-down body to its limits. "I'm coming, Sarah!" he yelled.

Where was she! She had been right here; he was sure of it. Ryan spun in circles. "Sarah!" he called.

Another break in the fog allowed him a short glimpse. He could make it. "I'm coming, Sarah," Ryan said. He couldn't make out her face, but he was getting closer, he could feel it.

Then she disappeared. "No!" he screamed. "Sarah!"

He began to sink, slowly, as though the sea wanted him to endure the pain for as long as possible. He was underwater, surrounded by darkness, his lungs tightening with every passing second...

Ryan shot up, gasping for breath. The images of the nightmare were still fresh in his mind, as if they were being projected onto the television in front of him. Why couldn't he see her face?

He shuffled his legs over the edge of the bed and planted his feet on the cold floor. He leaned over and ran his hands through his hair. The pain in his eye and ribs had become an afterthought, as he knew it would. He lifted his neck, the simple movement becoming harder and harder with each passing day. A faint light snuck around the edges of the curtains, crawling along the floor toward his bare feet. He watched the day begin from another motel room. He was beginning to lose count.

2

Sophie's arm exploded out of the ocean and raced through the cool morning air like a jet. It splashed back down through the water with ease, slowing slightly as it fought through a persistent resistance beneath the surface. She repeated the motion with the other arm, all the while her legs kicking furiously. The ocean was calm today, like an undisturbed indoor pool, and her out-stretched body cut through it like a knife. Every movement, every stroke was made with purpose, as if it were her last. This wasn't a Sunday drive. This was a race, and not one for the average weekend swimmer. She was competing against herself from yesterday morning, and she was winning by a full length.

She tilted her head to the left and took a deep breath. Through tinted goggles, Sophie stared straight into the rising sun. A perfect circle resting on the ocean's edge. She absorbed the scenery before plunging back into the water. For now, the sun was her only fan, cheering her forward as it spectated from a cloudless sky. But her aspirations were higher than that, her motivation unwavering. Calling on another shot of energy, Sophie doubled her efforts.

Stealing another breath, she watched a school of dolphins

rainbow the horizon. She put her head down and smiled underwater.

After four inspired strokes, Sophie checked her status in the race. When the fins reappeared, they were well ahead, surging forward with ease and patience as Sophie struggled to keep up. She smiled as she inhaled a deep breath. If there was a heaven, she was closer than anyone to it right now.

Once the dolphins were out of range, Sophie pulled up and came to a stop. Her arms and legs swayed back and forth as if conducting an underwater orchestra as she effortlessly treaded water. She had reached the north end of the boardwalk, her turn-around point. From about thirty yards out to sea—comfortably beyond any waves threatening to crash—Sophie was easily able to make out the forms of a few umbrellas popping up on the sand like blooming flowers. Some red, some blue, some rainbow-colored. But only a few. The north end was rarely overcrowded, the vacationers usually keeping to the south side where the condominiums and arcades soaked up money like a sponge. That was what she loved about her little town, she reflected as she floated with the ease of a buoy. It never took on the feel of a strictly tourist destination, as so many other beaches along the coast had. For her, the small-town charm remained intact year-round. One only had to know where to be and when.

But enough rest. She knew the sights and landmarks. It was time to head back.

The one and a half miles back to her house went by too quickly, as it always did. Before she knew it, Sophie was back on dry land.

As the sand changed texture from firm to soft under her feet, Sophie pulled off her goggles. She had to squint as her eyes adjusted to the unfiltered morning light. Tearing off her cap, she released a waterfall of mahogany brown hair that tumbled down to the small of her back, as dry as it had been before she entered the water. The strengthening light glistened off the back of her navy-blue swimsuit as she strode toward the smallest house on the beach.

Before reaching the weather-worn walkway that led to her house, Sophie turned and gazed out into the ocean. She raised her head slightly, closed her eyes, and breathed in deeply. Releasing the breath, Sophie opened her eyes and said, "I'll see *you* later."

She turned and jogged up the walk. She rounded the pool and headed for the outside shower behind the garage. She rarely used the shower in her bathroom. Her father used to ask why, but Sophie had only mirrored his confused expression. "Why not?" she would say. He was the weird one. Who in their right mind would choose an indoor shower over an outdoor one? The only conclusion she had been able to come to was that most people didn't have the option. She felt bad for those people.

After a quick rinse and an even quicker dry, she hustled up the short staircase that led up to the back deck. With a towel wrapped securely around her chest, clearing each step two at a time, she slid inside to get ready for work. She almost slipped on the hardwood floor of her bedroom as she rounded the bedpost. "Whoops," she giggled, and continued. She brushed on some make-up for appearances sake, threw on her orange tank top, and slipped into a pair of jean shorts. It wasn't her ideal outfit, but there were worse work uniforms in the world.

Within a few short minutes, Sophie was ready to hit the road. She ran back outside, having spent more than enough time indoors already, and skipped down the steps on the opposite side of the deck toward her father's workshop.

She breezed into the shop like a gust of wind. Her father was bent over a worktable like a mad scientist attempting to recreate life. Only, he was attempting to bring a piece of wood to life. A much more difficult proposition, Sophie often joked.

"Bye, Daddy," she said behind his ear. "Off to work. Don't forget to eat."

Like a doctor performing surgery, he didn't bother to look up as he shaved another imperceptibly thin slice of wood off his patient. "Will do, Sweetheart," he said. "Love you. Be safe. And slow down, would ya? You're making me dizzy."

Sophie smiled. "Never."

Before shutting the door on her way out, she peeked around it and said, "Love you more," then shut the door before he had a chance to respond. She laughed as she made her way to her bike. He usually got the better of her at that game, but not today. Today she was unstoppable.

The smile fell into a frown as she thought about how much she would miss him. A flood of memories rose. But she shook her head and pushed the pedal under her right foot, surging the bike into motion. He would be alright. It had been a long time, and she had stayed with him. But it was time, and he understood.

The pavement raced by beneath the wheels like a blur. The pine trees and mansions on either side of the road were left behind like unwanted memories. Her hair held on for dear life as it flapped behind her like a cape. The air was warm now, and it felt like a blow dryer was blasting in her face as she leaned forward in the seat like a pro, elbows tight to her sides.

After a mile and a half, the road curved to the right before colliding with the beginning of the boardwalk, then curved back to the left, like the colorful warped straws Sophie used to play with as a kid.

She took a deep breath as she coasted down First Street. It was never one distinct smell, but rather a mixture of many. Fresh flowers lining the streets. Sand and salt twisting through the avenues. Freshly baked pizza from around the corner. Mrs. Virginia's perfume chasing her from the screened-in porch Sophie had just passed. They were all different and yet the same, wrestling in the wind, working together to make her town smell like a memory. Yeah, she would miss this place.

Before reaching the Avenue—the town's main drag that separated locals from vacationers—Sophie turned left and coasted toward the boardwalk. Single-family homes dominated this part of town, a mixture of grand Victorian and cottage style structures. Giant oak trees lined the sidewalks, their leaf-burdened branches creating a tunnel that fed directly into the sand.

She pulled up a few yards short of the boardwalk, jumping off the bike as it skidded to a stop. She opened the rotting wooden gate that led into the narrow alley behind the restaurant. It smelled like garbage, but she had become used to it over the years. She rested the bike up against the wall without chaining it and made her way into the building from the back.

Sophie strode through the kitchen, waving to Nicolai the chef as she went. She pushed through the swinging door that led into the bar and got right to work.

"You're late," the familiar voice of Skip Finnigan said.

Startled, Sophie almost dropped one of the saltshakers she was putting out on the bar. He was busy at the register counting the cash from last night and didn't bother to look up. Sometimes it seemed like all he did was count money.

Skip was the son of Mr. Finnigan—she still didn't know his first name—who started the restaurant over fifty years ago. The food and beverage industry was all Skip knew, and he took full control a few years ago after his father suffered a stroke.

"Skip, it's nine-thirty," said Sophie, turning to face her boss. He was huge. His stomach almost touched the register while his backside nearly grazed the liquor counter. He wore long khaki shorts and a green Finn's Bar and Grille t-shirt, the logo stretched to its limit across his chest. He turned to Sophie, glaring with his tired eyes.

"Yeah?" he said. His voice sounded like it had been run through a shredder. The smell of stale cigarettes accompanied his question.

"I don't start 'til ten," she answered, already bored by the pointless conversation. "I'm thirty minutes early," she added, just in case the math was too much.

He looked at Sophie for a long moment. She didn't know if he was going to laugh or lose his mind.

"Well, what are you waiting for? Get to it," he ordered. He returned his attention back to the register.

She grinned. Sophie didn't really need to work. And she didn't have to put up with Skip's shit, unlike everyone else that worked at Finn's. But she loved bartending. She loved listening to ten conversations at once while she made three drinks at a time. It was fast-paced, her kind of work. And she never had to sit down.

She made her way around to the outside of the bar, pulling the stools down and planting them right side up as she moved. The interior of the restaurant was too tight, and Sophie had said as much to Skip. Why not expand? "Waste of money," he'd answered. She knew it didn't really matter. Finn's was the kind of place locals simply wouldn't allow to fail. Come to think of it, they would probably complain if anything changed.

"I'm gonna need you to work tomorrow night," Skip said from the opposite side of the bar. "Rachel can't work." Once again, he didn't bother looking up from the cash in his hand.

"Skip, I told you, I'm done with nights."

"Since when?" he asked, looking up.

"Since, like, a month ago. And don't forget I'm leaving at the end of the summer. So, you'll have to get someone else to work the out-of-season shifts. You'll probably have to start looking soon, too. They suck."

Skip zipped the money into a blue cash bag and laid it on the bar in front of her. "Okay, how much?" he said.

Sophie laughed. She pushed the money back across the bar. "Money can't buy what I'm after," she said, smirking.

He narrowed his eyes. "Maybe I should just fire you now."

"By all means," she countered. "It'll give me more time to train." She rested her hand on her hip.

He glared at Sophie, and she glared back. Finally, Skip scooped up the bag of cash and turned to go. "Make me some money today," he said over his shoulder as he disappeared through the saloon-style door.

"Aye, aye Cap," she said to his back, complete with a salute.

By 10:15, Sophie was finished with her opening duties. The restaurant didn't open until eleven, so she decided to do the opening work for the server that was scheduled as well. It had become a bit of a routine, and the younger servers had come to expect their work to be done before arriving. Maybe that was why they always seemed to be late when she worked. And hungover. But she didn't mind. She'd much rather do simple side-work than sit around scrolling through her phone like everyone else.

She finished the server's work with time to spare as well. Grudgingly, she took a seat in one of the window booths and watched the boardwalk until she could unlock the doors. Over the shallow dunes, more and more umbrellas were popping up by the second, making it harder and harder to see the sand from her elevated level. A family of three strolled along the boardwalk, distracting her view. They gazed around at everything, unwilling to miss a single sight. They were on the wrong side of town, she thought. Nothing up here but an old restaurant and the same antique and consignment stores on every block.

She rested her head against the back of the booth. She had a feeling it was going to be a slow day.

By three o'clock, she had checked everything off her closing list.

An elderly couple lingered at the far end of the bar. Sophie watched the levels of their wine glasses like a hawk. The server, dejected over having probably made less than twenty dollars, leaned up against the front door, like a puppy begging to be let out.

The bell hanging from the door rang as it opened, and the young server nearly fell through the threshold. The incoming customer caught him by the shoulders.

"Sorry, man," the server said and moved aside as the man eased by.

"No problem," the man replied without breaking stride. He wore a pair of Ray-Ban style sunglasses, a plain white shirt, and faded blue jeans. Long black hair fell around his face and he was desperately in need of a shave. He seemed to be favoring his right side.

He made his way to the middle of the bar and eased onto a stool. The movement appeared to be painful. Sophie grabbed a coaster and a menu and moved to meet him.

"Hey," she said brightly. "I'm Sophie. Welcome to Finn's. What can I get for you? Half price—"

"Your cheapest whiskey," he interrupted. "Please."

"Rocks?" she asked.

"Sure."

As he spoke, he removed the sunglasses and Sophie was unable to hide her surprise when she saw the swollen eye hiding underneath. He didn't meet her eye but sensed her shock. "It's not as bad as it looks," he said in a soft voice, almost a whisper, as if his vocal cords were still half asleep.

She wasn't sure whether to laugh or not, so she busied herself with making the drink. She reached down and pulled a bottle from the rail, simultaneously grabbing a rocks glass and scooping it full of ice. As she poured out a generous portion, she realized she'd forgotten to card him.

"Do you have your ID on you?" she asked. "Sorry, we have to."

"No problem," he answered. "Not worth losing your job over."

He winced as he reached into his back pocket. He handed her the ID and Sophie held it between her index finger and thumb as she studied the birth date. It took her a moment. She'd never seen a Maine license before. Twenty-five? She looked back at the man in real time. It was hard to believe he was only two years older than she was. She would have believed him if he'd told her he was thirty-five.

He must have assumed she wasn't buying the resemblance. "It's me, I promise," he said. "Just a long time ago."

Sophie looked at him, then back at the picture. They were the same person, she was sure. And yet, they weren't. The person in the picture had short, clean-cut hair, like a businessman, and a face as smooth as a baby's. But the most distinguishable feature was the smile. He had a great smile, with kind, caring eyes. The eyes staring blankly at her from across the bar were... dead. It was like looking into a starless, midnight sky.

She handed the card back to him. "I believe you," she said and slid the glass toward his hand.

"Thanks," he replied. He took down half the drink in one sip. She almost gagged. "I'm Ryan, by the way," he said after returning the glass to its coaster. "I didn't mean to be rude, cutting you off like that."

"Oh, no problem," she answered. Actually, it *was* kind of rude, now that she thought about it. She hated it when people did that.

"I hate it when people do that," he said.

Weird.

Sophie lingered a moment, and an easy quiet filled the space between them. Before coming to work for Skip, she'd never been very good at small talk. It had seemed like a waste of time to her. But she'd quickly realized it was worth the effort to improve her conversational skills. The awkward silences between bartender and patron could be deafening sometimes.

But she had a feeling the man before her wasn't much interested in small talk. The problem was that *she* was. Something about him made her curious. She looked down the bar and checked on the couple drinking wine. Drink levels still unchanged. She was convinced the two elderly folks were having a telepathic conversation; they hadn't said one word to each other since arriving.

She turned back to Ryan as he was finishing up what she assumed would not be his last drink. He pushed the empty glass forward. She scooped a few cubes into the glass and re-filled it.

"Rough night?" she said as she poured.

"What makes you say that?"

She couldn't tell if he was kidding, his tone refusing to deviate from its sunken path. "Oh, I don't know," she said. "Maybe because it looks like you ran into a brick wall. Twice."

He chuckled. It was more like a short exhale, but enough to put her at ease. He rested his forearms on the bar and wrapped both hands around the glass, interlocking his fingers as if afraid it might run away. His hands were calloused and dry, cracking between the thumb and forefingers. "Well," he said, bringing her attention back to his face. "I don't think I was *that* drunk. But yeah, it was a rough night."

She checked back on the couple at the far end. No change. "So," she said. "What brings you to town? I don't think I've seen you before."

He set his glass down and looked around the bar, then back to her. "Yeah, must be hard keeping track of everyone," he said.

She smiled. "It's not usually this slow."

"No doubt," he said, unconvinced. After a moment, he said, "A rough night."

"Huh?"

"A rough night brought me to town."

"Oh, right," she said, nodding. When she realized he wasn't going to elaborate, Sophie pulled the damp rag hanging from her back pocket and wiped down an already clean area of the bar a few feet away.

She inched her way back to the middle of the bar. "So, are you here on vacation?" she tried. "What do you do?"

He set his drink down again, patiently, as if she'd interrupted a conversation he had been having with the glass. "No," he said. "I'm not on vacation. Just passing through. And I guess you could say I'm in between jobs." He took another sip.

"Where are ya headed?" she asked.

"Not sure. Maybe South America."

"That's pretty far south."

"Not far enough," he answered. The deep amber of the whiskey held his gaze. She took the opportunity to study him some more while giving the weight of his statement the silence it deserved. His eyes raised to hers, aware he was being watched closer than he would've liked. She shifted her vision. They were quiet again.

"Well, I envy you," she said after a few moments.

He nearly spit out a mouth full of whiskey as he began to laugh. This time it was a series of short, quick exhales. It could have been mistaken for a whimper. He reached for a cocktail napkin a few inches from Sophie's hand and wiped his mouth. As quickly as the random spell had come over him, it disappeared, and his composure was restored. He reached for his side and winced; the laugh being apparently costly.

"What's so funny?" Sophie asked, genuinely confused.

He crumpled up the napkin and laid it next to the glass. "Nothing," he said, keeping his eyes low.

Sophie glanced back down the bar. The elderly husband was glaring at her, shooting her the familiar look that suggested he had been waiting for his check for hours. She rolled her eyes and turned back to her mysterious guest. "I'll be back to check on you," she said.

"Where should I smoke?" he asked before she had a chance to move a step.

"Out on the deck," she said, pointing. "No one will bother you."

"Thanks," he said. He slid off the stool, grabbing his drink before slipping outside.

After getting rid of Mr. and Mrs. Grinch, who, astonishingly, tipped twenty-five percent, Sophie decided to re-stock what she'd already re-stocked. She'd given up on trying to figure out the beat-up stranger and left him to his drinks.

At 4:15, Lindsay arrived to relieve Sophie. It was a miracle the girl was only fifteen minutes late this time. And, as always, Lindsay rushed behind the bar, feigning apology as she shuffled through her purse for a wine key she had forgotten, again.

"Sorry, Soph," she said as she dug deeper into the labyrinth that was her purse. Unlike many girls who claimed it, Lindsay really did keep her entire life in there.

"Don't worry about it," Sophie said. *I'm used to it*, she thought. "You're all set for tonight."

"How was today?" Lindsay asked, giving up on the purse and rushing over to the register as if she were robbing the place and running out of time.

"Slow."

"Bummer."

"Totally."

That was usually the extent of their conversation.

Sophie didn't mind Lindsay. Most of the other servers and

bartenders found her annoying, but that didn't stop them from hooking up with her. Lindsay was the kind of bartender who would do anything for a tip, and she didn't hide it. If the bleached blonde hair and inch-thick make-up didn't give her away, one simply had to lower his or her gaze to the mountain of cleavage bulging out of her chest. A V was cut down the middle of her tank top, for good measure.

Sophie turned to Ryan, who showed absolutely zero interest in the girls' exchange and slid his bill across the bar. Wincing at the pain of the movement again, he reached back into his pocket and pulled out two twenties. "I'll grab your change," Sophie said, scooping up the bills.

"Keep it," he said casually.

Sophie glanced back down at the check. "You sure?" she asked. He nodded. "Thanks," she said. "Hope you feel better." She gathered her things to go. He tilted his glass towards her before taking another sip.

"So, you coming out with us tonight?" asked Lindsay before Sophie had a chance to swim through the swinging doors.

"Not tonight," she answered. "Early morning tomorrow." She could almost feel the water already.

"It's always an early morning for you," Lindsay said as she made her way over to Ryan. Sophie shrugged. Maybe that's why she was always on time. "You'll come around eventually," Lindsay went on. "Just don't forget about me when you're a big star."

"Don't hold your breath," Sophie said. She pushed through the doorway and rushed through the kitchen before Lindsay had a chance to prolong the conversation.

In seconds, Sophie was back on her bike. As she pedaled along what felt like an uphill return journey, her mind backtracked to the man at the bar. She couldn't bring herself to refer to him as a young man, even if he was only twenty-five. Something about him betrayed a temporal past, as though he had already lived a full life and was patiently waiting around for it to end. She pictured him as a traveling gambler who had experienced so many ups and downs through the years, he'd finally decided staying in place was the safer option. Except, she would be surprised if she ever saw him again.

Despite the offensive resistance of the wind, Sophie made it home in no time. After skidding the bike to a stop, she jogged over to the workshop and pushed open the door. She gazed fondly at her frustrated father.

"Hey, Daddy," she announced. "How's it going?"

He looked at his daughter with a helpless expression. "I think I'm getting worse, Sweetheart."

Sophie jogged over and kissed him on the cheek. "Nah," she said. You're a rock star. You just don't know it yet."

"Yeah, a washed-up rock star who can't even fill up a coffee house."

Sophie laughed. "Well, I'll always be your biggest fan."

"Thanks," he said, softening his tired features. He stood and wiped his hands with a rag. "How was work?"

"The same," she answered. She considered telling him about the sad man at the bar but decided to save it for another time. She was late for a date. "I'm gonna go for a swim," she said, leaning over the worktable to kiss him on the cheek again.

"Okay," he said. "Don't forget, lasagna for dinner," he called as she fluttered past him toward the open back door.

"I won't. Love you."

"Love you more, Sweetie."

She Superman changed into her swimsuit and raced down the walk. She couldn't see the sun, but she felt it behind her, like a fond childhood memory. Lifting her head to the cloudless sky, Sophie inhaled deeply. She could breathe again.

She exhaled slowly and opened her eyes. "I've missed you," she said. A small wave crashed.

The only invitation she needed.

3

"And then I transferred to WVU. I think it was the right decision. I mean, Florida was fun, don't get me wrong, but I needed to focus on a career, you know? Not just partying all the time. I mean, every weekend was like spring break down there, so I miss that. And..."

Ryan raised the glass to his mouth, staring over it, and passed her, not even attempting to hide his disinterest.

"I totally know what you mean," she continued, as if he had responded. "It gets boring. I wish I could just go from town to town like you." Ryan didn't even remember telling her anything about himself. What was her name? Linda? Laura? Whatever, it was late, and he was sufficiently wasted.

The inside of the restaurant was never more than half full during Ryan's seven-hour stretch at Finn's, and the people who came and went either didn't notice him or pretended not to notice. It made no difference. The ability to be completely alone in a crowd of people was an art form he had mastered.

As Linda continued to ramble on about wasted years and undergrad regrets, Ryan turned his attention to the bartender from earlier.

Maybe it was her eyes, he thought, wondering why she remained in his memory. They were the first thing he'd noticed after sliding into the familiar dim ambience of another bar. He'd never seen eyes so green. And there was an unmistakable flame flickering behind them, like Greek fire, an obvious passion glittering under the surface. And her hair was as brown and smooth as the bar. Her skin was unusually pale for someone who lived at the beach. Her arms and legs were long, just long enough to be noticeably long. Now that he thought about it, all her features were long. Her fingers seemed to stretch out forever, gracefully dancing along the bar. Her neck formed a formidable platform that held up her narrow, high cheek-boned face. He might have had a couple inches on her height, but not her wingspan. He surprised himself by how much he had picked up on in so little time.

Ryan's mind jumped to the surrounding town and what his plans might be moving forward. After spending most of the morning cleaning shattered glass out of his Jeep, he'd decided to take a walk around. It didn't take long for him to gather that it was a vacation town fit for families and retired elderly couples. It was a place for memories and sunrises and smiles. No place for someone like him.

And he couldn't help noticing the coastal getaway had a bit of an identity crisis. The Avenue seemed to evenly split the town in half between commercial and residential. Ancient Victorian houses on one side and modern condominiums on the other. The restaurant he'd wandered into was a bit confusing as well. Inside, Finn's had the look of an Irish Pub Ryan might have seen on any random street corner in Boston. While outside, the patio was adorned with picnic tables painted in blues and oranges as though a Jimmy Buffet concert had thrown up on it. No doubt an attempt to lure in ignorant vacationers searching for a more colorful experience.

It seemed the only available work would be either cleaning hotel rooms or cleaning dishes, two things he would prefer to take a break from. Not that he was in a position to be picky, but a few days off sounded much better than cleaning up after people. He figured he would hang around for a week—he'd already paid the nice man at the Seabreeze—then drive south until he ran out of gas, sell his car, and go from there.

"And that's how I wound up in Vegas."

Ryan allowed her to come into focus. "That is insane," he said.

"I know, right? I mean—"

"I'm gonna sneak out for a smoke," he said, cutting her off.

"Ugh, jealous," she said.

He slid off the stool and made for the door.

Ryan weaved through the maze of tables over to the lone ashtray in the corner. He put his glass down, lit a cigarette, and blew a long stream of smoke into the lamp-lit night. He chased the drag with a long sip of cheap whiskey. He closed his eyes and breathed out slowly.

Turning to face the dwindling crowd, he scanned the scene lazily. A family of three, the two young parents struggling to control their spirited toddler girl. A twenty-something couple obviously not on speaking terms. A four-top of old men drinking Coronas. The mother of the young girl glanced at Ryan then turned away quickly, hoping he hadn't caught her eye. His gaze remained on her for a moment, blank and unchanging. He took another drag and looked away.

He leaned on the low railing, back hunched and forearms planted firmly on the rough wood. Strange how quiet this side of town was. He imagined a tumbleweed rolling by in the light breeze, illuminated only by the weak light of the lampposts that were spaced about twenty feet apart along the boardwalk. Toward the south, the lights seemed taller and brighter, suggesting the party was just getting started. It appeared distant, though, like a light at the end of a long dark tunnel.

He seriously considered hopping over the railing and strolling north into the darkness. Anything to get away from the talkative bartender. Plus, it would save him some much-needed cash.

Before the idea had any time to ferment, Ryan heard a raspy voice behind him.

"Spare a smoke, my man?" it said.

Ryan glanced over his shoulder, unwilling to commit to a full turn until he was sure the man had addressed him. But Ryan was the only one smoking. Rising to his full height, Ryan turned to see a bald man of at least seventy-five smiling at him with dirty, yellow-stained teeth. The top of the man's bald head had so many wrinkles, it looked like a skin-colored brain. The wrinkles continued down his forehead and around his eyes like branches on an ancient tree. A white goatee came to a point a few inches below his chin. He wore a light blue shirt, opened to mid-chest unfortunately, and sand-colored shorts. No shoes.

"Let me guess, that's your last one," he said after Ryan failed to respond.

Ryan reached into his pocket and pulled out a half-empty pack. "Here you go," he said, handing the pack to the older man.

Ryan reached in his other pocket for a lighter, but the man said, "I'm good," and pulled a book of matches from his front pocket. Ryan had a fleeting thought that the man probably had a full pack of cigarettes in his pocket as well. But he quickly lost the thought as he watched the old man, in one fluid motion, using only one hand, flip a match around the pack and scrape it against the back with his thumb, as if he were snapping his fingers. A small flame exploded then weakened as he lit the cigarette. "Thanks," he said as he waved out the match and handed the pack back to Ryan.

"Cool trick," Ryan said.

"I'll teach it to you some other time," the stranger replied, smoke escaping his mouth as he spoke. "You'd look like an infant trying to do it right now."

No argument there, Ryan thought.

"That's quite a shiner you have there," the man said, pointing to Ryan's eye.

"Thanks," Ryan muttered. He wasn't in the mood.

"I'm Paul," the man introduced, strategically changing the subject. "But everyone calls me Old Man." He held out his hand.

"Ryan," said Ryan. He shook the man's hand.

"So, what brings you to Quicksand, Ryan," Old Man asked.

"I'm sorry?" Ryan replied, resuming his preferred position.

"Quicksand Beach," Old Man clarified after sucking down half a pint glass of dark beer in one gulp. "That's where you are, my friend."

Ryan turned his head slightly so he could see Old Man's profile. It wasn't any more flattering from this angle. "I thought the town was called—"

"Man," Old Man interrupted. "I've been trying to get them to officially change the name for years. Politicians, though. What are ya gonna do?"

Ryan shrugged.

"But make no mistake," Old Man continued. "You are in Quicksand Beach, buddy. And good luck gettin' out."

Ryan would be willing to bet his car that wasn't the first time Old Man had said that. And he could tell by the grin on the man's face that he was proud of his cleverness.

"Yup," Old Man went on, relaxing further as though he had roped in an avid listener. "I've spent my whole life here. Seen a lotta people come, and very few go. This place is like...Well it's like Quicksand, you see? Something about it just doesn't let go." His features turned sour. "Bastards wouldn't even give me a street name. I mean, how many Quicksand Avenues have you heard of?"

Ryan shrugged.

"Exactly. But they think another Washington, or Madison Avenue is going to set them apart," Old Man scoffed. He paused, then said, "I'm just tryin' to help, ya know?"

Ryan nodded, acting as though he was absorbing the information.

"Anyway," Old Man said. "So, what brings you to town?"

"Just passing through," Ryan answered, his eyes distant, staring through the wall of black beyond the waves.

Old man shifted his position, so he was still leaning against the railing, but now facing Ryan. He studied Ryan for a moment. "Might not be that easy to leave. Like I said—"

"I'll manage," Ryan interrupted. In his travels, Ryan's respect for his elders had seen a gradual decline. Or maybe it was his respect for all things. Either way, he didn't care what Old Man thought of his manners.

Old Man didn't seem to care either. "Maybe," he answered. "But the water, it's like a voice, begging us to stay. And if we try to leave, sometimes it shows us how powerful it really is."

Ryan watched a small wave crash onto shore and retreat into the ocean. "The water took everything from me," he said in a moment of weakness.

"Well," said Old Man, grinning. "Maybe it's about time it gives something back." And with that Old Man crushed out his cigarette and rose to leave. "I'll see you around, Ryan. Thanks for the smoke." He patted Ryan on the back as he turned to go.

No, you won't, Ryan thought. He lifted the small glass to his mouth and drained it in one gulp.

He was floating down a wide, angry river. Smooth walls of black rock flanked either side of the channel, rising higher than Ryan could see. He was traveling fast, too fast, with no control over where he went. White water splashed his face relentlessly, and like him, it searched in vain for a way out.

"Ryan!" Sarah yelled.

He tried to focus through the onslaught of freezing cold water that continued to force its way into his eyes and mouth.

"Sarah! I'm coming!" he tried to scream over the waves.

"Ryan! Help! I'm scared," her voice rolled over the waves and slammed into him harder than any amount of water ever could.

Ryan tried to swim towards her voice, but it was hopeless. The water was flowing faster than he could swim. He could see her, though, twenty feet up ahead. "Hold on, Sarah!"

"Please, Ryan!"

Please, God. Stop.

As he rounded a bend, Ryan noticed a drop off up ahead. No more water, just endless gray sky. He could hear the roar of water crashing onto more water, like thunder, a hundred feet below. Time slowed to a crawl as he watched her beautiful hair slip over the edge. "No!" he screamed as loud as he could manage. He closed his eyes before going over the edge...

"Help! Help!"

Ryan's eyes shot open, and he swallowed a deep breath, as though he'd been shocked back to life. A gray sky hung low over his head, like a concrete ceiling.

In an instant, the world was turned on around him. Seagulls cried, waves crashed, and the wind howled. He sat up and looked around. The boardwalk, and his memory, were nowhere in sight. He was alone on the beach.

But he could have sworn he'd heard someone screaming. *Must have been in the dream,* he thought. He rubbed his eyes with the heels of his hands and tried to piece together another blackout.

The sound came again. Terrified screams that drowned out the wind and waves, piercing through Ryan's eardrums. He whipped his head around, searching for the source. Through white-capped waves and bloodshot eyes, he thought he saw something yellow floating in the water, like a volleyball. Narrowing his eyes, Ryan was able to make out a figure that seemed to be struggling, just past the breaking waves.

Without another thought, he jumped up and ran toward the surf, hastily ripping off his sandy shirt and jeans as he rushed into the water.

Ignoring any lingering pain in his side, Ryan plunged into the ocean. He leapt over an incoming wave and dove under the next one. They were coming hard and fast, one after another. But Ryan, as if possessed, cut through them with ease, rising and falling as they lifted him into the air then dropped him back into the ocean's unforgiving embrace. There were no obstacles or invisible forces holding him back. He felt as if he were being towed by a boat toward the struggling figure.

Those screams again, high pitched like Sarah's. Ryan pushed himself harder, clawing through the water. His eyes were red and wide, and a little crazy. *Not this time.*

The ocean opened enough to allow Ryan a clear view of the struggling figure before him. She was only about ten feet away, facing the horizon. He was going to make it. He was going to save her, and she was going to be okay. Everything was going to be okay.

Ten feet away now. Seven feet. Five feet.

He pulled up short.

Blinded by towering waves and an uncontrollable sense of adrenaline, Ryan had nearly failed to notice the change in temperature, as well as the color of the water. He wished he had failed to notice. Until now, the only fear Ryan had known was that he might not make it in time to save the girl. However, staring straight into what was undoubtedly a pool of blood that was flowing from the floating girl, Ryan was suddenly afraid for his own life. Frozen, his mind fought for clarity.

No, he was too close. He swatted aside the fear, and in three swift strokes, covered the short distance between him and the girl.

When he was close enough to grab hold of her, the look of terror in her eyes multiplied the fear in his heart. Her body floated lifelessly.

"Come on," he said, hooking his arms under hers. "I've got you. It's going to be okay."

"Please," the girl whispered. "Please get me out of the water."

Ryan began paddling toward shore. He had scarcely enough time to catch a breath as wave after wave washed over him, but his attention remained fixed on the sand that seemed so close.

He glanced back for a moment. Only a few feet away, inches under the surface, Ryan watched, eyes wide and horrified as a shadow of a shark slowly swam by. It disappeared an instant later. He thrashed and splashed wildly as he pulled the fading girl with every ounce of energy he had toward the safety of the shore.

"Come on!" he yelled, half to the girl and half to himself.

He felt like he had been in the water for hours when a towering wave rose up before him, like outspread wings come to guide him and the girl to land. Caught in the unbreakable grip of the wave, the two bodies rolled, end over end, as if they were tumbling down a steep cliff. He couldn't breathe or see or hear. Finally, the firm sand caught the two of them as they washed up onto the surf together. Somehow through the suffocating ride, Ryan was able to keep his grip secured around her waist. The top half of her body lay strewn across his chest while her lower half remained in the shallow foam of the surf.

Ryan slid out from under her. He dragged her body up onto softer sand, out of reach of the breaking waves. A stream of red thread through the retreating water.

Breathing heavily, Ryan finally allowed himself a glance at the damage. The shark's bite had taken more than half of her lower left thigh, and nearly all of her upper calf. Below the knee, her leg seemed to be attached by threads of skin. Blood poured from the wound profusely, staining the sand around it.

"Oh my God," Ryan said, his eyes wide, glued to the poor girl's leg. He searched around for something, anything. But what? He didn't have a cell phone, and he sure as hell was no doctor. He caught sight of his discarded clothes not far away. He jumped up and ran to them and hustled back to the girl. Hands shaking, Ryan knelt beside her and covered as much of the wound as he could with the t-shirt. He might as well have used a tissue. The blood instantly soaked through the light fabric and onto Ryan's hands.

"Shit," he said.

"Is it bad?" the girl asked, lifting her head to try to see for herself. "I can't feel anything," she said. She was shaking.

Ryan returned his attention to her pleading face. Tears streaked down the creases around her eyes. Her skin was ghost white, and shock was frozen into her features. He pushed her shoulders back down to the sand.

"It's not that bad," Ryan lied. "It's going to be alright, Sarah. We're going to get you out of here." Ryan tore off her swimmer's cap and slid his hand under her head. "Hold on. You'll be alright."

But she wasn't going to be alright. They were all alone.

"Sophie!" a new voice screamed through the wind. "Oh my God, Sophie."

Ryan looked up to see an elderly woman running toward them. Her gray hair was electric in the wind and her nightgown as white as Sophie's face. Ryan stayed where he was, unable, or unwilling to budge from Sophie's side.

Sophie?

When the woman reached them, she fell to the sand beside Ryan, ignoring him for the moment. "Sophie? Sophie, dear? Can you hear me?" the woman said. She pulled back the blood-soaked shirt and gasped when she saw the damage. Ryan could tell it was everything she could do not to break down into tears. "John!" she screamed behind her. "Call an ambulance!"

"Mrs. Ginny," Sophie whispered. "I'm scared."

The woman stroked Sophie's forehead. "Everything will be alright, Sophie."

Ryan watched in a daze as an elderly man hustled toward the trio with an armful of towels. "They're on their way!" he shouted through the wind that blew his plaid pajama pants and white t-shirt tight against his body.

"Keep pressure on the wound," the older woman said, acknowledging Ryan for the first time. Ryan pressed his hands into the drenched t-shirt, grateful for something to do. "John!" she screamed again. The older man had finally caught up and was standing right beside her.

"Take the shirt off the wound," he said. He knelt calmly. Ryan was pressing down so hard, the man had to pry his hands off. "Take this," he said, handing Ryan a clean towel. "I am going to tie this one," he held up another towel, "around her thigh. I need you to keep constant pressure on the wound. Do you understand?" Ryan nodded. "You're doing great, try to stay focused." His tone was soft, yet as determined as Ryan had ever heard. Trying to steady his hands, Ryan pressed the towel into the wound as the man worked around Sophie's thigh like a surgeon.

Ryan tried to mirror his calm demeanor, but he couldn't help blaming himself. The girl was going to die because he was too slow.

"Sophie, darling," said the man. "Can you hear me?"

Her expression flashed recognition, but her eyes were tired. She nodded almost imperceptibly. "Mr. John," she said in a whisper. "I'm really scared."

"Help is on the way," he said. "Everything is going to be alright. I just need you to be strong for a little longer." He brushed his ancient hand over her forehead.

Ryan heard the faint song of sirens in the distance. The sound continued to grow in strength until it drowned out the positive affirmations the elderly couple were speaking into Sophie's blank eyes.

Ryan felt a pair of strong arms pull him away from the scene. He'd been so lost in his task that he hadn't even noticed the team of paramedics that now surrounded Sophie.

He stumbled backwards as the men and women went to work.

He felt as though he was watching the scene unfold on a television screen, as if he wasn't even there. Bodies rushing to and from the ambulance, a controlled kind of chaos playing out before his eyes as Sophie's body disappeared under the swarm of paramedics. What could he do, except watch? He'd imagined himself in this scenario countless times. Dreamed of it. But like in his dreams, he was helpless, forced to watch from afar.

The elderly woman and her husband were speaking with one of the paramedics off to the side, but Ryan couldn't make out the conversation. Everything had become eerily silent, and it seemed as though everyone was moving in slow motion. Standing there on the beach, half-naked and soaking wet, he suddenly felt cold. The wind brought with it a light spray from the ocean that felt like snowflakes against his shivering skin. He looked down at his hands. Her blood.

When Ryan looked up again, a crowd had begun to gather. A fit of rage swelled up inside him when he saw a man taking pictures with his phone. Unable to control himself, Ryan rushed the man, swatted the phone from his hands, and shoved him to the sand.

"What do you think this is, a fucking zoo?" Ryan yelled. The man scrambled around in the sand, searching for footing. Ryan was about to pounce when a warm, gentle hand fell on his shoulder. He turned to see the older man who had been so collected during the ordeal standing as calmly as ever behind him.

"Easy," said the man. "Come on, let's get you cleaned up." He slid his hand down to Ryan's back and led him toward one of the homes that loomed high over the beach. Ryan turned back one more time to see the ambulance speeding away.

"I'm sorry," Ryan said as he followed the man up a series of wooden steps to a massive deck area. "I don't know what got into me."

"There's an outside shower over there," the man said, ignoring Ryan's apology. "I'll get you some dry clothes."

Ryan meandered, head down, like a zombie to the shower.

He felt like he was showering in a fire. Watered down blood spilled from his body and swirled around the drain before falling through the nail-head-sized holes. Twice in as many days. After a few minutes, he turned the shower off and dried himself. The man was waiting on the deck with a pair of sweatpants and a t-shirt.

Now that Ryan could focus his attention on the older man, he was able to make out deep wrinkles around patient eyes that followed a narrow face down to a pointed chin. Long silver hair slid past elvish ears and fell halfway down a long neck.

"You okay?" he asked when Ryan reached him.

Ryan nodded. "Yeah, I'm alright."

The man introduced himself and his wife as John and Ginny Palmer. Ryan returned the introduction. "She'll be alright," John said as he gazed out at the small crowd on the sand.

"How do you know?" Ryan asked.

"She's strong," he answered. Ryan believed him.

Ryan glanced back out to the beach. John's wife was bounding up the steps faster than Ryan would have thought possible for someone her age. When she reached the two men she said breathlessly, "We need to get to the hospital, John."

John nodded. "You're welcome to come along, Ryan."

Ryan declined, citing that he simply needed to get back.

"Let us give you a ride," Mrs. Palmer pressed. Her voice was friendly and light, a miracle, considering she was fighting tears, panic, and hysteria on three fronts. Ryan hadn't considered how he would make it back to the motel, but a car ride was preferable to walking. He could hardly stand upright as it was. As graciously as he could manage, he accepted.

The ride took too long. Fortunately, the Palmer's didn't ask Ryan what he was doing on the beach so early. That was a question he was desperately trying to figure out for himself, along with a dozen others. But at the moment, his fragile mind simply wasn't capable of entertaining such thoughts as he rested his head against the window. He stared blankly through half-closed eyes at the blur of pine trees racing by. A couple times, for no apparent reason, Ryan glanced into the rearview mirror from his spot in the back seat, and every time he looked, John was looking back at him. It was uncomfortable, as if he were being scrutinized through a magnifying glass.

After what seemed an eternity, they arrived back at the motel. Ryan never thought he'd be so happy to see such a plain-looking building. He got out and thanked them for the ride. Before he got to the door, he remembered something and jogged back to the car. Mrs. Palmer opened her window.

"If at all possible," Ryan said. "Do you think you could not tell anyone my name?"

"But you may have saved Sophie's life," said Mrs. Palmer. "You're a hero. You deserve to be recognized."

"Please," Ryan said, his tone betraying desperation.

John answered for the two of them. "Of course," he said." If that's what you want, we'll respect it. It's the least we can do." He looked at his wife, who, after a moment nodded in agreement.

"Thank you."

"Get some sleep," John said over his wife's shoulder as Ryan walked to his door.

He eased into the dark room and lumbered over to the bed. He sat down heavily and ran his hands through his still-damp hair.

"What the hell just happened," he whispered aloud. He lay back on the sheets, and all at once, pure exhaustion fell over him like a blanket, and Ryan collapsed into a dreamless sleep.

4

The world was blurry, as though she were looking through a pair of glasses that belonged to someone else. But after a few moments, her surroundings became clear. A cold white ceiling. Fluids running through an IV and into her arm. A wash sink to her right. A television mounted to the wall before her.

Confusion.

Then it came back all at once, the memories rapidly sketching themselves into her fragile head too quickly. Flashes of white teeth and massive black eyes gripped her consciousness. Heavy breaths assaulted her lungs. Tears flooded her eyes.

Her lips quivered.

"Dad," she whispered. "Dad?"

He was fast asleep in a cushioned chair beside the bed. He awoke with a start at the sound of her voice.

His eyes were red, his features worn. "Sweetheart," he said softly. He leaned forward. "You're awake. Thank God." He took Sophie's hand in both of his and squeezed.

"Dad," Sophie said. She could feel her composure wobbling on a wire, threatening to fall into a sea of panic. "Dad, how bad is it?"

His expression changed, then changed again quickly, but Sophie had caught it. He was afraid. Her father gripped her hand even tighter. "Sophie," he said. "Sweetheart, you're lucky to be alive. It's a miracle you even—"

"Dad," Sophie said. Her eyes widened. "Tell me. How bad is it?"

He closed his eyes. When he opened them, tears threatened to spill over onto his cheeks. "They weren't able to save your leg."

"No."

"Sweetie, I'm so sorry. But it's going to be okay. I—"

"No, please. Dad, please."

"Sweetheart listen to me. Look at me."

"Please."

The dam was shattered, and tears gushed from Sophie's eyes. As the sobs increased, she allowed her left hand to travel down her waist and along her thigh. Her chest heaved with each breath.

"Sophie, don't," her father said. He attempted to block the path of her hand. "Please, don't."

"I have to," she said, and he released his grip. Her hand traced on top of the white sheet. Her gaze remained fixed on the ceiling. When her fingers made it to the end of her thigh, they abruptly dropped off, and instead of touching her knee, she now felt the unwelcome softness of the bed's surface.

She ripped the sheet off her body before her father could protest and stared down in horror at the heavily wrapped stump that used to be her left leg.

She screamed at the top of her lungs.

Sophie could scarcely make out the sound of her father's voice beside her. "Sophie," he pleaded. "Sophie. Please calm down,

Sweetheart. Please." He was on his feet, hovering over top of her. She thrashed back and forth, wailing uncontrollably as he tried to steady her.

"Sophie, please," he said softly. "Look at me, Sweetheart, I'm right here. You're safe now." She could see the pain in his eyes and feel it in his voice. But she didn't care. She couldn't stop screaming. More images of cold eyes and razor-sharp teeth flashed through her like electricity, jolting her body this way and that.

She could hear other voices, male and female all around her, begging her to calm down. She felt like a caged animal.

Then she began to feel weak and tired. As if shades were being drawn over her face, her eyelids became heavy and she stopped struggling. Before the world went dark, the last thing she remembered was her father, a few feet away, weeping.

Six days later, on a hot, cloudless Saturday afternoon, Sophie was finally released from the doctor's care and allowed to go home. As her father had pushed her wheelchair through the doors, she'd been barraged by a throng of reporters. Dozens of questions all at once and blinding camera flashes. Sophie had put her head down and begged her father to get her out of there.

Now, as the monotonous hum of cool air leaked from the truck's air vents and thick rubber rumbled along Coastal Highway, all she could think about was how she would never again feel the wind wash over her face as she cruised on two wheels down the road. Like everyone else, now she would have to settle for the weak breeze of an air conditioning system.

She could feel her father's eyes sneak in her direction every few seconds, as if he feared she might suddenly open the door and fall out. She considered it.

The truck slowed to a crawl and turned into the driveway.

Her father pulled around the oval-shaped drive and stopped in front of the porch steps.

She opened the door and slid off the seat. The fabric of her sweatpants where her left leg should have been lagged behind as her right leg landed heavily onto the pavement.

"Hang on," her father said, and he jumped out of the front seat and ran around back to grab the wheelchair.

Sophie stood beside the truck, holding onto the side-view mirror for balance. A slight breeze blew the hollow leg of her pants.

A sudden urge to walk up the steps gripped her, and, without another thought, Sophie gave in. She fired her left glute muscle and moved that side of her body forward, just as she would to take a step. Just as she had every day for her entire life.

She fell like dead weight onto the driveway, scraping her hands as she caught herself before any real damage could be done. It hurt, but not as badly as it should have. The strength of the painkillers wouldn't wear off for a while still.

"Sophie!" her father cried. He rushed to her side.

"I'm fine," she said. She pushed herself onto her knee. He helped her up and guided her into the wheelchair.

"What were you thinking?" he scolded. "You could have—"

"I'm fine, Dad."

She pushed the wheelchair toward the cobblestoned path that cut between the house and garage. She followed the curve of the path around to the pool deck where she stopped inches from the edge of the water. Her father followed like a shadow, ready to materialize if needed.

"Do you want me to help you up the steps?" he asked.

"No."

His eyes burned into her cheek as he lingered beside the wheelchair. He said, "I'll have a ramp put in tomo—"

"No," Sophie said again. "I'm not handicapped."

He knelt beside her and leaned his face in front of hers so she couldn't escape his stare. She looked right through him. She could hear his breath. "I know that, Sweetie," he said. "But the sooner we accept your situation, the sooner we can start to move past it."

Sophie focused her vision and the details on his face became clear. She looked hard at her father.

"Sweetheart," he said, "you know I feel everything you feel."

"Leave me alone!" Sophie snapped, and he recoiled, as if she'd slapped him. By the look on his face, she could tell he would have welcomed a physical blow.

He took his time standing up and backed away. His feet shuffled along the stone. "People will be coming over soon," he said. "To welcome you home," he added. His footfall faded as he easily climbed the steps and went inside.

Welcome me home.

Sophie peered into the clear water before her. White light danced along the surface to a rhythm she failed to follow. Beyond the pool, tall grass swayed in a light breeze as if slow dancing atop the shallow dunes to a song she couldn't hear anymore. In the distance, a calm ocean stirred as dozens of seagulls lounged on the surface, sometimes indistinguishable from the white of the waves. A lone dolphin fin arced beyond the seagulls. Everything was just how she'd left it, free and natural. And it would continue to stay that way. But she had changed. The world wasn't beautiful anymore. A view that had once befit purity now appeared tainted. The water looked cold, the grass was brittle and weak, and the seagulls' cries were like static to her ears.

Sophie had always considered herself strong-willed. Adversity had been just another form of exercise. When life had taken an abruptly arduous turn, she'd powered through it, as if it were another wave in her path. Now, the darkness she had so valiantly kept at bay over the last three years with every stroke, every breath, and every step, had finally crawled its way in through an open window that she didn't even care to get up and close.

She was tired of fighting.

5

Ryan awoke to a loud knock at the door and a ruthless pounding against the inside of his temple. He sat up too quickly and was forced to wait out a wave of nausea.

His vision had yet to adapt to the ambient gloom, and the air around him was heavy, contaminated with the smell of lingering cigarette ash, stale beer, and liquor fumes. He rolled to his right and tumbled over the side of the bed. He landed with a thump and an involuntary, "Ugh," escaped his dry mouth.

He struggled to his feet. It had been a bad week, even by his standards, and his entire body ached from a marathon of heavy drinking. He limped toward the yellow light that trimmed the closed curtain by the door.

He peeked outside. An older man, wearing a faded blue button-down shirt and sand-colored shorts, waited patiently outside Ryan's door. Thick, dirty blonde hair fell short of attentive ears. A sand-sprinkled five o'clock shadow clung to a wide, sun-tanned face.

Did he know this person?

Before Ryan had a chance to move, the man cocked his head to the side, as if sensing he was being watched.

His vision now somewhat acclimated to the lightless room, Ryan lumbered to the door and turned the knob, opening it a quarter of the way, about the width of his dwindling frame. A blinding reflection of the setting sun bounced off a nearby windshield in the parking lot, forcing Ryan to raise a hand in protest. Mercifully, the stranger stepped to his right, shielding the light from Ryan's pale face.

"Thanks," said Ryan.

"No problem."

The voice was familiar.

Quiet fell between them while Ryan attempted to swim through the cavities of his flooded memory.

The man peered over Ryan's shoulder. "Looks like you've been having a good time," he said.

Ryan frowned. "Can I help you?"

"Looks like that eye healed up well, too," the man observed. "How are your ribs feeling?"

Recognition breathed to life inside Ryan's mind.

"You don't remember me, do you?" the man persisted.

"Sure, sure I do," Ryan answered as he ran his hand through his greasy hair. "From the other night. Tom, right?"

"Ted."

"Of course, sorry."

"You never have to apologize to me," said Ted. *Kind of a weird thing to say*, Ryan thought. "Do you have a minute?" Ted asked.

Ryan was having trouble reading Ted's expression. The man's eyes drooped at the sides, betraying sadness. However, he didn't seem sad. He seemed nervous.

"Um," Ryan answered, feeling trapped. "Yeah, sure," he said.

He shuffled back inside, grabbed the pack of cigarettes on the bed then moved through the barrier between light and dark, shutting the door behind him. Just outside Ryan's door were two plastic chairs on either side of a circular plastic table, with a circular plastic ashtray in the middle. Ted took a seat and crossed his legs. Ryan followed suit, slumping into the chair. He lit a cigarette. A one-story, single-family home on the opposite side of Main Street was half bathed in what Ryan guessed was late, and still very hot, afternoon sun. Light spilled out over the crowded parking lot of the Seabreeze Motel, which had filled up around Ryan's beat-up Jeep as the week had worn on.

"So," Ted began. "How's the job search going?"

"Um, not great," Ryan said. He hadn't filled out a single application. Once Ted was gone, and after a few more hours of sleep, Ryan was planning on enjoying the view of the town from his rearview mirror.

"That's too bad," Ted said casually.

"Eh," Ryan let out. "Wasn't meant to be, I guess."

Ted let out a short laugh. "I disagree," he said.

Ryan frowned. "What can I do for you, Ted?" he asked, not attempting to mask his impatience.

Ted looked down at his fingers as his thumbs played hide and seek with each other. Ryan flicked the last of the ash into the overflowing tray.

Finally, Ted looked over at Ryan and said, "The girl you saved last week is my daughter."

Ryan stopped his hand an inch away from his face before taking another drag, as if someone had pressed the pause button on his life. Sophie was Ted's daughter? He was too stunned to respond.

"Don't worry," said Ted. "I'm the only one who knows it was you." Then he added, "Besides John and Ginny, of course. And my brother-in-law. But that's it."

Ryan didn't really care who knew now. It didn't matter, he was leaving town.

"How's she doing?" he asked.

"She's alive," Ted answered.

Ryan knew that. Ginny Palmer had stopped by the motel earlier in the week to pass along the good news.

"It's gonna be a long recovery process, but she'll be alright," Ted went on.

"That's good to hear," Ryan said.

Ted nodded. "I've been struggling with how to thank you properly. But I don't think I can do it here. The main reason I came by was to invite you over to the house for dinner tonight."

Taken aback, Ryan said, "Um." He hesitated. "I don't know. I'm planning on leaving tonight. I really appreciate it, but—"

"Please," Ted interrupted, and there it was, only for a split second, but Ryan caught it. It wasn't nervousness or sadness as he'd assumed, but desperation. This man was desperate, Ryan realized in that fleeting instant. "I need to *show* you how much it means to me, what you did," Ted went on. "And it would mean a lot to Sophie to be able to thank you in person."

Ryan exhaled. How could he say no to that?

"I'm in a bit of a rush," he tried.

"It won't take long," Ted persisted. But there was no need. Ryan had already made up his mind.

"Okay," said Ryan, nodding. Ted seemed visibly relieved. "I'll have to get cleaned up. You want to give me directions?"

Ted settled into his chair and smiled. "No need, I'll wait. The house is only a few minutes away. You can follow me."

"Well alright," said Ryan, defeated.

Ryan followed close behind Ted's truck. When he'd made this drive in the back of the Palmer's Mercedes his mind had been too preoccupied to notice the pretentious size of the mansions lining the ocean side of the road. Each one seemed bigger than the last, and they all looked as though they could comfortably sleep at least twenty. The driveways were well hidden from his view by tall, immaculately landscaped bushes, and he assumed they weren't home to 95 Jeep Cherokees. The massive homes glared down their shingled noses in judgment at the small cottages that hid behind the pine trees on the other side of the road.

About a quarter mile after they passed the Palmer's residence, Ted's truck turned right into what looked like an empty lot between two mammoth-sized, cedar-sided homes. But when he pulled into the drive, Ryan was surprised to see three small structures incongruously sandwiched between their overachieving neighbors.

To his left, on the north side of the property was obviously the garage, painted a deep ocean blue with a single massive white door. A staircase climbed up the side to what Ryan assumed might be a second story or some kind of loft area. The structure to his right was almost a mirror image of the garage, but its function wasn't so obvious. Instead of a garage door, an enormous rectangular window stretched nearly the entire length of the façade. The setting sun created a glare, obscuring his view of what might reside inside.

Sandwiched between the outer buildings was the main house,

painted the same rich blue. A white deck elevated the structure about five feet from the ground and wrapped around the entire single story of the beachside dwelling. White trim framed the windows and a pyramid-shaped roof stretched out over the porch in all directions. Ryan thought the place looked more like a bungalow, or guest house compared to one of the neighboring mansions. He decided it was the other houses that surrounded Ted and Sophie's that were out of place. This was what a beach house should look like.

Ted's truck pulled to a stop in front of the mystery building on the right. Ryan circled the driveway around to the garage so he could make a quick escape if needed.

Ted was waiting on the opposite side of the house. "Over here," he said with a wave.

Ryan entered the small building with the big window and stopped inside the doorway. He looked around in wonder. The window concentrated a thick stream of golden yellow light from the setting sun which lit up a million specks of dust that swam up into the safety of the wooden rafters hovering above. Two circular skylights on either side of the vaulted ceiling gazed down like giant baby blue eyes. In the middle of the sawdust-covered cement floor were two large worktables. Between the tables, a lone, unfinished rocking chair rested in the evening glow. To his left, hung on the wall, were more hand tools than Ryan had ever seen in one place, at least a dozen different saws of varying size, more chisels than he cared to count, and a seemingly unnecessary number of hammers, as well as a variety of tools he couldn't name. A thin counter lined the wall beneath the tools where more tools lay haphazardly like toys on a living room floor. The opposite side of the room housed the power tools: a band saw, a table saw, a belt sander, and a drill press. Everything was highlighted by the honeyed glow of the fading day. It was a beautiful room. But what grabbed his attention the most was the complete openness of the ocean side of the room. It was as if the builders had forgotten to build a wall on the east side, and it opened like a painting before his eyes, inviting him to take a seat and gaze wondrously for hours out at the rolling dunes and endless Atlantic Ocean beyond.

The room's ambience had a calming effect on Ryan. He didn't feel hungover, or tired, but instead, he felt relaxed. And the atmosphere wrapped around him like a warm blanket. He couldn't help but feel safe. He tried to dispel the foreign sense of security.

Ted leaned against one of the worktables, arms crossed, watching patiently as Ryan drank in his surroundings.

After enough exploration, Ryan said, "So you build furniture for a living."

"Not really," Ted answered. "Like I told you, I'm retired." Ryan had forgotten. "This is more of a hobby," he added, "or obsession, depending on who you ask."

Ryan walked along the line of the counter, inspecting the tools on the wall more carefully as he tried to figure out why he was there.

"Well, it's not *just* a hobby, I guess," Ted continued. "I sell some stuff to a woman with a small shop in town, but I don't make much from it."

Ryan came across a framed photograph on the wall. In the picture, a younger Ted stood with his arm around a woman who appeared in almost every way to be Sophie. Long arms, long legs, and those impossibly green eyes. It couldn't be Sophie, though, as Ted's face looked at least twenty years younger, lacking the deep creases around the eyes and sporting a boyish grin. The pair was standing in front of the house only a few feet away from where Ryan stood. But the house was a pale yellow, instead of deep blue.

"That's Sophie's mother and I after we bought the place, not long after Sophie was born," Ted's voice came from directly over Ryan's right shoulder, the older man having crept up on him. "The resemblance is incredible, isn't it?"

"Had me fooled," Ryan answered, unable to tear his eyes away. Unavoidable questions entered his mind, the worst of which he was unwilling to ask.

"She passed away three years ago," Ted said. "Pancreatic cancer." He heard Ted's listless footfall behind him as the man returned to his position beside the table. Ryan turned around and leaned against the counter.

"I'm sorry," Ryan said. It just slipped out. He knew full well how meaningless those words were.

Ted looked out through the open wall, crossed his arms, and took a deep breath. "That's partly why I wanted to bring you here," he said, returning his attention to Ryan. "I want to give you some background on our family; how and why we came to be here. I know I said it wouldn't take long, but if you don't mind…"

He didn't know if it was some spell the workshop had cast upon him, or what, but Ryan found himself more than willing to stick around for a little longer. He felt he owed the man at least that much. "Not at all," Ryan answered as he rested his palms on the table behind him.

After a short pause, Ted began.

"We haven't always lived here. Sophie's mother and I met in college. I was from a suburb of D.C. and she was from here," he raised his hand and gestured through the walls to the surrounding town. "After college, a friend of mine and I started a construction company that took off way faster than we could have anticipated, and it wasn't long before I could comfortably build a house of my own. I never had a very good relationship with my folks, but I won't get into that. Suffice to say, they live in Arizona now and I haven't spoken to them in years. My wife's parents died in a car crash during her senior year. So, it was really just the two of us from the start." He looked at the wood shavings at his feet, lost in a memory. "Anyway," he went on. "Sophie's mother made the move to D.C. and we got married. But I knew how much she loved it here, and not long after I built our house out there, I bought this place." Ted wiped some dust from the top of the table and Ryan watched it float for a few seconds before disappearing into a shadow. "She had grown up in the Pines across the street and always dreamed about having a beachside place," he said. Ted grinned, more to himself.

Ryan stood as still as a statue as Ted reminisced about a blissful past. It wasn't long ago that Ryan would have envied Ted and his wife, two people in love, with homes in the city and the coast. He had often imagined himself in similar circumstances over the years. But that picture had faded, worn, and weathered like an old beach chair. It was a memory he had locked away in a room he'd forgotten about.

"So, Sophie grew up here in the summers and back in Maryland during the school year," Ted went on. "She always considered this place her real home, though. She used to say she could breathe better here. Her love for the water was difficult to understand." Ted stopped to let out a short laugh. "When she was a kid, she used to swear she could talk to dolphins." Ryan smiled politely. "I think I envied her a little," Ted continued, "because I simply couldn't understand the love she held for it. But her mother could." Ted smiled, and Ryan couldn't help but smile as well.

"When she was diagnosed five years ago, our world was shattered. I revolved around my wife. She was so smart—much smarter than me—and beautiful, and funny, and strong." Ted stopped again, the memory demanding silence. After a few seconds, he went on. "Sophie had just begun her freshman year at Maryland on a full swimming scholarship. But she didn't hesitate to drop out and come with us when we decided to move here permanently. In fact, it was Sophie's idea. You see, the form of cancer Sarah had— Sophie's mother's name was Sarah." A thick knot formed in Ryan's stomach as he fought against the pang of emotion. "The form of cancer she had offered little hope at more than a few years, and Sophie and I knew she would be happier here. And who knew, maybe something in the water could have saved her?" Ted chuckled at the suggestion, as if he knew it was far-fetched. But Ryan could tell the man had probably put more hope in that than any medical treatment she might have had.

A wave crashed in the distance, the sound slipping into the workshop, taking a look around, then swimming back out as Ted searched for what to say next. "Sarah held on for two years. But when she died, I died," he admitted. The smile evaporated from Ted's face. "I was supposed to be the strong one, the one who consoled Sophie and reassured her everything would be alright. But I didn't, I couldn't. I fell into a dark place I couldn't climb out of." He shook his head, as if he still hadn't forgiven himself for his weakness. "At least not by myself. It was Sophie, she brought me back. She consoled me and told me everything was going to be okay. I'll never forget how young I felt, and how much older she seemed, like our roles were reversed. She picked me up, dusted me off, and said, 'I can't do this without you.'" A wet glaze appeared in Ted's eyes.

"This," he said, gesturing to the room around them, "was all Sophie's idea. The two things Sophie's mother loved more than anything were watching her daughter swim, and furniture. She was an interior designer, by the way. Did I tell you that?" he asked. Ryan shook his head, the most drastic movement he'd made since the story began. "Well, she loved furniture, all kinds. She used to read so many books on histories of French or Persian or English furniture. I mean dull stuff that would put most people to sleep," he joked. Ryan believed that. He couldn't imagine reading that stuff. "But for some reason, she loved it, worshipped it even," he went on. "So, Sophie suggested I build furniture. I had sold my half of the business and had no intention of going back. My life was here now. But I was a little apprehensive because, although I have a construction background, I was actually embarrassingly average at building stuff." Ryan couldn't help but frown. "You're not kidding," Ted said. "But something incredible happened after I had the shop built. I began to heal. With every leg and armrest and nightstand I built, I felt myself being put back together." He looked directly into Ryan's eyes. "Sophie said she couldn't do it without me," he said. "But the truth is she could have, she has her mother's strength. It's me who couldn't have done it without her," Ted confessed. He paused, then said, "I can't live without her."

Understanding washed through Ryan.

"You didn't only save Sophie's life last week, Ryan, you saved mine as well," said Ted. "I wouldn't have survived losing her." And as sincerely as Ryan had ever heard, Ted said, "Thank you." Ryan held Sophie's father's gaze for as long as he could.

"You're welcome," Ryan said. It seemed a weak response to such a well-delivered thank you, but he couldn't think of anything else to say. He could have told Ted there was no need to thank him, and that maybe Sophie's attack happened because he showed up in town, bringing with him an enveloping cloud of misery and heartache. But that would have been insulting.

Ted nodded. "There's something else I think you should know before we go inside." A grave expression masked Ted's usually friendly face. "You see," Ted said. "Sophie wasn't just swimming for the fun of it, that morning you found her. I mean, don't get me wrong, there's no doubt she was having the time of her life. But she was training." Ryan searched through the dying light to try to find a change in Ted's features. "Sophie gave up a lot when she left college, and she gave up even more to take care of me after her mother passed. Over the past three years, though, she's been swimming every day, pushing herself. I finally convinced her to take the next step, and at the end of August, she was going to make the trip to Colorado and train for the Olympic trials, with a world-class coach and everything." He stopped, and Ryan could hear the tears in Ted's voice as the man said, "If I hadn't been so weak, she would have left a long time ago. And this never would have happened." Silence followed. "Swimming was everything to Sophie," he continued. "And I'm afraid this will destroy her. But more than that, I'm afraid I won't be able to help her." Ted walked over to the open wall and dug his hands into his pockets. Ryan watched, silent, wishing he could say something profound.

After tumbling around like wrestlers, all Ryan's thoughts could produce were, "I don't know what to say, Ted."

Ted turned around, his frame not quite a complete silhouette against the navy blue of the Atlantic in the distance. "You don't have to say anything," Ted replied. "I asked you to listen, and you did." Ted walked to Ryan and gently squeezed his shoulder. "How about dinner? You must be starving."

6

Nostalgia met Ryan when he entered through the front door of the house. He wasn't prepared for the vivid flash of childhood memories at the beach that accompanied the smell. He should have known; all beach houses hold that familiar scent of salted air, fine sand, and the ocean, as if they all three had been shaken up in a bottle and sprayed on the walls.

Ted led him into a small foyer. The ceiling was low, and a single lamp sprinkled the room with a studious light. Dark brown hardwood floors squeaked beneath Ryan's boots. A small blue bench was between a closed door and an open arched hallway that led somewhere he couldn't see. To his left was another narrow archway that led into what appeared to be a library. To his right, yet another archway led into a billiards room. The foyer offered a labyrinthine effect; Ryan wasn't sure where to go. Ted took the lead and ushered him through the first hallway Ryan had noticed.

The hallway opened into the *Great Room*, Ted announced as they walked. A long, narrow island separated the kitchen from the living area. If Ted hadn't just informed Ryan of his late wife's love of furniture, Ryan might have been surprised by what he saw. An intricately carved wooden couch with tan upholstery that looked like something out of a colonial mansion he'd visited in high school, and two equally impressive antique, high-backed chairs huddled around a dark brown coffee table with claws for feet that clung to a dizzyingly designed rug. A large fireplace presided over the furniture, and although the house held the distinct scent of ocean air, Ryan thought the living room betrayed an atmosphere more akin to the countryside. That was until he looked out the floor-to-ceiling window walls that hugged the blue and gray stone hearth. The view of the ocean was even more impressive than that of the workshop.

Sophie was standing on the deck, leaning against the railing. An immobile wheelchair idled beside her. She wore a loose, white long-sleeved shirt and a pair of baggy sweatpants. She seemed to be favoring her right leg.

Ted's voice brought him back inside. "Well, I'm gonna get dinner started. Shouldn't take too long. How do you feel about lasagna?" he asked. Ryan nodded. "Great. Help yourself through the doors. The handle's over there." He pointed with a kitchen knife. "It kind of blends in with the windows," he said. Ryan nodded again, afraid his voice might contaminate the delicate scenery.

Careful not to touch the furniture, he weaved his way toward the back door. He found the clear handle and pulled. Nothing happened. He pushed. Nothing happened. "It slides," Ted called from behind him. Ryan slid the giant door open and stepped onto the deck.

A gentle breeze had picked up outside, and the sun had dipped below the tree line behind the house, leaving the deck in shadow.

He studied Sophie from the ground up as he inched toward the railing. He stopped in his tracks when a gust of wind blew the bottom half of her left sweat pant leg to the side, as if it were hollow. Realization rocked him back a step as he quickly tried to take in the scene before him. Ryan hadn't been told, and for some reason hadn't asked whether or not the doctors had been able to save her leg. He was suddenly aware of how ill-prepared he was. The urge to flee grabbed him.

Before he could act on the thought, Sophie said, "Hi," without turning her head.

"Hey," Ryan answered. Tentatively, he moved to her side, keeping a safe distance of a couple feet between her. He rested his arms on the railing. A rectangular swimming pool was sunken into the ground between the deck and the dunes. A wooden walkway as straight as a ruler but perhaps not as sturdy parted the sand and led to the private beach not more than thirty yards away.

When it was obvious Sophie wasn't planning on responding, Ryan asked, "Do you remember me?"

Sophie looked at him for the first time, her eyes dull and tired. The roaring emerald flames he remembered now reduced to weakening embers. "Whiskey on the rocks, right?" she said.

"You're good with names," Ryan said, and despite herself, Sophie laughed. But it was transient, and she quickly retreated inward.

Ryan understood right away why Ted was so worried; he could see it in Sophie's profile as soon as the opportunity arose. He knew that look, it was his look, and he saw it every day when he passed by a mirror. But his was bought and paid for, unreturnable. He hoped she was only trying it on for size and that she was aware it didn't fit. Her face seemed paler as well, as if it hadn't seen the sun since the attack. Her hair lay matted to her long neck.

"How are you feeling?" he tried.

"Handicapped," she said, lowering her gaze to the surface of the pool.

"Incredible place you have here," said Ryan, attempting to maneuver the conversation elsewhere. At the bar last week, she had been the one struggling to keep the conversation afloat, but now he felt the need to steer it this way or that, attempting to avoid any potholes or awkward turns. It was uncomfortable, like trying to learn a new language.

"Were you scared?" Sophie asked, ignoring his statement. "That morning?"

Ryan looked at her profile. She winced and he noticed a bead of sweat dribble down her eye and along her cheek. He wondered how long she had been out there standing on one leg.

"I was terrified," he answered. He would never forget the fear he felt when he saw that shadow swim by. He could only imagine how scared Sophie was.

"Me too," she said softly. After a pause, she said, "So I guess my dad gave you the rundown in his workshop? Since you two have been here for like an hour already."

"Yeah," Ryan answered. "I mean, he just told me about your mom and your swimming career."

"What swimming career?" she hissed. "Sorry," she said quickly. "It hasn't been easy. I mean, it's not like I had a back-up plan." She laughed mockingly at her own words and contrition stabbed Ryan. "But what do you care," she finished.

What did he care? That was a good question. All he knew was that she needed to be okay. "I'm sorry this happened to you, Sophie," Ryan said. "It's not fair."

"What does it matter," she whispered, "whether it's fair or not?"

Ryan turned away, his eyes rolling over the sand and into the foamy surf. "It doesn't," he said.

She stumbled, and reflexively, he moved to catch her as she fell towards him. His left hand went low, and through the fabric of her sweatpants, Ryan could feel the soft underside of her left thigh, where her knee should have been. With his right hand, he caught her shoulder. Her body tensed at his touch. He could feel her suppress a grunt from the pain. They both froze, caught in an awkward embrace.

He helped her upright and she slid down into the wheelchair beside her. She looked forward, refusing to meet his eyes.

"I'm so sorry," Ryan said. "I didn't mean to—"

"It's fine," Sophie said, cutting him off. She was shaking.

Ryan turned away, searching for something, anything to do.

Mercifully, Ted opened the door and announced dinner was ready with a smile.

Darkness having fallen, bringing with it cooler air, Ted suggested they eat outside. Along with three lounge chairs, a circular glass table furnished the back deck, accompanied by three white wicker chairs with blue cushions. Ted lit a few tiki torches that lined the railing, giving the scene an uncomfortably romantic feel.

When Ted offered to help Sophie into her chair, she said, "I got it, Dad." Ted seemed to be walking on eggshells in her presence, his gestures obsequious.

When Sophie sat down Ryan couldn't help but look at the

empty leg of her sweatpants. It looked like the hay had been removed from a scarecrow's leg. She caught his eye and scooted herself in further, hiding her legs under the table.

Thankfully, Ted offered Ryan a beer.

Before diving into the meal, Ted surprised him by giving a short speech. "I just want to officially welcome you to our humble home, Ryan, and thank you for being here," he said. "It means a lot to both of us." Ryan raised his drink in thanks. What about the Palmer's? Or the doctors? Where were they? He felt the older man was giving him too much credit, but he kept his mouth shut. It would all be over soon.

The beer was awful, but the food was delicious, and Ryan helped himself to more than one serving. Sophie and Ted watched him scarf down the lasagna as if he hadn't eaten in days.

"Eat much?" Ted joked.

Ryan stopped chewing. "No," he answered with a straight face. After a moment, Ryan said, "Everything's delicious, by the way," belatedly finding his manners.

"Thanks," Ted said. "Sophie usually cooks, but—"

"But I can't walk," Sophie finished for him. Ted sighed and Ryan settled in for another awkward silence. The sound of waves crashing filled the air for a few minutes.

"So," Ted finally said. "Ryan, what's your story? I know you're from Maine?"

Sophie kept her eyes low and Ryan set down his fork as he carefully formed an answer in his head before speaking. "Yes," he said.

Ted waited for him to elaborate. When it was clear Ryan had no intention of doing so, Ted said, "I hear it's beautiful up there."

"Sometimes."

If Ted had assumed a lively conversation would accompany the meal, he should have invited someone else. "How about school?" he tried. "You can't be much older than Sophie."

"I graduated two years ago with a finance degree," Ryan answered. It was a little more detailed of an answer than he usually preferred.

"No kidding?" Ted said, a little too enthusiastically. It wasn't that interesting. "Play any sports?"

"I played soccer for three years," Ryan responded. Sophie lifted her head and gave Ryan a measured look, as if deciding whether to believe him.

"What division?" she asked.

"Division 1," Ryan answered.

"No kidding?" Ted said again.

Ryan nodded.

"So, what are you doing here?" Sophie asked. Her challenging tone was unmistakable.

"What do you mean?" said Ryan.

"Well, you have a finance degree, you are, or were, clearly an accomplished athlete. What brought you here?"

Hadn't he already lied to her about this when they first met? He tried to remember what he had said. "Like I said," he answered, somehow remembering. "Just passing through."

"On your way to South America?" she said sarcastically.

"Sophie," Ted said, embarrassed.

Ryan was unfazed by her tone. "I don't know where I'll head next."

"Must be nice," Sophie said.

"What's that?"

"Picking up whenever you want. No responsibilities."

"Sophie, please," Ted snapped.

Ryan caught Sophie's eye. "I wouldn't recommend it," he said.

Ted attempted to keep the conversation afloat, but the ship was irreparable, and the tone had been set. And Ryan realized something he had overlooked; Sophie didn't want to be there any more than he did, and she certainly had no interest in thanking him face to face as Ted had led him to believe. What did the man hope to accomplish?

While Sophie brooded, and Ted searched for something to say, Ryan asked if he could have another beer. "Help yourself," Ted answered. "There should be a couple more in the fridge."

As Ryan opened the sliding glass door to rejoin Ted and Sophie, he heard Sophie say, "Absolutely not," then the conversation ended abruptly as Ryan took his seat. A few minutes later, Sophie announced she was tired and wanted to go to bed. Ryan watched as Ted looked on helplessly while Sophie struggled out of her chair and slid into the wheelchair. It was obvious Ted wanted nothing more than to help, and Ryan felt the urge as well, but he knew by now how Sophie would react. She stopped before passing Ryan, half of her face cast in the orange glow of a nearby torch. "Thanks for coming," she said. She didn't meet his eye. He followed her dejected form as she opened the door and rolled inside, disappearing behind the glare against the glass.

It couldn't have been any later than nine-thirty when Ted walked Ryan out to the front porch. Ted settled heavily into a rocking chair. Ryan lit a much-needed cigarette, leaned against the railing, and exhaled into the still night. A floodlight overhead spread out across the pavement and fell upon a small tree in the center of the circular driveway. Ryan recalled a framed sketch he'd glanced at in the hallway leading to the living room. It had been labeled the *Tree of Life*. He wondered if it was the same tree.

"I'm sorry about Sophie," Ted said from over Ryan's shoulder. Ryan turned around. Ted was rubbing his eyes, his hands sliding down his cheeks before falling by the side.

"Don't worry about it," Ryan answered. "I understand," he added. Then he said, "You could have told me about her leg, though."

Ted sighed. "I know, and I am sorry about that. I just didn't want to scare you off."

Ryan understood.

"So, where to next?" Ted asked.

"Why does everyone keep asking me that?" Ryan said. He made an instinctual move toward the steps.

"Well, if you answered honestly, we might stop," Ted said as he rose from the rocker and joined Ryan.

"Nowhere," answered Ryan. "That's where I'm going."

Ted's voice adopted a more serious tone. "Look, I don't know what you're running from, and I don't know what happened. That's your business and I understand your reluctance to share it. But if there's anything, anything at all that I can do, ever, please don't hesitate."

"I appreciate it, Ted," Ryan said. He extended his hand. Ted took it warmly, then pulled Ryan into his powerful frame, hugging him hard.

"Take care of yourself," Ted implored. He released Ryan and held him at arm's length, staring deep into his dark eyes.

Ryan nodded. He pulled away from Ted's grip and walked

down the steps toward his Jeep, which blended in with the darkness like a black cat. "Try not to break down on any dark roads," Ted called behind him.

Ryan lifted a hand and waved. "I'll know who to call."

Sophie lay with her back propped up against the wicker headboard of her bed. To Sophie, a bedroom had always been simply a place to sleep, to recharge. Nothing more. She had never paid much attention to decor; a simple white dresser, the same twin-sized bed she had been sleeping in for years, and two nightstands on either side were all she needed. Now, as she scanned the shadowed blue walls and white trimmed curtained windows, she realized she was going to be spending more time than ever in this bed.

To her, the walls were now a dull white under cold fluorescent light. The bed was narrow, and the windows barred. At least her prison had a view.

She pulled back the thin sheet covering her lower body and stared blankly at the empty space beside her right calf. Where skin, muscle, and bone should have been, only white fabric lay, tousled and wrinkled like her hair. And yet, it hurt. She could *feel* her leg there, and swear she was moving her toes; swear the muscle in her calf was flexing. The doctor called it phantom pain and assured her it was completely normal. It was a sick joke is what it was. Her hand slid down along the tan compression sock—used to prevent swelling—that was secured tightly to her stump. The doctors called it the "residual limb." She closed her fingers around the end of the residual limb and closed her eyes, begging to wake up.

Her father's soft knock at the door startled her, and Sophie threw the sheet back over her legs. "Yeah?" she said.

The door squeaked as it opened. He sat down on the edge of the bed and looked through the open door into the living room. His slow breathing drove her crazy.

"I know this is hard for you, Sophie," he said. "But I wish you would have been a little more appreciative towards Ryan tonight."

Sophie stared straight ahead. "I told you I didn't want to see him. I begged you not to bring him here."

"Sophie, he saved your life. Why can't you—"

"No," Sophie cut in. "The doctors saved my life. He's a drunk who happened to pass out in the right place for once. Or wrong place, depending on how you look at it." She met his eye. "And I don't know what you two talked about when I left, but he is not staying here."

He looked at Sophie like she was a stranger, like he was trying to remember where he'd seen her before. "Soph, can you hear yourself?" he pleaded. "Where's the girl who never judged, and looked for the best in people?"

She turned away.

He stood up, and Sophie watched with envy as her father walked to the door. Turning back, he said, "I think there's more to him than that. And if you gave him a chance, you'd see it too."

"Well, we'll never know, will we?" she said. "Can you close the door? I'm tired." She slid down the headboard and pulled the blanket up to her chest. She could hear his heart break with the creak of the door as it closed.

7

"Another one?" the bartender asked.

"Yeah, thanks," Ryan answered. He pushed his empty glass forward.

Ryan didn't want to be back at Finn's. He would have been more than happy to crawl back into his little cave at the motel, satisfied with a full stomach and weakening headache. But how was he supposed to know that liquor stores were closed on Sundays? He didn't even know it was Sunday.

Unlike last week, this time he was met by a standing room only crowd and the ear-drum-destroying sound of a four-piece band playing outside to a group of overly excited twenty-somethings.

But that was a couple hours ago, and now that he was a few sips into his seventh course, the cacophonous noise of the crowd sounded more like distant waves breaking against a forgiving beach, the ambient energy dispelled. But something wouldn't let him be. No matter how hard he tried or how many drinks he ordered, Ryan couldn't stop thinking about Sophie and Ted. Relief, guilt, and apprehension mixed inside him like a potent cocktail. As badly as he felt the need to get back on the road, he couldn't help feeling like he was leaving a job halfway through the first day.

But what could he possibly have to offer? How could he do anything except worsen the situation? The dying light in Sophie's eyes and the pain behind Ted's had awoken something in him, though, something that had been in dreamless hibernation for so long, he'd forgotten it was there. He didn't even know what to call it, but he felt it, like a soft tap on the shoulder. But when he turned to search for the source, it was gone, lost in an overflowing crowd. He thought about Ted's workshop, how the setting sun clung to that rocking chair like glue, and how the clouds passed by overhead through the skylights like curious birds.

He finished his drink and pushed the empty glass forward, longing for the mindless mixture to run its course. Ted's workshop was too pure, too warm, and the scent had followed him around like an annoying fly. Finn's, conversely, like any other watering hole, was already contaminated and welcomed Ryan like an old friend. The assortment of spilled liquor and beer along the bar mats hung heavy in the air. The smoke from a faraway cigarette weaved through the crowd and snuck up his nose. This is where he belonged.

"Hey, can I get ten lemon drops?" a young girl said through slurred speech as she squeezed in between Ryan and an empty stool. Ryan glanced at her and she caught his eye, narrowing hers invitingly. She couldn't have been any older than twenty-one, if that. She wore a low-cut tank top and cut-off jean shorts that frayed high on her thighs. The bartender drenched a shaker full of ice with cheap vodka. "Want to buy me a shot?" the girl said to Ryan.

Ryan looked at the row of shot glasses lined along the bar. "Looks like you're all set," he said.

"I don't even like vodka?" she said in a tone that suggested it was a question. "Jager's my drink?" She leaned closer to him and batted her eyelashes, a move that might have worked had it not looked more like a bug had flown into her eyes. "So, what do you say?" she persisted.

"Maybe next time," Ryan answered. He knew trouble when he saw it.

"What the hell is this?" an angry voice said. Ryan turned his head slightly to see a young man, presumably the girl's boyfriend, emerge from the crowd. He was short and stocky, and a pink t-shirt stuck to his chest and arms like paint. He looked pissed. "We have one little argument and you're already trying to pick up the first douche bag you see?" he said.

"Jesus, Ray. We were just talking?" She was really the only one talking.

Ryan watched the exchange, entertained for the moment.

"You better back off, bro," Ray said to Ryan. He pushed his chest out, letting everyone in the bar know just how serious he was.

Ryan tried to measure the younger man as he considered how to respond. He had seen both of these people many times in different forms. But the situation rarely changed, and he knew exactly what to say to either calm them down or rile them up. He decided on the latter. "Maybe you should keep a closer eye on your slutty girlfriend," he said. It's not that he was confident he could win the fight. Far from it. He just didn't care.

"What did you just say?" The boyfriend took a step toward Ryan.

"Well look who's still in town," croaked a raspy voice. Ryan turned to see the wrinkly face and bald head of Old Man strategically maneuvering its way between Ryan and the boyfriend.

"Hey, old man," Ray said. "Do you mind?"

"Take a hike, buddy," Old Man said over his shoulder. "I have some drinkin' to do with my friend here."

"Do you want these shots, or not?" the bartender called over the confrontation.

The girl reached for the tray of shots as if it were a gallon of water in a desert. The liquor spilled and splashed as she moved. Her boyfriend took her arm and said, "I better not see you again," pointing to Ryan as they disappeared into the crowd.

Ryan turned his attention to Old Man, the memory of the young couple already fading in his mind like a brief introduction.

"I had a feeling you'd still be hanging around this sleepy town," Old Man said, resting his elbows on the bar.

"Not for long," Ryan said. "Thanks for stepping in."

"As badass as that shiner looked on you last week, I figured your face could use a rest," Old Man said. "Tommy," he called to the bartender. "Two shots of Tanqueray." He turned back to Ryan.

"Tanqueray?" Ryan asked incredulously.

"Why not?" Old Man responded, confused.

"I don't think I've ever actually had a shot of gin," Ryan answered.

"You don't know what you're missing." Ryan doubted that. "So, I guess you made it home alright the other night," Old Man said.

Ryan frowned. "Yeah, why not?" he asked. The bartender set two small shot glasses filled to the brim on the bar.

"Well," Old Man said. "Last I saw, you were jumping the railing outside and heading north along the beach."

Ryan sensed Old Man's skepticism. "I made it home alright, thanks," he replied.

"Funny," Old Man continued, as if Ryan hadn't said anything. "I heard a local girl was attacked by a bull shark up that way the next morning. And supposedly a mystery man, or woman, I suppose, pulled her out of the water. Saved her life, but no one knows who he is. You know anything about that?"

"I heard about it, like everyone else. Pretty wild."

Old Man lowered his gaze, as if peering over a pair of spectacles, allowing Ryan time to amend his statement. But after a moment, Old Man relented and said, "Rumor had it she was planning on leaving town, off to try out for the Olympic swim team. Like I said, Quicksand Beach doesn't let go so easily."

Before Ryan could catch himself, he said, "It was a shark attack, not quicksand. And it ruined her life."

Old Man smiled. "Maybe," he said, unperturbed by Ryan's challenging tone. "Or maybe it saved it," he offered. Ryan resisted the urge to take the bait, instead taking his frustration out on the half-empty glass of whiskey in front of him. The shots of gin remained unnoticed. "Anyway," Old Man went on. "Have you decided to stay for a while? Or are you still planning on taking off?"

Ryan ran a hand through his hair. "I'm outta here first thing in the morning. Even if I have to wade through your quicksand."

"Well," Old Man said, reaching for the untouched shot glasses. He held one out to Ryan and Ryan reluctantly accepted. "Here's to the next step in your journey." He raised the tiny glass. Ryan lifted his a few inches off the bar in salute and threw down the shot.

8

He awoke to a spider web of intense light weaving its way across his half-open eyelids. It wasn't like him to leave the curtain open. Rolling over to his side, Ryan turned his back on the new day, unwilling to even consider getting up yet.

His nose kissed a fabric that felt like silk. It tickled a little. He had almost fallen back to sleep when the realization struck that no such fabric inhabited his small motel room. Cautiously, he opened his eyes. Centimeters from his face was the beige-colored backrest of a couch. Ignoring the pounding chorus in his head, Ryan rolled over, lifting his hand, and shading his fragile eyes from the sun. A fan overhead, suspended from a triangularly vaulted ceiling spun round and round like spokes on a wheel, adding to his nausea.

He swung his legs over the side of the couch, his bare feet landing safely on the warm rug. He leaned forward and crushed his head into his palms.

No further exploration was needed; he knew where he was. The bluestone fireplace looked down on him with contempt, as if insulted by Ryan's intrusion. The massive windows on either side felt no contrition over the unnecessary amount of light they allowed to assault him without mercy. Even the couch seemed to rustle beneath his jeans in annoyance.

He was so astonished, so shockingly bewildered that he actually felt calm, as if he were over it already, resigned to his fate. It was so irresponsible and so embarrassing that, out of necessity, he couldn't afford to care.

At least after the morning he saved Sophie, he had experienced dreamlike flashes of dark sand and rough waves, brief slideshows of the previous night's events. At the moment, he couldn't remember a thing, as if hours had been deleted from his memory, the backspace button having been held down for too long. The last thing he remembered was taking that shot of Tanqueray with the old man. He nearly vomited right there on the rug at the thought. Was Old Man right? Was there some invisible force that wouldn't allow him to leave this place? How else could he explain the outrageous coincidences that seemed to be attached to him like a leech?

Angry voices vibrated through the glass, and Ryan shifted his position to find their source. Sophie and Ted were talking on the back deck, both forms lit by a sunrise that hadn't climbed very far up the sky yet. He couldn't make out what they were saying, but Sophie was throwing her arms around in the air recklessly from her wheelchair while Ted leaned over the railing, shaking his head. Ryan's stomach plummeted as the gravity of the situation took hold. His insouciant demeanor gave way to fear.

Creating as little noise as possible, Ryan lifted himself up and tip-toed around the couch, creeping toward the dark hallway that he remembered led into the small foyer. He peeked over his shoulder periodically to check that the coast was still clear.

When he emerged out of the hallway, he crept to the door and turned the knob slowly, as if he were twisting the dial of a safe he was trying to crack.

Palpable humidity and oven-like heat met Ryan like a slap across the face as he stepped onto the front porch. A trickle of sweat ran down his cheek and across his jaw and hung on for dear life to the edge of his chin before falling with an audible splash onto the white floorboards. As uncomfortable as the morning's heat was, it paled in comparison to the crushing view.

His Jeep was nowhere to be found, and suddenly Ryan felt heavy, as if the heat were physically pushing his shoulders down. He thought about walking, but he could hardly stand. And his car could be in the ocean for all he knew. So, with every option his suspect intellect was capable of concocting exhausted, Ryan took a seat in a nearby rocking chair and fumbled in his pockets for the only consolation he could manage. He lit the cigarette, blew out a thick cloud, and waited.

He didn't have to wait long, and after a couple drags, Ted exploded through the front door, his eyes searching the driveway and beyond frantically before falling upon Ryan's lounging form. Ted sighed, as if relieved. He fell into the chair to Ryan's right.

"Morning," said Ted, as if it were just another day. "Thought you might have made a run for it."

"It crossed my mind," Ryan answered, bewildered by Ted's bright tone.

"Oh, hold on," said Ted. He jumped up and disappeared back into the house. A moment later, he returned with two coffee mugs in either hand. "Sorry, didn't know how you liked it, so it's black," Ted said as he returned to his chair. He placed Ryan's mug on the small wicker table between them.

Ryan didn't know what to say. He felt like a Neanderthal as he picked up the mug in confusion and sipped. His eyes squinted in Ted's direction, deciding if this was all some kind of game the older man was playing. The coffee was like a glass of water to him after two days in an endless desert. He nearly forgot where he was.

Ted reminded him. "So, I guess you're wondering what you're doing here?" he asked. He put down his mug and crossed his legs.

"Look, before you say anything," Ryan opened. "I just want to apologize in advance for what I might have done. Whatever that may be." He paused. "It was a long night. I think."

"Do you remember anything?" Ted asked.

Ryan took another sip of coffee while he considered how to respond. "Honestly," he said. "No. The last thing I remember is taking shots of gin with some old man. Then nothing. So again, I apologize for any inconvenience I might have caused." He felt like he was apologizing to the court for a public drunkenness charge.

"An old man?" Ted asked. "At Finn's?" Ryan nodded. Sophie's father was mysteriously pensive for a moment. "Was he bald, with a goatee? And was he an old man or was his name, Old Man?"

"His name was Old Man," Ryan answered. "You know him?"

"Ryan," he said gravely. "Old Man died ten years ago. He's kind of a local legend."

Ryan's face sunk and he went cold, despite the heat. He stared straight ahead, unable to move or think.

A chuckle came from Ted's direction. He turned to see Ted desperately trying to smother a laugh. Then all at once, it exploded, the convulsions rocking Ted's chair back and forth. "I'm sorry," Ted said through quickened breaths. "I couldn't resist."

Ryan stared, horrified. "Are you kidding me?" he said.

"Old Man is alive and well. He's just a crazy drunk," Ted said, trying to calm himself down. "You should have seen your face."

"That's not funny," Ryan said, refusing to see the humor. "You scared the hell out of me. I actually thought I'd had an entire conversation with a ghost for a second." He let out an exaggerated breath.

Ted calmed himself enough to formulate an uninterrupted response. "Sorry, but I thought it would be a good idea to soften the mood," Ted explained. He took a sip of coffee. "You don't have to apologize for anything. Nothing happened. Well, something happened, but nothing you need to apologize to me and Sophie for."

"Really?"

"Really," Ted confirmed, a smile still plastered across his face.

Ryan relaxed a little. "So, how did I get here?"

Ted lifted his mug, tipped it to his lips, and placed it back on the table. A pale brown ring had formed on the coaster under the mug. "You remember the brother-in-law I told you about?" Ted said. "Who knows that you saved Sophie?"

"Sure," Ryan lied.

"Well, I probably forgot to mention that he's the local sheriff in town," he said. Ted watched Ryan's reaction like a professor as the information settled in. Ryan gave little away. He was surprised, sure, but he was too busy racking at his mind in frustration, desperately begging it to give him something, anything to work with. "He stopped you just before you reached the bridge that leads out of town," Ted went on.

"I was driving?" Ryan asked, a little more astonished than he felt.

"Yeah," Ted said. "And you're lucky Kevin stopped you. Had

it been anyone else, you would definitely be in a jail cell right now."

Ryan glanced around the porch. He enjoyed another sip of coffee. He imagined how he would have felt waking up in that scenario as opposed to the one he presently found himself in. Suddenly the heat didn't feel so oppressive, the headache so painful, or the company so intimidating.

Ryan cocked his head to the side. "I'm grateful, for sure," he said. "But I still don't understand why I'm here."

"When Kevin realized who you were, he called me," Ted clarified. "You were basically incoherent, and he asked me what I thought he should do. I told him to bring you here," he explained. Ted shrugged as he finished, as if that decision was standard protocol.

Ryan's head remained cocked. "Why?"

"Why what?"

"Why would you tell him to bring me here? Why not tell him to take me back to the motel?"

Ted sighed and trained his eyes on the floorboards. "Look, Ryan," he said. "I've never been one to give much credence to coincidence. Things just happen, nothing we can do about it. At least, that's what I've always thought. But, admittedly, I had trouble sleeping last night because that line of thought has been, well, not so straight since I met you." Ted stopped, and Ryan tried to imagine where he could be going with this. Ted continued, "I guess what I'm saying is, I don't think it's a coincidence that you're here, that you saved Sophie, and that I came across you that night on the side of the road. And I think there may be a connection to all of this that I can't see yet."

Ryan swallowed Ted's speech and chased it down with a long

sip of coffee. He had considered this himself. But it didn't mean there was anything to it. "So," Ryan said. "You brought me here because you don't believe in coincidences anymore?"

Ted smiled. "No. I had Kevin bring you here because I want to offer you a job. And a place to stay for a while. Until you have a better idea where you're going."

"I'm sorry?" Ryan managed.

"I was hoping you would consider staying here with me and Sophie for a while," Ted reiterated. "I could use some help in the shop."

"Building furniture?" Ryan asked, stalling.

Ted nodded. "It might not seem like the most exciting job in the world, but you'd be surprised. You might even enjoy it. Who knows?"

Ryan stared at the floor as he considered. "I can't imagine Sophie would be on board with the idea," he said.

Ted's mood sunk at the mention of his daughter, allowing Ryan a good idea of what the two were arguing about on the back deck. "Sophie isn't capable of seeing through her grief right now," Ted said. "But in time, I'm sure she'll come around."

Ryan stood up, nearly fainted, and walked to the railing for support. "I appreciate the offer, Ted," he said. "But I'm not sure if it's a good idea."

He heard Ted's footfall creep up beside him. "What do you have to lose?" Ted asked. "You said yourself you didn't have any plans or an idea of where to go." Maybe that's why Ted kept asking him. "So, what's the harm in hanging around here for a couple weeks while you figure out a more concrete plan?"

"A couple weeks?" Ryan asked. For some reason associating a

number with the idea made him feel a little better about it, as if there were an expiration date.

"Or however long you want to stay," Ted mediated.

"You don't even know me."

"You saved my daughter's life. What more do I need to know?"

"I'd be more trouble than I'm worth. And you obviously have your hands full already."

"You have no idea what you're worth. And let me be the judge of how full my hands are."

Ryan paused, searching for another excuse he couldn't find. Ted seemed poised, determined. Ryan felt tired and defeated. He looked down at the pavement. He visualized the oval-shaped driveway straightening out before him like a snake stretching after a long winter. It cut through the green forest and leapt over the bay. He didn't know where that road led, and yet he knew exactly where it led. And for the first time in two years, he didn't want to follow it. Maybe it was exhaustion or dehydration. Or maybe that road wasn't there anymore. Maybe he'd come as far as he was meant to come, and no matter how hard he tried to imagine otherwise, that driveway led right back to where he stood.

He turned to Ted and said, "I don't know a damn thing about making furniture."

Ted straightened up, clasped his hands together, and smiled. "Well, we'd better get started then."

Part Two

9

The midday sun poured through the skylights as Ryan pushed the sanding block forward and backward over a fresh piece of oak. His body swayed over the wood, the motion rhythmic. Steady. His shirt was soaked through with sweat, and he was forced to pause every few strokes to wipe his brow. Every gust of wind that blew into the shop was like a splash of cold water on his face. A stray strand of hair untucked itself from his ear and dangled in his peripherals as he moved. Dust swirled around his face, forcing him to measure his breaths carefully.

After a few more inspired passes, he stopped. He ran his calloused fingers along the smoothened wood, decided it was as ready as it would ever be, and placed the curved piece beside the other three of identical length and width.

He walked outside, lifting his shirt so the breeze could kiss his bare stomach. A narrow patio overlooked the ocean, furnished with two unfinished chairs, and covered by a shallow awning. A log still wrapped in bark was squeezed between the chairs. Ryan took a seat and leaned forward. Ted and Sophie wouldn't be home for another half hour or so.

He leaned back and crossed his legs, grateful for the shade the awning provided. It had been six weeks since he started working with Ted, and as he closed his eyes and let out a deep breath, he allowed himself to reflect on his time there.

The fact that there were only two bedrooms in the house was a concern. To Ryan's relief, though, Ted informed him on the first day that a small loft had been built above the garage a couple years back. Ted pointed out the advantages with a realtor's optimism. It was bright, cozy, and private he'd said.

The only entrance to the loft was a staircase that climbed up the side of the garage. A white door opened to a narrow space with white carpet. A single twin mattress was shoved against the wall. No frame or box spring. There was room for a small nightstand on either side of the bed, but nothing more. A wooden railing looked down onto the carless garage floor below. A large circular window faced the ocean, the only portal to the outside world.

Ted had originally intended the space to be used as a guest room of sorts, but he'd given up the project after Sophie's mother died. The room was bare and excruciatingly hot at all times. It was still more than Ryan needed.

Ted insisted right away that he wasn't Ryan's boss, and that Ryan should approach it as more of a partnership.

"Woodworking is a deeply personal experience," Ted would say. "You need to find your own way and your own style. And I can help you get there. But ultimately, you're the only one who can figure it out." That was all well and good, but Ryan required some kind of fundamental instruction. And although Ryan was good with numbers, and the fractional math required for measurements was as easy as breathing, he struggled to comprehend Ted's aphoristic way of delivering a lesson, and the man's metaphors tended to bounce off the walls like tennis balls, lacking any concrete direction.

"Building furniture is a lot like life," Ted said one day. "It takes patience, and focus. You can't rush it, you know? Let it come to you. Like a soccer game, right?" What? "Or," he'd persist, "it's a lot like love. Every piece might not fit together perfectly at first. You might miscalculate something. But when it all comes together, it can last forever." He was trying so hard.

Ted had an unorthodox approach to Ryan's drinking habits as well. When Ted sensed Ryan had been drinking—and he *always* knew—he would simply tell Ryan to take the rest of the day off. He was so casual about it, and Ryan didn't know whether to quit, or thank him.

Early on, Ryan took a lot of days off. His progress was slow.

Sleepless nights continued to inhabit his life as well. His time at Ted and Sophie's house was failing to offer him the peace he was searching for. And every night, he would lie awake, considering how best to leave.

Then two things happened, two things that would change everything.

About a week after moving into the loft above the garage, while Ted and Ryan worked quietly on an overcast day, Ted said abruptly, "Hey, I've been trying to figure out the best way to say this." Ryan stopped what he was doing and looked up. "Kevin insisted he look into your background, just to make sure you weren't wanted for murder or anything."

"Sure," Ryan said. A tempest gathered inside him.

"Of course, nothing came up," he said. "Your record's cleaner than mine. Not even a speeding ticket. But he did come across some old articles." Ted paused to gauge Ryan's reaction. When Ryan didn't respond, Ted said, "Ryan, I'm so sorry. No one should have to go through something like that. If there's—"

"Have you told Sophie?" Ryan interrupted, his face a mask of indifference.

"No. It's not my place. I know that. I just wanted to let you know I'm here, you know, if you ever want to talk."

"Thanks, Ted," Ryan said, and that was the end of the conversation.

Later that night, while he considered how early he should take off in the morning, a loud crash came from the workshop. Ryan crept to the back of the shop and peeked his head around the opening. What he saw arrested him. Ted was on his knees, crying. A single naked bulb hung over the older man's head, spotlighting his hunched form. Ryan watched, unable to turn away as Ted looked up at a photograph on the wall, tears pouring down his cheeks and along his neck. "I don't know what to do," he whispered. "I'm not as strong as you." He crushed his palms to his face and wept as his wife's face smiled down on him.

Something changed in Ryan that night. He knew Ted was struggling to keep it together every day. He knew the man felt like his family was falling apart. And Ryan also knew that he was right, that slowly but surely, Sophie was moving beyond anyone's reach. But until he had witnessed what it was doing to Ted, he had chosen to ignore it. He couldn't anymore, and lying awake that night in bed, Ryan decided he was going to start working for his stay.

He started in the library.

It was a small room, easily the smallest in the house. Two antique armchairs upholstered in cardinal red flanked a short, square coffee table. All four walls were smothered in floor-to-ceiling bookshelves, and other than the arched entrance, the only portal to the outside world was a lonely window on the west wall, squeezed tightly between the crowded shelves on either side.

As he scanned the spines, though, Ryan amended his initial assessment of the room's size. Sophie's mother collected indiscriminately: Jules Verne, Anne Rice, Edgar Allen Poe, Dickens, Dumas, Austen, along with countless volumes on furniture making and various histories of the craft. It became apparent that, although his eyes begged to differ, there were no walls restricting that room. Only doors. Every spine was another hallway, and every page another portal. The seemingly narrow space stretched out infinitely in all directions. He could only imagine the places Sophie's mother had traveled to in those armchairs.

He began his education with a large volume claiming to contain everything he needed to know about the fundamentals of furniture making. And with a determined sense of inspiration, he dove in headfirst. Instead of whiskey with his morning coffee, Ryan complimented the caffeine with textbooks and history volumes. During Ted and Sophie's absences, which hovered around two hours a day, when Ryan would normally substitute work for cocktails and cigarettes, he instead poured over a History of French Furniture while practicing carving techniques on discarded slivers of wood. Where his nights had previously been filled to the brim with heavy drinking in his gloomily lit loft, they were now accompanied by small letters on large, heavy pages, companions that proved to be just as entertaining, and much less destructive.

As the days turned like pages and a language previously foreign to him began to take form, Ted's obscure comparisons started to make sense. Understanding dawned on Ryan like a controlled sunrise climbing the sky at a pace he could follow with ease. He was by no means a prodigy, but he could comfortably call himself a beginner, a term that suggested he was going somewhere. Moving forward.

More unexpected than his unforeseen comprehension of the finer points of woodworking was the relationship he felt he was forming with Ted's wife. It was strange, and terrifying at first, but the more he read and the more time he spent in the library, the more he felt he knew her. He appreciated her love of furniture, her love of books, and her passion for all things beautiful. Those passions and those loves were not his, though, and Ryan would never see the world in the magnificent light that she was able to. He didn't envy her for it, but rather respected her.

His nights continued to be invaded with nightmares that showed no signs of abating, but some days, although rare, were filled with daydreams of a world he had previously turned a blind eye to. Those days he wasn't quite so alone.

On one of those days, about a month into Ryan's stay, while he was bent over a worktable littered with chisels, scrap wood and an opened book, he heard a knock at the door of the shop. The knob twisted, and a woman Ryan had never seen before entered the sun-drenched room. She could have been thirty-five or forty-five, or any age in between. She walked in and floated along the edges of the interior, scanning the walls, and smiling at the skylights, apparently oblivious to Ryan's presence. He watched her in silence for a few moments, too stunned to speak just yet.

Ted had told Ryan that while he and Sophie were gone, he was in charge and implored him to act as though the place was his. And Ryan had done a respectable job, until now. The woman commanded the room, and Ryan's attention, as if she owned both, as though she had come home early and was inspecting the work her employees had done.

But more impressive than her silky, dominating presence was her statuesque figure. Long, wavy auburn hair framed a sharp, porcelain face with friendly yet intimidating dark brown eyes. And she seemed tall, but Ryan assumed everyone else just felt small around her.

Her manner was befitting of someone who spent her entire life within walking distance of the ocean. An air of relaxation emanated from her like perfume, and a blinding ambient iridescence pulsed around her, rendering the sunlight irrelevant. A sea foam green cotton dress fell to the floor, skimming the sawdust-covered cement as she glided.

She spoke first. "Hello," she said in a voice as soft and light as a feather.

Ryan struggled to recover. "If you're looking for an interview," he said. "The girl doesn't live here." He had rehearsed and used that line many times over the first few weeks as reporters and journalists had swarmed the property daily. Fortunately, Ted and Sophie were usually gone, so it was up to Ryan to turn them away. Easier said than done, but as the weeks passed, their uninvited visits became less frequent. And although this woman looked nothing like a reporter, he couldn't think of anything else to say.

She smiled, her cheekbones rising with the corners of her mouth. "I'm not a reporter," she said. She stopped in front of the west window and pulled her hands behind her back, peering at Ryan curiously. "My name is Laura. I own the store that sells Ted's pieces." Then she added, "And yours, I guess." She smiled again.

"Oh, sorry about that," Ryan fumbled. "You really don't look anything like a reporter. But I," he paused, at a loss for words. "Sorry," he finished clumsily.

She smirked, making Ryan feel like he'd said something childish. "I understand," she said.

"I'm—"

"Ryan. I know," she cut in effortlessly. She floated to the edge of the table directly opposite Ryan and laid her slender hands over the rough surface. "I'm sorry it took so long for us to finally meet," she said. So was he. "Sophie's mom was my best friend. I want to thank you for what you did."

Her eyes were penetratingly kind, and Ryan didn't dare contradict her. "I wish people would stop thanking me," he said. "They give me too much credit."

"Maybe you don't give yourself enough," Laura said, raising an eyebrow. She pulled a slip of paper from out of thin air and placed it on the middle of the table, exactly halfway between her and Ryan. "It was nice meeting you, Ryan. Can you give this to Ted and tell him I dropped by?"

Ryan nodded, and like a rare bird, Laura flew out the door as gracefully as she'd glided in. He picked up the slip and turned it over. His brow furrowed when he saw the number on the check. He didn't know many hobbies that paid that well.

As the days mingled with weeks, Ryan's relationship with Ted began to border perilously close to friendship, and despite his hesitance, a comfortability in Ted's presence settled over him. They joked, laughed, made fun of one another, and, as Ted had promised, Ryan began to feel more like a partner every day. And Ted never brought up what he had learned about Ryan's past again, a simple gesture that meant more to him than Ted knew.

And though he had only met Laura once, and exchanged only a handful of words, he felt a seed planted there for a potential friendship. He even felt like he was forming a bond with Sophie's mother, with every word read, and page turned.

Ironically, it was his relationship with Sophie—the one person he felt he needed to befriend—that was stuck in neutral. If anything, it was picking up speed in reverse. Rarely did they speak, and if the need arose, never more than a "sorry" or "good morning" or "hey" was exchanged. Seldom did Ryan even see her. She was like a ghost, a shadow that disappeared around the corner before he could glimpse a full view. But he heard her all the time. At first, it was the wheelchair rolling along the deck. After that, it was the crutches thumping heavily up and down the stairs. Then it was a cane, to accompany the temporary prosthetic she had been fitted with about five weeks after the attack.

He often wondered, just by being there, if he was making the situation worse.

"I'm done, Dad. I'm not going back," Sophie's angry voice whipped around the corner, waking Ryan from his reverie. He hadn't heard the truck pull in.

A car door slammed.

"Sophie," said Ted. "They're just trying to help you come to terms with everything."

"No," she challenged. "They're trying to convince me my life doesn't have to change. That's bullshit and you know it. I'm not going back," she hissed. It was the bitter voice Ryan had come to know as Sophie's. The bright, excited melody he'd heard in the bar the first day they met was long gone, lost at sea somewhere with the fire and ambition which had emanated from her like a torch.

"You're not thinking straight. We can—"

"Don't patronize me. I'm thinking as clearly as ever."

"What about your stretches and exercises?" said Ted. You need to strengthen your leg."

"What leg, Dad? What leg!"

"Sophie," he began. But she was working her way up the steps, and an instant later, Ryan heard the front door slam.

Ryan walked back into the shop as Ted entered through the side door. At first, Ted failed to notice him, and Ryan had a moment to look the older man over. Ted seemed as though he had aged six years in six weeks. It was getting harder and harder for Ryan to watch, like an over-the-hill boxer who kept getting up when the crowd was begging him to stay down.

Ted moved to the table and ran his fingers along the wood Ryan had recently finished sanding. Acknowledging Ryan's presence for the first time, he said, "Looks like your table is coming along well. Maybe I should start reading those books of yours. You're gonna be better than me in no time."

"Come on," Ryan said. "We both know you can't read." Ted smirked, lowering his gaze. "Everything alright?" Ryan asked.

Ted sighed. "No," he answered, and after a painful pause, he continued, "She's refusing to go back to the support group meetings. Says they're a waste of time." He let out a dejected breath.

"She doesn't do her exercises. She sleeps all day. And you want to know the funny thing? She's still healing at an accelerated rate." He laughed sarcastically. "The doctor still says she could be fitted for a more permanent prosthetic within a couple weeks, even though she half-asses her physical therapy sessions. She says it doesn't matter whether she walks a little better in two weeks or two years, she'll still never run, or swim like before." He rubbed his eyes and shook his head. "And," he said, "on top of all that, now she's starting to hang out with those losers from the bar." Since being fitted with her temporary prosthetic, Ryan had noticed Sophie spending more time with the annoying bartender. "I'm losing her all over again," Ted finished.

They were quiet for a while, and Ted leaned over the table, studying a sketch he had done for an Adirondack chair. The sun illuminated every inch of the shop, but he was cast in shadow, as if an opaque umbrella hovered over his head.

"Hey," Ted said, straightening up. "Have I ever told you how making furniture is a lot like sex?"

Ryan smiled. "Yeah, many times."

"You have to take it slow. You know? Feel it out. All wood's different. Requires a unique touch. Sometimes it doesn't fit and—"

"I get it," Ryan laughed.

Ted's world was crumbling around him. Legs and arms didn't fit as smoothly into the joints he cut. Glue wasn't quite as strong as it used to be. And yet he still found time to make a joke. It couldn't be easy, and Ryan's veneration for Ted increased with every joke, as well as every sigh.

10

Later that evening, as daylight faded and the sharp shadows of the trees and houses lengthened to a point, Sophie stood on the back deck waiting for a call. She gripped the railing hard, partly for support and partly for a physical release. Nearly all her weight burdened the right side of her body, as if she were trying to push her foot through the floor.

Her gaze slumped to the pool a few feet below. The water was a mirror, calm and still. Motionless, like her. She followed the shadows along the boardwalk toward the sand. The last remaining beachgoers were packing up their things. In the distance, an explosion of cloud erupted above the horizon, smaller shreds of white surrounding it like debris.

The fact that she was losing her mind was not lost on Sophie. She knew she was going about this all wrong. She knew she should have been grateful to be alive. She knew it killed her dad to see her so weak, so fragile, and so resentful, all the things she had worked so hard not to be. She knew she should be diving headfirst into her recovery and fighting this calamity with every breath. But she was tired, tired of trying to be strong. What was the point? To what end?

The people at the support group said that, eventually, she would be able to live a life similar to the one that seemed a distant memory now. They didn't understand. Sure, they had suffered similar tragedies—worse in some cases—but they didn't understand her love for the water, her *need* for it. They didn't know what she saw every time she dove into the pre-dawn waves. It was like going back in time every morning, blissful memories swimming around and embracing her like a warm light, and with every stroke and every breath, she came one step closer to a future that promised a peace most people only dreamed of. Now, as she stared blankly ahead at the ocean, it looked cold.

Sophie thought about all those miracle stories she'd seen on TV, the inspirational one's that Hollywood sunk its greedy fangs into and drained dry. People making incredible recoveries out of impossible odds. What about the people who didn't come out of it stronger? What about the people who just wasted away in despair? What about people like her? Stories like hers wouldn't attract too many viewers, she assumed.

Out of the corner of her eye, she caught Ryan exiting the workshop. He lit yet another cigarette—probably his eighteenth of the day already—and stretched his arms wide as if preparing for an embrace. He looked like a caveman, with his long hair and lengthening beard. Her father was convinced there was something more to him, something Sophie couldn't see. But what her father failed to see was the constant reminder that Ryan was, just as blatant as the scarred stump she now called her left leg. Why was he still there?

Her phone vibrated in her pocket. "Hey, I'm here," Lindsay's high voice said on the other line.

"Okay. Coming," Sophie replied. Ever since Sophie had upgraded to a temporary prosthetic that allowed her to limp around with a cane, she'd decided to take Lindsay up on those invites she had ignored for so long. It wasn't like Sophie had anything better to do, and the alcohol had a way of numbing her mind to the point of blissful unconsciousness. The lifestyle drastically slowed her recovery, potentially severely damaging it, but it helped the nights race by and allowed her to sleep the days away as if they'd never happened. It was a coward's way out, she knew. She was well aware of how pathetic she had become. Maybe she had been a coward the whole time. Maybe this is who she really was. Maybe she didn't care anymore.

"What the hell?" said Ted.

Ryan looked up, temporarily losing focus. The razor-sharp teeth of his saw narrowly missed his index finger before plummeting into the tabletop. Ted ran to the window, paused, then stormed out of the side door. Confused, Ryan stepped to the window. Ted was waving his arms frantically as the annoying bartender's smart cart zipped around the driveway and out onto Coastal Highway. Exasperated, Ted dropped his hands and lowered his head as his daughter disappeared around the corner.

"Do you want me to go back?" Lindsay asked.

"No, keep driving," Sophie replied indifferently, any remaining guilt flying out the open window like a piece of loose trash.

She tried to settle into Lindsay's suffocating ride. She wasn't the type to get claustrophobic, but this was pushing it. Lindsay insisted the car was cozy and had character, not to mention energy efficient. Sophie didn't care if it ran on laughter, the lack of legroom was enough to make her want to yank the steering wheel into oncoming traffic.

"Thanks for dressing up," Lindsay said. She scanned Sophie head to toe, patiently, as if she weren't driving sixty miles an hour.

Sophie didn't respond. She looked down at the navy-blue tank top and gray sweatpants that nearly covered the tennis shoes she wore. The shoe on her prosthetic foot was angled in slightly, making it look as though she were pigeon-toed. She shrugged. Who was she trying to impress? Her hair was pulled back in a messy bun and her face was make-up-less. Really not much different than how she had always dressed.

Lindsay, however, dressed as though her future ex-husband might be right around the next corner, her blonde hair straightened to the breaking point and enough make-up for two hiding her face. "You never know who's gonna be there," she would say before anyone had a chance to judge.

Except, Sophie did know who was going to be there; the same people who were there every night.

Lindsay yanked the wheel and turned into the dense forest of pine trees. The pine needles created a barrier against the setting sun, scarce threads of yellow and orange flickering through like strobe lights. Houses along either side of the road sat back and blended into the trees. At the end of the avenue, backing up to the bay was a narrow two-story house. A colorful assortment of cars overflowed the driveway and spilled out onto the road, forcing what little traffic there was to slow to a crawl.

Lindsay managed to weave the little go-cart through the crowd and brought it to a screeching halt a few feet from the house. Sophie limped toward the porch using her cane. With every step, her prosthetic struggled to catch up while her right leg waited impatiently. Every step was a chore. And although the doctor assured her the permanent prosthetic would be less bulky, the temporary one she donned now felt like a cinder block was attached to her thigh, her muscles aching in ways they never had before.

Lindsay bounded up the steps while Sophie clung to the wobbly railing and inched her way up, taking one calculated step at a time. Her prosthetic had to swing to the side to clear each step.

When they entered through the front door, they were greeted with cheers, as well as a wall of smoke that stung Sophie's eyes, like too much chlorine in a pool.

Lindsay knew the excitement was geared toward Sophie, but that didn't stop her from taking the lead, and a quick bow, as if she were strutting down her own private red carpet. Sophie knew the already drunk crowd couldn't have cared less about her. They wanted to hang out with the girl who got attacked by a shark.

"That's wild," one would say.

"My absolute worst nightmare," another would offer.

Sophie was fascinating to the crowd. "What did it feel like?" they would ask. She never answered, but that didn't stop them from pressing.

Through the smoke, Sophie observed an intense game of beer pong being played while spectators crowded the table like bees to honey. On the other side of the room, a girl was unhooking her bra while the rest of the table looked on, eyes wide and glazed over during a game of strip poker. Drool cascaded from the lucky men at the table's mouths. Fortunately, the overcast ambience of the room obscured Sophie's view. Tucked away in the corner, oblivious to the show they were missing, were two young men sunken into a cigarette-stained couch, controllers molded into their hands while armored soldiers killed each other on a massive flat-screen TV. A two-foot bong rested on the coffee table within arm's reach.

It was like watching three separate movies at the same time, all of which she had a confident idea of the ending.

A shadow moved toward Sophie through the smoke, materializing in front of her like an apparition.

"Hey, Soph," a tall young man with long, curly blond hair and no shirt said. He extended a red cup filled with cheap beer from a dented keg in the corner. It took her a moment to find a name for the tan face. Geoff, that's right. She'd made the mistake of allowing him to kiss her a few nights ago.

Lindsay thought Sophie was crazy not to indulge Geoff. Supposedly every girl in town would have loved to be in Sophie's position. Sophie didn't see it.

"Come on," Geoff said, taking Sophie's arm. "There's a bonfire outside."

Sophie shrugged his arm off. She didn't want to feed the fire. But outside was preferable to the intoxicating aroma of inside, so she followed Geoff through the minefield of empty beer cans and discarded clothing. She breathed in the cool evening air when she stepped outside onto the screened-in back porch, and Geoff waited as patiently as a butler while Sophie navigated the treacherous terrain of fallen chairs and skim boards that covered the creaky floorboards. He offered her a hand when she reached the steps, which she accepted grudgingly.

The grass backed up to the bay, and as Sophie made her way toward the small group huddled around the fire, she looked out over the water. The setting sun had nearly fallen below the tree line on the far side of the bay.

The bonfire was still in its infancy as Sophie approached, and it reminded her of a fading childhood memory. Countless nights on the beach with her mother, the two of them studying a dying fire after everyone else had gone inside. "How many people do you imagine wish they would have spent more time on the beach?" she would ask Sophie. "Not me," she would say. Sophie felt so close to her mother on those nights. It was like they were the only two people in the world. It was a memory she used to lean on for support. Now it felt more like sticking a branding iron into a wound.

Everyone cheered when they noticed Sophie. "The party's here!" someone yelled. She waved halfheartedly.

The group had formed a tight circle around the fire. They lounged in beach chairs, plastic Adirondack chairs, and rocking chairs, while some sat on the bare grass. Geoff, as obsequious as ever, pulled up a flower-printed beach chair for Sophie and held onto the back while she settled in. Before she sat down, Geoff slipped a cushion underneath her. "Don't want your butt getting too sore," he said. He sat next to her on the grass.

"Thanks," she said. With luck, she wouldn't have to get up for the rest of the night.

"Hey, Soph," someone said from across the fire. Sophie peered through the flames, trying to put a name to the face. Tyler, she thought. Or maybe it was Taylor. "We were just talking about how easy or hard it would be to hop around on one leg," he said. He looked to his friend for support. "Jason thinks it would be hard, but

I told him I could do it all day." Sophie's breath quickened as a chuckle ran through the crowd. "Figured you could be the judge for us," he finished.

Sophie said, "Um—"

"I mean," Tyler went on, "how hard could it be?" He jumped up from his chair and started hopping around on one leg. The crowd roared with laughter as he struggled to stay balanced. One of his friends shoved him towards the fire and he was forced to use his other leg to stop himself from falling in. Everyone laughed. "Alright," he said. "I guess it's not as easy as I thought."

A few others tried and failed to balance on one leg as well.

And with that, Sophie began drinking heavily. Her goal was to get as drunk as possible in as little time as possible. The feat took little more than an hour to accomplish. By the time twilight had come and gone, and darkness had formed its thick barrier around the group, Sophie was suddenly interested in what her guard dog had to say. Geoff had managed to keep everyone else at a distance while he attempted to convince Sophie that he genuinely cared about her and blah, blah, blah. At first, that was all she heard. Then, as if a switch had been turned on, or off, his words began to make sense. She wouldn't remember any of it, but at that moment, on the wrong side of the highway, he was indulging her with the most interesting information she had ever heard in her life.

She was a different person. She didn't feel resentful or angry. She felt nothing.

She felt she now understood why people drank so much. It gave them the opportunity to be someone else, someone more charismatic, or interesting, or confident. Or worthless. She didn't necessarily want to be any of those things, but she sure as hell didn't want to be herself. It was like she was stepping out of her skin, naked and unconscious, without a care in the world. No regrets or dreams. She knew it wouldn't last, and tomorrow she would crawl back into her hole like everyone else. But for now, she could pretend as though two real feet touched the ground.

It was a little after midnight. Ryan lay propped up in a lounge chair on the back deck, one leg draped over the edge and one pulled up to serve as a backboard for the heavy volume weighing into his lap. A dwindling cigarette dangled from his fingers and smoke drifted into the glow of the floodlight overhead, then disappeared into the star heavy night. On the floor to his right was a pint-sized bottle of whiskey, so close he need only let his arm fall to grab it. The crashing waves were like background music, an oceanic symphony that swam through his head like a well-made cocktail he didn't even know he was drinking.

He was exhausted from another long day, and he was drunk. The sleep he dreaded should have taken hold hours ago, and yet here he was, a hundred pages into a three-inch-thick dictionary of various kinds of furniture. It was a mystery he might never solve, but Ryan was fascinated by all of it.

The low hum of a car's engine crept around the corner, drawing Ryan's attention away from the page. A moment later, he heard a car door open and close—the time in between extended—followed by Sophie's familiar footfall against the front porch steps. The front door opened and closed, again, the action taking longer than what would be considered normal. An instant later, a loud crash stormed through the glass behind him, followed by an intense vibration in the floorboards. It sounded as though all the billiard balls had been dropped to the hardwood at the same time. Startled, Ryan jumped up from his reclined position and hastily slid open the glass door.

The house was dark except for a single light illuminating the narrow hallway. Sophie lay curled up, motionless under the spotlight. As Ryan started toward her, Ted exploded out of his bedroom door. He raced through the living room, into the hallway, and fell to the floor beside his daughter before Ryan could take two steps. Sophie and Ted, draped in the yellow-filled archway, seemed distant. It was as if Ryan were watching a staged tragedy play out from the back row.

As he crept forward, Ryan heard what he thought was a whimper escaping from Sophie's hidden lips, but as he drew closer, he realized it was laughter. And when he passed under the archway into the light, he heard her say through slurred speech and eerie giggles, "I. Can't. Get. Up."

Ted looked up at Ryan, light glistening off panicked eyes. "Can you help me get her up?"

Ryan leaned down and hooked his arms under Sophie's right shoulder while her father lifted from the opposite side. Together, they threw her arms around their shoulders and walked her out of the hallway, like soldiers carrying a fallen comrade. Her feet hissed as they dragged along the floor. "I can't even walk," Sophie chuckled as the two men carried her into the darkness of the living room. Ted opened her bedroom door and they laid her down on the bed softly, as if afraid she might break.

Ryan backed up and stood in the doorway.

"Can you hit that light?" Ted asked, pointing, his eyes never leaving Sophie. Ryan flipped the switch without a word. He watched as Ted rolled Sophie's pant leg up to her thigh and removed the prosthetic. Ryan turned away, feeling as though he were watching something he shouldn't be, something private that Sophie would be appalled to learn he had seen. Ted slid the compression sock off Sophie's thigh as well. "She's not supposed to sleep with this on," he said, as if he were a doctor instructing a new student.

By the time Ted finished, Sophie's laughter had abated, and Ryan could tell by her breathing, she had fallen into a drunken, hopefully dreamless sleep. Ted rose from the bed and pulled the covers over his daughter. He turned off the light and closed the door, his fingers lingering on the knob. He rested his hand on Ryan's shoulder. "Thank you," he said. Ryan nodded his head in the dark, unsure if Ted could make out the gesture.

When Ryan stepped back outside, the night seemed darker, the air heavier, and his thirst for knowledge had dissipated. He leaned down and scooped up the book that had fallen face down onto the deck. As he lifted it, two loose sheets of different-sized paper fell from the pages. He took a seat on the edge of the lounge chair and picked them up. The first page was the size of any standard notebook paper but was blank and lacked any lines. When he turned it over and held it up to the light, he could make out a sketch drawing of a girl exiting the ocean, caught forever in the shallow surf. She was frozen mid-stride, one foot submerged while the other hovered just above the water. A wave was poised to crash behind her. It only took Ryan an instant to see Sophie, her slender frame unmistakable. The right side of her body was expertly shaded in a way to suggest the sun that day was high off the left. No color was needed, the desired effect captured beautifully. Sophie's head was tilted to the side and she was smiling, as if posing for a picture for someone else, seemingly unaware she was being sketched. All at once, she looked strong, graceful, and happy.

There was no signature identifying the artist, but Ryan assumed the only hand capable of portraying Sophie in such a light belonged to her mother. A moment later, his suspicion was confirmed.

He flipped over the second sheet, also lineless, but half the size and a tan color that reminded him of ancient parchment. A single paragraph filled the sheet with attractively feminine handwriting. Ryan hesitated, again, afraid he might be invading a deeply private world. But his curiosity had been ignited, and his eyes, as if of a mind of their own, began racing left to right.

I watched Sophia swim today. How many more days I will be able to witness such perfection is uncertain. But that's okay. I will leave this world knowing that I never once took for granted the gift of seeing her as she is in the water. I will never forget the first time her father and I took her into the ocean, the way she laughed. The way she smiled. In some ways, she hasn't changed at all, and every time she dives into the waves, I see my little girl, laughing and splashing in the water as if for the first time. But she isn't a little girl anymore, and I couldn't be prouder of the woman she's become. Her confidence is contagious, her light warm, her beauty breathtaking. Her athletic drive she inherited from her father, and she always said she wished she could have received more of my artistic talent and eye for what's beautiful. But the truth is, Sophia taught me to see a world I never knew existed, colors few ever have the privilege of experiencing. I began seeing the world through her eyes the day she was born, and that day, I realized how blind to all things beautiful I really was. The world is hers now, and the ocean is her playground. And I will sit here, watching my little girl grow in grace and strength forever. No, I'm not afraid to die. How could I be when I know exactly what heaven will look like?

Ryan let his hand fall by his side, clutching the small sheet like a lifeline. He looked out into the darkness. He could picture Sophie striding out of the water, just as she was in the sketch, her emerald eyes like green flares. He wanted to know her, the girl Sophie's mother described. The girl he saw that day in the bar. He wanted to speak with her and sit beside her on the sand.

Ryan tried to imagine the two women together as he settled back and fell into a dreamless sleep.

11

Sophie felt cornered, like a mental patient weary of the medicine her nurses offered. She was seated in a white wicker chair. Her hands were clasped together, and her eyes were low, as though she were praying. Her head throbbed, and she longed for the comfort of her bed.

Laura stood, her posture casual. Easy. Her arms stretched out forever along the railing. She wore a T-shirt and jeans. Flip flops left her feet exposed. Jealousy seeped into Sophie's soul as she studied her mother's best friend out of the corner of her eye. She wanted to vomit it up, or sneeze it out, the foreign emotion like a virus.

Mrs. Ginny sat beside Sophie, a little too close. The urge to shift her body a little to the right tugged at Sophie's shirt. But she couldn't give in. It would hurt the older woman too much.

Every second was torture. She was screaming inside. Outside she was mute.

"You look great," said Laura. She was trying so hard to hide her pity, but Sophie could feel it emanating from her like a strong wind off the ocean.

Sophie didn't respond. Her gaze remained low. She tried a subtle smirk to let Laura know she had heard her.

Mrs. Ginny leaned forward and took Sophie's hand in hers. "Are you feeling any better?" she asked.

Sophie tilted her head toward Mrs. Ginny and nodded. "A little," she said.

The first awkward silence Sophie had ever experienced in the company of either of them followed. A circle of seagulls complained nearby. The neighbor's dog barked. A family's laughter rode the breeze. It killed her to be so short with the two women.

Twisting her long neck, Laura looked out over the water, searching the waves for the perfect thing to say. Sophie followed her gaze, knowing she wouldn't find it.

Laura turned to Mrs. Ginny and said, "Did you hear about the young man who lost his leg in the war?" Sophie allowed her eyes to move in Laura's direction.

"No, I don't think I did," Mrs. Ginny replied, eager to hear more.

"I don't remember the number," Laura continued. "But he has run something like a hundred marathons in a short period of time. Broken all kinds of records."

Mrs. Ginny widened her eyes. "No kidding!"

Laura nodded, then addressed Sophie. "I've heard all kinds of stories about people who have suffered tragic accidents. How they have done extraordinary things."

Sophie sighed. "Yeah," she said. "I've heard some of those stories."

"You could do something like that, Sophie," Mrs. Ginny offered. "You could do things no one could even dream of."

"I used to think that," Sophie said. She felt Mrs. Ginny look up at Laura, the two women exchanging worried looks.

Laura moved to the seat on Sophie's right and lowered herself. She placed her hand on Sophie's knee. "You will feel that way again, Soph," she said. "I know it." She leaned forward and kissed Sophie's forehead. Sophie remained in a state of silent stasis.

"I will never forget what your mother said to me a long time ago," Mrs. Ginny said, still holding Sophie's hand. Sophie winced at the mention of her mother. "Remember how we used to watch you swim?" *Please stop.* "One day we were watching you swim, and I told her how strong you were. I told her I'd never seen anything like it," she remembered. Mrs. Ginny paused, searching Sophie's expression. "Do you know what she told me?" she asked. Sophie shook her head, but she knew. "She told me your strength didn't come from your arms and legs." She paused for effect. "She said it came from your heart." Mrs. Ginny placed her palm over Sophie's chest. "She had been saying that ever since you were a little girl. You don't need anything else, do you? Your heart is so big."

Sophie looked up for the first time into Mrs. Ginny's eyes. "I needed my legs," she said. The sides of Mrs. Ginny's eyes fell. "I'm tired," Sophie said. She removed her hand from under the older woman's and reached for her crutches.

Laura jumped up and snatched them before Sophie could protest. She didn't have the energy, anyway. Laura handed her the crutches as Sophie rose from her chair. "Thanks," Sophie whispered. She made for the door.

"Can we come see you tomorrow?" Laura asked.

"I think I have a doctor's appointment," Sophie lied.

"The next day, then," Mrs. Ginny said.

Sophie pulled the handle and stepped inside.

"We love you, Soph," Laura said. "If there's anything you—"
Sophie slid the door closed on the rest of the sentence.

When she reached her bed, she allowed the crutches to fall away from her body as she fell onto the mattress. She wept quietly into her pillow until she fell asleep.

Ryan was bent over a worktable. He was attempting to decipher the barely legible handwriting that accompanied a variety of sketches strewn throughout the surface like puzzle pieces. The breeze was strong enough that afternoon that he was forced to plant his forearms on the sheets of paper so they wouldn't blow away. His attention was elsewhere, though, and he was only pretending to be entirely focused on his work. Outside on the grass, just beyond the awning, Ted and John Palmer were deep in conversation. Earlier in the day, Laura and Mrs. Palmer had come to see Sophie, and judging by the length of the visit, Ryan assumed they had been unsuccessful in their attempt to revive the old Sophie.

The scene before Ryan fascinated him. Ted seemed so much younger next to John. And although Mr. Palmer was Ted's senior by at least thirty years, Ryan thought the older man carried himself as though he were three hundred years Ted's senior. Ted soaked in every syllable Mr. Palmer uttered as though it were a lifeline.

"It gets harder and harder every day, John," Ryan heard Ted say. The voices were muffled by the wind, and Ryan needed to fill in the blanks occasionally. Ted's hands were in his pockets and his shoulders were high, under his ears, as though he were bracing against a bitter winter wind. Ryan had come to know it as his tired posture; Ted slept less than he did.

John Palmer nodded. "These are uncharted waters we're in, Ted," he said. His voice was deep and friendly. And unlike Ted, John stood straight, shoulders back and chin up, his hands folded in front of him, as though he were standing at attention. The posture didn't appear forced, but natural, as if he had been standing that way for his entire adult life. "I can't imagine it's going to get any easier, either," he said.

John turned his head enough to force Ryan's gaze back to the page.

"That's what scares me," said Ted. "I don't know her like this. I don't know what she's capable of."

John nodded. "I don't know that anyone has ever known what Sophie is capable of," the older man offered. "Good or bad," he added. He stopped. "Although," he said. "I believe she'll not only come out of this stronger, but eventually, she will have found a part of herself along the way she never knew she needed." Ryan let those words sink in.

Ted sighed and lifted his head to the sky. "I hope you're right, John," he said.

John turned to Ted and rested his ancient hand on the younger man's tensed shoulder. Ted's frame relaxed at the touch. "Give it time," said John.

Ted looked up at John, like a son would to a father. "I'm afraid she's running out of time."

John smiled. "I know it seems that way. But we have to be patient," he advised. John glanced over his shoulder at Ryan again. Ryan dipped his head back down to the table. "Besides," he said. "I think you have another card here that's yet to be played."

"What do you mean?" Ted asked.

They were silent, and Ryan sensed something unspoken was said between them.

A moment later, John announced his departure, waved to Ryan, and disappeared over the dunes.

On his way back to the loft that evening, Ryan heard a deafening crash from inside, followed by a terrifying scream.

Dropping the paperback book in his hand, Ryan sprinted along the pool deck and bounded up the porch steps. He slid through the half-open sliding glass door, hurdled over the couch, flew into Sophie's bedroom, and burst through the bathroom door before a thought had time to form.

"Oh my God, get out!" Sophie yelled, her eyes wide and pleading.

Ryan froze, his feet cemented to the floor, eyes locked on Sophie's struggling form. A bath towel lay wrinkled over the trunk of her body as she held onto the side of the bathtub like it was the edge of a pool. Drops of water escaped from the showerhead above her. Exposed and naked, Sophie slipped on the wet tile as she struggled to regain her footing. Her residual limb stood out like a light bulb in pure darkness, and the pink of the scar crawled up her thigh on two sides. Still, he failed to formulate a coherent thought.

"Get out!" Sophie screamed.

Finally finding his voice, Ryan said, "I'm so sorry." He closed his eyes and flung his hand up to cover them instinctually. "I heard you scream. I thought you were hurt."

"Please get out," she begged. "Please." Her voice cracked with the last plea.

Ryan backed out of the bathroom and closed the door. He opened his eyes. "I'm so sorry, Sophie," he said through the door. "Really, I swear, I thought you were hurt." The sound of shuffling feet and wet skin on porcelain phased through the door. Ryan waited for a response. "Are you alright?" he pressed after a few seconds.

"Please," she said, her voice softer now, defeated. "Please just go."

He dropped his head.

In a daze, Ryan walked back outside, down the porch steps, and up the stairs to the loft.

He lay down on the bed and stared into the ceiling for hours.

12

Early the next morning Ryan and Ted sat out on the workshop patio drinking coffee. It had become an informal tradition ever since Ryan had decided to take more of an interest in the woodcraft trade, and it offered Ted the opportunity to run through the agenda for the day. This morning, however, the conversation was scarce, and the two men sipped in silence as the sun rose.

The oppressive heat wave that had plagued the beach had relented, and a cool breeze off the water was a welcome luxury. When the sun had risen high enough so they were completely shrouded in shade, Ted finally said, "So, how are you doing?"

Ryan looked over at Ted. He would be surprised if more than an hour of sleep had visited the older man the previous night, the bags under his eyes drooping into his cheeks as he slumped in his chair.

"Don't worry about me," Ryan answered.

"Hey," Ted said, lifting himself more upright. "I'm just looking out for my investment. You've been a godsend helping out around here. Just want to make sure I don't wake up one morning to see that beat-up old Jeep of yours gone." He smirked before taking a long sip out of his short mug.

Ryan gazed out over the water. A thin cloud hovered above the horizon, as if a jet had just flown by. "Don't worry about that either," Ryan said. "I'm not going anywhere." He took a sip of coffee. "I can't leave you here alone, anyway. You might hurt yourself. You know, throw out your back or fall down the stairs."

Ted laughed. "I'm not that old yet, asshole," he said. "But seriously, it's been a huge help having you around. I hope you know that." Ryan nodded. "And I know it's not easy," Ted went on, "being here with me and Sophie. But I just want you to know how much it means to me." Ryan nodded again and tipped the mug to his mouth, savoring the bitter taste.

Ted rose from his chair and stretched. He patted Ryan on the shoulder. "Let's build some furniture," he said. "How about we work on carving today?"

Ryan stood and followed Ted into the workshop. "I told you, I'm no artist," he said. Taking measurements, cutting, sanding, and gluing were one thing, but carving designs into wood was a whole new monster, and all the books in the world couldn't steady his hand.

Ted turned around. A golden yellow cascade poured down through the skylights onto his face. "We're all artists, Ryan. Some just take a little longer to figure it out."

Sophie was curled up on the floor of her bathroom that afternoon. Stale beer and vodka hung heavy in the air around her. She had lost count of how many times she'd vomited.

She tried to sit up, using the rim of the toilet for support, but her hand slipped, and she fell back down to the tiles, all her energy having been spent on throwing up all morning.

Spouts of uncontrollable weeping came and went with regularity. She begged it to stop, ridiculed herself for having made such a terrible decision then swore to never drink again. Then she would look down at the scar on the stump that remained of her leg, the disgusting scar that crawled up the sides of her thigh like a smile, laughing at her misfortune. When that happened, Sophie begged for the convulsions again, pleaded for the pain to take her mind away from the real nightmare.

A knock at the door startled her. She had almost finally fallen asleep.

"Sophie?" her father said.

She didn't respond. If she was lucky, he might think she'd left earlier.

"Sophie, I know you're in there," he persisted. "Your physical therapy appointment is in an hour. Just wanted to make sure you remembered."

"Shit," Sophie whispered into the toxic air. She'd completely forgotten about it. "I thought that was on Tuesday," Sophie said, hoping he had made a mistake.

"It is Tuesday, Sophie," he answered.

Sophie closed the lid of the toilet, threw her arms over it, and with all her strength lifted herself onto the seat. She slammed her elbows into her thighs and crushed the heels of her hands to her bloodshot eyes.

"Are you alright in there, Sweetie?" he asked.

"Yeah, Dad. I'm fine."

"You sure? Why is the door locked?"

"I'm not feeling well, Dad," she said. "I can't make it to the appointment today."

"Sophie," he said, defeated already. "You've already missed too many. The prosthetist will push back the date for your permanent fitting."

Sophie stared at the floor. "So?" she said.

"So?" he replied, astonished, although he shouldn't have been. "Don't you want to walk? Or swim again? You know they make waterproof prosthetics. I don't get it?"

"I know you don't get it, Dad, that's why I can't talk to you about it," she said, and as soon as the words left her mouth, she regretted them, but she refused to take them back.

She heard him sigh through the door. "What are you afraid of, Sweetie?"

Sophie was quiet. After a few moments, she heard his familiar footfall fade as he retreated into the living room. Another spasm began to announce itself. She fell to the floor and threw back the seat. She heaved and heaved, but only tears dripped into the water.

Late that night, Ryan lay back on his favorite lounge chair, eyes closed, an open book resting on his chest. A light breeze trotted off the ocean and rolled over him like a blanket, and the repetitive melody of the crashing waves had almost sung him to sleep when the sound of unfamiliar footsteps running up the steps forced him awake. In the dim light, he was only able to catch a glimpse of the stranger as she briskly skipped past him, slid open the glass door, and disappeared into the house. He wasn't sure whether the girl had seen him or not.

A moment later, a door from inside opened and closed. Ryan threw his legs over the edge of the chair and sat up, unsure what to do. Although a glimpse was all he had managed, he was certain he'd never seen the girl before.

After a few confusing seconds, she popped her head outside.

"Where's Sophie?" she demanded.

Ryan looked up, but the glare of the floodlight obscured his vision. He still couldn't make out any defining details. "Who are you?" he asked.

"Where is she?" the girl demanded again. Her voice was high and sharp, and a little intimidating.

Ryan relented. "She's out."

The girl frowned. "Sophie doesn't go out."

"Tell that to her," he said.

"I will. As soon as I see her," she replied. The girl stepped outside, her bare feet making as much noise as a feather against the wood. Standing over him, hands on hips, she glared at Ryan. One side of her head was shaved. The other side had straight, bleached blonde hair that fell well past her shoulders. A line of red streaked through the blonde in her hair, as if she had dragged a thin paintbrush through it. She was tall and thin, like Sophie, but not quite as athletic. A flattering red dress fell invitingly just below her hip. Black leggings with a rip that ran from mid-thigh down to mid-calf justified the dress's lack of length. Her dark blue eyes were serious. "Well, where's Mr. Galloway?" she persisted.

"Asleep, I think," Ryan answered. When she didn't respond right away, Ryan said, "Anything else?"

"Ugh, no," she said. She floated around Ryan's chair and fell into the vacant one beside him. Her movements were graceful, as if she were constantly dancing to a love song only she could hear. She turned to Ryan. "Who are you?" she asked.

"Ryan," he answered.

"Ryan Monroe?"

Ryan frowned. "How do you know that?"

"Psychic," she said with a shrug.

Ryan waited for a serious answer.

Abruptly, she started laughing. "I'm just messing with you," she said. I know who you are. I know you saved Sophie's life and I know you work here with Mr. Galloway. I probably know more about you than you do."

"How do you know all that?" he asked.

"I'm sorry," she said, crossing her legs. "I'm such a bitch, I know. I'm Liv Palmer, John and Ginny's granddaughter." She extended her hand.

Ryan hesitated, studying her another moment, then reached out and took the soft, slender hand. It felt like velvet. "That makes a little more sense," he said.

"And I know you want to remain anonymous and all that. So," she pinched her thumb and forefinger together and slid them across her lips. She turned an imaginary key, managing to make the movement sensual, and Ryan's eyes lingered on her full lips after she threw the key away.

"I don't care about that anymore," he said. It was kind of true. When she didn't respond, he asked, "How did you get here?"

"I walked," she answered flatly, as if the conversation was already boring her. "My grandparent's place is only a few houses down." Ryan forgot it was so close. He should probably make a visit sometime. He noticed her eyes fall on the bottle of whiskey between them. "Couldn't invite me?" she asked, grinning.

"If I'd known you existed," he said. "I would have."

She smiled wryly, then changed the subject. "So, where's Sophie?"

Ryan picked up the bottle and unscrewed the top. No point in hiding it now. He took a long sip. "I have no idea," he answered. "Are you two friends? Why don't you call her?"

For the first time, Liv's bright façade lost its opacity and Ryan glimpsed sadness behind her eyes. "We used to be best friends," she said, her gaze fluttering into the darkness. "But that was a long time ago."

Ryan extended the bottle across the narrow space between them. She rested the rim on her lips and tilted her head back with the bottle, her eyes never leaving his.

She passed the bottle back to Ryan, his fingers grazing hers in the exchange. "You look like you need a drink," she said. "Wanna go out?"

Ryan looked down at the bottle in his hand then back to Liv and frowned.

"Alright, *I* need a drink," she tried again. "Wanna go out?"

He looked back down at the bottle then back to her again, still confused.

"Alright, fine," she said, exasperated. "I. Want. To. Go. Out. Are you coming or not?"

Ryan couldn't help but smile.

He returned her intense stare with a calculating one. In the six weeks since he'd been living there, Ryan had only left the property for the occasional run to the liquor store, and although he preferred the quiet and solitude that Ted's home offered, even he couldn't deny the attraction of a night away. Also, Liv's flammable personality promised to be illuminating in more ways than one. So, he accepted the invitation.

"I probably shouldn't drive, though," he noted.

"I'll drive," she said brightly. She hopped up and offered Ryan a hand. He smirked at the gesture and accepted.

They ended up at Finn's. It was a cool night and Liv decided they would sit outside on the patio. It was late, after midnight when they arrived, and the faint light of the lampposts showered specs of yellow mist onto a desolate boardwalk. Orange and blue lights slithered through the railings that separated the boardwalk from the restaurant's patio, casting a warm glow around Ryan and Liv.

A solo musician with an acoustic guitar under his arms, a harmonica strangling his neck, and a pained expression tattooed on his face played quietly to the small crowd gathered. The scene offered a campfire feel that might have put Ryan to sleep, had he not found himself opposite Liv Palmer.

"So, after I went off to New York to study dance, we grew apart," she said. Her dirty martini arrived, and she emptied half of it in one gulp. When Ryan raised an eyebrow, she said, "What? Last call is like an hour away. Anyway, you're one to talk."

"Fair enough."

"We were always so different," she went on. "She was the athlete, and I was the artist. But it didn't matter, you know? We never drifted apart early on, even in high school when, historically speaking, we should have hated each other. But when I went to college, everything changed. I fell in love with New York, and rarely came back." She sighed for the first time. "I haven't been back since Mrs. Galloway's funeral. Three years," she continued. She looked up from her drink, her eyes dispirited, a foreign look on her. "I think I may have screwed things up beyond repair between us," she finished.

Ryan nodded. He hoped she was wrong, for everyone's sake. After another comfortable silence—there was nothing awkward about being with Liv; she wouldn't allow it—she said, "And I guess I'm obligated to say thank you. You know, for saving her life."

"I guess I'm obligated to say you're welcome," he said. She grinned.

Ryan took a sip of whiskey and lit a cigarette. "Got one for me?" Liv asked. He passed her the pack. She placed one end between her lips and Ryan offered her the lighter. Ignoring his gesture, she leaned forward and waited expectantly. He leaned forward to meet her and sparked the lighter, the flame basking their skin in a sunset orange glow. He watched, hypnotized, as she inhaled and released a silky stream of smoke out of the corner of her mouth. She sat back and crossed her legs. Ryan stayed where he was, elbows planted like pillars to the smooth surface of the table, his eyes unable to stray from hers.

After a few alternating drags and healthy sips of liquor between the two, Ryan asked, "So, why are you here now?"

Liv shrugged. "I quit my job at the studio and decided to spend the rest of the summer down here. Figured I'd put it off long enough." Ryan nodded. "What about you?" she said. "Just a traveling furniture maker who happened to run into a fellow craftsman?"

"Not exactly."

"Just stumbled into town to save the day?"

"Something like that."

"'Not exactly.' 'Something like that.' Wow," she said, feigning astonishment. "What else can it say?"

Ryan smiled. "It prefers to listen."

She grinned again. It was seductive and playful, its meaning undeniable. "Well, can it dance?"

"It most certainly cannot," he answered quickly. That was one order he would not follow.

"Too bad," she said, frowning.

Liv crushed out her half-smoked cigarette, emptied the martini glass, and rose out of her chair. She brushed past Ryan—his head following her as if attached to her hips by a string—and glided onto the small, empty dance floor. Every set of eyes on the patio turned in unison as Liv began swaying back and forth to the lonely musician's melancholy tune. Ryan watched, mesmerized as Liv dipped herself backwards, her hair grazing the floor. She moved like water to the drowsy rhythm, her form ethereal through a cloud of exhaled smoke. A young server stopped in his tracks on his way back inside, forgetting that he worked there for a moment. A lone passerby from the boardwalk stopped and leaned into the railing like a curious child trying to get a better view. Ryan noticed Liv's eyes were closed; she was somewhere else, somewhere every single person lucky enough to witness the magic wished they could be.

And for those sixty seconds, amnesia abducted Ryan's mind. For those sixty seconds, he forgot where he came from and how he'd come to be there. It didn't matter. She was dancing, and he was grateful for a front-row seat.

***

Liv slowed the car and pulled into a driveway that wasn't Ted's.

She turned off the engine and twisted in her seat to face him, her slumped form a silhouette against the faint porch light.

"I guess I'll walk back?" he said.

Liv leaned over the center console and kissed him, her lips finding his like a magnet. Instinctively, Ryan's right arm slid around her small waist as she pressed her chest into his shoulder, forcing him to turn in his seat. She smelled of vodka and perfume, and his senses were immediately overwhelmed, a longing desire he'd forgotten was there taking hold like a vice. His mouth opened with hers as her body's rhythm sped up, his hand sliding over her hip and down her thigh.

She pulled away, retreating only a few inches after allowing her lips to linger over his for a calculated second. He could feel her warm breath on his face in the dark, and the heavy beat of his heart pounded like a drum in the silence.

"Want to come inside?" she whispered. "The place is a castle. No one would even know you're here."

The words hung between them while the obvious response refused to escape his mouth. Had her lips never left his, he wouldn't have stood a chance, but granted a moment to think, inexplicable reluctance took hold, his conscience reappearing after hibernation. She sat back and waited patiently.

"I don't know if that's a good idea," Ryan finally managed, and as soon as the words left his mouth, he regretted them, but he couldn't take them back. Everything about the night, from the moment he saw her, insinuated the offer she now presented so casually. And almost every particle of his being begged for it. Almost. The minute part that pulled him away, the part he thought he'd left behind told him he needed to get back to the house. It was subtle, but powerful, like a strong current he was oblivious to, dragging him out to sea.

"Because you're in love with Sophie," she said simply, not in the least offended by his rejection.

"What?" he blurted. "No, of course not. What makes you say that?"

Liv shrugged. "I'm just trying to figure out what you're still doing here. You say you were just passing through before you met her and Mr. Galloway. And yet here you are, living in their house. Doesn't make a whole lot of sense."

She was right, it didn't make sense. But it didn't mean he was in love with Sophie.

"I mean, I feel for her and Ted," he tried. "But I'm not in love with her."

Liv shrugged again. "Suit yourself," she said. Let me know if you change your mind." And with that, she opened the door and slid out of the car.

Ryan got out and watched her walk to the front door. She turned around before twisting the knob and said, "You can find your way back, right?" Ryan nodded. "See you around," she said, and disappeared into the house, leaving Ryan outside to wonder whether he had just made a terrible mistake. In another life, he thought, he would have gladly let her break his heart.

Ryan came off the beach and up the walkway to a darkened house.

The stars were bright, and a cool green light floated under the pool's surface as he skirted the edge.

The motion floodlight from the deck sprung to life as he passed.

"Well, look who it is," Sophie said. "My knight in shining armor." Her speech was slow, slurred, and painfully sarcastic.

Ryan peered through the thin slits in the railing, his eyesight hovering inches above the deck's surface. Sophie lay back on the same lounge chair Ryan had been keeping warm earlier in the night, her arms and right leg hanging limp over the sides. The left pant leg of her sweatpants hung over the edge as well, loose and swaying in the breeze. Her prosthetic was discarded on the floorboards like a piece of clothing. From his angle, the socket of the prosthetic looked like a thigh-sized eggshell that had been cracked in half. A twelve-inch metal rod ran from the bottom of the socket down to a rubber foot attached at the other end. It looked nothing like a real leg, but as he understood, it was only temporary.

"I couldn't get inside," she said. "Door's locked."

Ryan sighed. He turned around and walked up the steps. When he walked past Sophie, her eyes looked through him as he moved to the door. He gripped the handle and pulled. The glass slid so easily, a gust of wind could have opened it.

"Oh," Sophie said, amazed. "You pull it. Who would've thought?"

Ryan left the door open and eased into the chair next to her. Sophie's head fell to the side, as if her neck muscles had suddenly stopped working. She looked at him. He couldn't meet her eyes, so lifeless and devoid of emotion.

The floodlight switched off, leaving them in the midnight blue of a moon and star-flooded night.

"Sorry about the fake leg," she said. Ryan turned to face her. "Hope you don't mind."

"Not even a little bit," Ryan answered.

"You want to see it?" she asked.

"See what?"

"My stump. You know you do."

"No," he said.

"Why not?" she said, feigning offense.

"Because you don't want to show me."

"What do you know about what I want," she said. She lifted herself up and began rolling the left leg of her sweatpants up. "Besides," she said. "Not like you haven't seen everything already." She rocked back and forth, unsteady as she moved.

Ryan put his hand on hers. "Please," he said. "Don't."

She fell back against the cushioned headrest. "Aw, are you scared?" she asked.

"Terrified," he answered, begging his memory to forget her expression of cold indifference. Absently, Ryan registered that it had already been the longest conversation he'd had with Sophie since that afternoon in the bar.

She squinted and tears swelled in the narrow slits of her eyes. Her face fell, her mood changing direction on a dime. "Me too," she whispered, and her apathetic façade gave way to the fear boiling under the surface.

He looked away, unable to face the helplessness he felt. When he turned back, she was asleep, her breaths slow and light. Without hesitating, Ryan stood up. He leaned down and scooped her slender frame in his arms, cradling her like a baby. He needed to adjust his grip slightly so that her left thigh didn't hang limp, but other than that, it was no harder than carrying a small child.

Sophie's head rested softly against his chest as Ryan stepped through the open door. He moved quietly through the living room, the skylights overhead providing a cool blue glow over the slumbering furniture. He nudged her half-open door wide enough for the two to slide through comfortably.

With concentrated care, Ryan placed her onto the bed. He knew as well as anyone that a tornado would struggle to wake her up in her state, but he insisted on treating her as though her sleep was as fragile as her thinning body. He pulled the comforter up to her chest, as though he were tucking in a child, the thought freezing him mid-motion as he peered down at her peaceful face. He lingered a few moments, watching the blanket rise and fall with her chest. He hoped her dreams offered the blissful release that eluded him every night.

"Goodnight, Sophie," he whispered.

Before falling into the swirling riptide of his nightmares that night, Ryan studied the sketch of Sophie and re-read the note. Maybe the image of Sophie gliding through the surf, or her mother's description would plant a more hopeful seed in his mind before falling asleep.

It didn't work.

13

The next morning, not long before noon, the sun was high over the workshop and the clouds low over the water. A strong breeze blew through the shop into Ryan's back, urging him forward as he pushed a hand planer over the face of a two-inch-thick piece of walnut. Thin shavings fell as lightly as feathers and lay at his feet like a pile of sand-colored ribbons. Beside him, the rhythm of Ted's impossibly sharp saw harmonized with the steady scrape of Ryan's measured movements as the two unwittingly created a sound all their own.

Ted's instrument stopped. "So, I'm thinking we should carve claws into the feet of the chairs and table," he said. "Make it look like they're grabbing hold of the floor, you know?"

Ryan stopped, wiped his brow, and stood up straight. He looked at Ted and shrugged. "Okay," he said. "What, like a Lion's claw?"

"No," Ted said. "The legs aren't going to be thick enough. Maybe more like a fox claw."

"A fox claw?" Ryan said incredulously. "What does a fox claw look like? I thought they had paws."

"What, they don't teach you that in your books?" Ted asked, grinning.

"You're talking about biology, not woodworking."

"Well, you're gonna be carving them, so figure it out."

Ryan looked down, pensive. "Are foxes' dogs?"

"Dogs?"

"Yeah, like canines."

Ted frowned. "Look, forget about the damn fox. Just carve a small claw."

"Woah, that sounds an awful lot like an order," Ryan replied. "Partner."

Ted laughed. "Toss me that chisel," he said, pointing to the table behind Ryan. Ryan grabbed the chisel, walked over to Ted, and placed it on the table. Ted changed the subject. "Hey, do you mind taking the finished stuff to Laura's shop this afternoon?"

Ryan had never delivered furniture to Laura, and he wondered why Ted offered him the job now. "Yeah, sure," he answered with a shrug. "You taking Sophie to an appointment, or something?"

Ted was thoughtful, as if he were trying to figure out the safest way to proceed. "Actually," he started. "I was thinking Sophie could go with you."

Ryan froze, his eyes blank while he tried to convince himself he'd misheard the man.

Sensing Ryan's reluctance, Ted pushed on. "I think it might be good for her, to get out of the house."

After allowing the words to sink in like lemon juice on a paper cut, Ryan said, "There's no way she'll go for it."

"She won't have a choice," Ted said. The sun lit up Ted's stern features as he leaned on the table like he was trying to push it through the cement. But under the determination, Ryan sensed the same desperation he'd noticed when Ted had come to his motel room that day. And although he and Ryan managed a joke or two throughout the workday, the weariness that weighed on Sophie's father clawed to the surface with ease, showing itself unabashedly. "She missed dinner again last night and didn't call. It's the least she can do," Ted trudged on. "And she has completely shut Laura out. Can you believe that?"

Ryan didn't answer. He could absolutely believe it, but he wasn't going to tell him that.

"Laura's always loved Sophie. She was like an aunt to her when Soph was a child," he explained. He started to ramble, as if it might offer some answers he had overlooked. "She hardly eats," he went on. "Sleeps all day. She's lost too much weight." He stopped and took three long, measured breaths. "I don't know what to do, Ryan," he said, his back turned to his young apprentice. Then he turned around and asked Ryan to do the unthinkable. "Maybe you could talk to her. I don't know, give her some advice. I don't want her to end up like—"

"Like me?" Ryan finished for him.

"That's not what I meant at all," Ted said, softening up a bit. "I'm just scared. I'm running out of ideas."

They were all scared, Ryan realized. Fear swam in the air like sawdust, seeping into their pores and poisoning their minds. The image of Sophie's tears was still vivid in his mind, and although he wanted to help, he was convinced his involvement would just make things worse. But when he looked up from the table and saw Ted's pleading eyes, he knew he couldn't deny the man.

"I think it's a bad idea," Ryan said. "But I'll give it a shot."

"Give what a shot?" a new voice asked brightly.

Their heads turned in unison as Liv Palmer danced into the

workshop. She wore a short orange summer dress and a wide smile, her hair swaying with her hips as she bounced on the balls of her bare feet like a ballerina. She winked at Ryan.

"Livy Palmer?" Ted gasped in astonishment.

"Hey, Mr. Galloway," she said with a smile.

Ryan watched as Ted rushed toward Liv and embraced her as if she were his own child, or a life raft in the open ocean. He held her tight, the hug extending well past what would be considered a casual greeting. Finally, Ted released her. "It's so good to see you!" he exclaimed. "Look how beautiful you are."

Trying and failing to hold Ted's gaze, Liv betrayed an air of embarrassment Ryan thought her to be incapable of. "Stop it, Mr. Galloway," she said, blushing.

"When did you get into town?" he asked.

"Last night," she answered. She looked to Ryan for some support. He waited quietly.

"Last night? And you couldn't come by for dinner?" Ted asked.

"I tried," she said. "But it was late, and everyone was asleep." She gave Ryan another one of her wry smiles.

Ted followed her eyes to Ryan and frowned, obviously aware of something not being said. But he chose not to push the subject. Instead, he said, "Well, it's great to see you. I'm sure Sophie will be excited." Ryan could tell by Ted's profile that he wasn't nearly as confident as he sounded.

"Where is she?" Liv asked.

"Inside resting," Ted said hastily. "But she and Ryan were just about to go into town to drop off a few pieces."

"Great," Liv said. "I haven't seen Laura yet." And just like that, she'd invited herself.

"I'll go get her," Ted announced, his mood having risen through the roof in a matter of seconds. "Ryan, you want to load the truck up?"

"You got it."

Ted rushed out of the shop like a kid let out of school for the summer, leaving Ryan and Liv alone.

Ryan traced his fingers along the smooth surface of what remained of the slab of walnut wood. The room was so quiet, he could hear a single piece of dust fall. Out of the corner of his eye, he felt Liv studying him with a mixture of humor and curiosity, as though she were pleasantly amused, but didn't know why. When he looked up, he couldn't help but notice that she inhabited the scenery so naturally. The open wall framed her body, while beyond, the dune grass rose to her hips and swayed like candle flames, playing hide and seek behind her slim torso. The ocean and sky met just above her shoulders, as though she was obliviously supporting its weight. Her blonde hair iridescent like its own sun. It appeared as though she had unknowingly walked into an overdone painting of a common seascape.

She shifted her weight from left to right, spoiling his concentration. "So, what the hell?" she said, frowning. "I got up early and everything, waiting for your call."

Ryan squinted as he tried to recall the previous night's events. Had they even exchanged numbers?

Liv laughed. "I'm just messin' with you," she said. "Look, you're sexy and mysterious and all. But the reality is, it wouldn't work. I think friendship's the way to go, don't you?"

Ryan steadied himself after the whiplash of Liv's idea at humor. Wasn't she the one who came on to him? And now she was making it seem as though he had tried and failed to seduce her, and she was letting him down easy. He didn't care, and yet he felt he'd been tossed to the curb, like he was being broken up with.

"That works for me," he finally answered. He welcomed an easy way out.

Ryan and Liv waited outside beside the truck, trying to filter the yelling match between Ted and Sophie that fazed through the walls of the house.

"Is it always like this?" Liv asked him.

"No," he answered. "Usually there are doors slamming."

A door slammed, and a few moments later, Sophie emerged from the front door, Ted following a safe distance behind. Sophie inched down the front steps, grudgingly gripping the railing for support. Her face wore a determined scowl.

When she reached the bottom, Liv rushed over to meet her. Ryan watched with curiosity as Liv threw her arms around Sophie.

"Hey girl. Lookin' good," Liv said brightly. Sophie's left hand remained on the cane, her right arm stiff by her side. It looked like Liv was hugging a statue. Ted looked on anxiously, waiting for Sophie to spring back to life at the sight of her old friend. Her chin hovering just above Liv's shoulder, Sophie looked through Ryan as if he weren't standing directly in her line of sight.

After the awkward hug, Liv slowed her pace to meet Sophie's as the two girls made for the truck. Sophie opened the door and Liv offered to help her into the front seat. "I'm fine," Sophie said.

"I don't mind," Liv replied. "Here, let me help," and she took Sophie's arm.

Sophie shoved Liv's arm away. "I got it, Jesus," she spat.

Liv stepped back, shocked. Ted's shoulders slumped. Ryan shuffled into the front seat and started the engine. Liv might have known the old Sophie as well as anyone, but she had a lot to learn about the stranger she now regarded with a mixture of pity and confusion.

Ted walked around to the driver's side window. "Take your time. Have fun." He tried a smile, but no one bought it.

Ryan pulled out of the driveway and started down Coastal Highway toward the center of town. He glanced into the rearview mirror. Liv lounged in the middle of the back seat, her feet resting on the center console beside Ryan's forearm. Her expression was pensive. Sophie had rolled her window up as soon as they'd pulled out of the driveway. She leaned her head against the glass. The trees flew by, but her eyes didn't follow. And although the sun was high and bright, spilling into the truck through every conceivable opening, Ryan knew Sophie was looking into a storm. He could hear the rain beating against the glass, the little drops tumbling down around her head.

It wasn't a long drive, but after a quarter of a mile, Ryan had already felt as though he'd been driving for hours.

Liv broke the painful silence first. "So, I'm starving," she said. "Where should we eat?"

"How do you do it?" said Sophie.

Ryan looked back into the rearview for some help. Liv spread her hands and shrugged her shoulders.

"How do I do what, Soph?" Liv asked hesitantly.

Sophie pried her head away from the glass and turned to Ryan, ignoring Liv. "How do you get drunk every day? I feel like death."

Ryan kept his eyes on the road, partly because it was the safe thing to do, and partly because he was afraid to meet her eyes, as if they might turn him to stone. He didn't need to think about his answer, though. "It's a lot easier than not getting drunk every day," he said.

For the first time since meeting her, Ryan noticed that Liv seemed content to spectate, as if she had underestimated the situation and needed to do some scouting before getting back in the game.

Sophie turned her attention back to the window. "I don't even know how I got into my bed last night," she said. "Did we have a conversation? Or was I dreaming?"

"We talked for a little," Ryan answered neutrally.

"About what?"

He hesitated. "Nothing important," he said. "I don't really remember, either." She looked him over for a long moment, and he wondered if she could tell he was lying.

After another wave of quiet filled the truck, Ryan said, "Speaking of drinking." Liv's head perked up in the back seat and she tilted her head questioningly through the mirror. Sophie stared into him expectantly. He steeled himself and continued. "Your dad is a little worried. A lot worried, actually. You should hear him, he's—"

"And you feel the need to tell me this, why?"

"I just thought maybe if you heard it from someone who's been there, you might, I don't know..." he trailed off.

"Been there?" she said. "Are you kidding me?" She turned her torso to face him now, like a cobra poised to strike.

"No," he said, flustered. "I mean, I just want to let you know how dangerous the road you're on is. Your dad asked me to—"

"Are you serious right now?" she said.

"I just—"

"I knew it," she cut in again. "I knew he would try to pull something like this. And from you of all people? Talking to me about drinking?" She was furious, her temper rising, and he felt like she was standing over him, scolding him like a nun.

"I thought maybe if you heard it from someone your own age, maybe—"

"I mean, it's almost funny," she pressed on, her words like venom. "You drink yourself stupid every day, and you actually thought I would listen to a word you said."

This was getting out of hand. "Look, I—"

"What, you think you're a hero because you pulled me from the water? I could smell the whiskey on you even then. Jesus." She had no intention of stopping. "My dad *must* be desperate to ask someone like you to—"

"Look, I'm sorry you didn't get to have your, 'This is for you, Mom,' moment on the podium, okay. But you—"

"What did you just say?" *What did he just say?*

Behind him, Ryan heard Liv catch her breath. He tried to backpedal. "I'm sorry. I didn't mean to—"

"Stop the car," Sophie said evenly, as if she were far past anger already.

The intersection of Main and the Avenue was coming up and the light was green. Mobs of vacationers thronged the sidewalks. "Come on," he tried. "We're almost there."

"Stop the car right now or I'll jump out," she said, again in a frighteningly nonchalant tone.

He glanced over at her. Her face was a sharply cut stone. Ryan pulled the truck to the curb and put it in park. Sophie opened her door and slid off the seat and onto the sidewalk.

"Sophie, come on," Ryan pleaded. "How are you going to get home?"

She looked up, and for the first time, he saw hatred in her eyes. They burned into him like a cigarette. "Nobody wants you here," she said. "Go drink yourself to death somewhere else."

It hurt more than he thought it could have.

"Soph, what's your problem," Liv said. She had leaned forward, her arms resting on the center console. "We're just trying to help."

Sophie's scalding stare darted to Liv. "I haven't seen you in what, three years?" she said. "And you show up six weeks after I almost died? You're not my friend, so stop trying to act like it. I don't need your help or want it. Save your pity and go back to New York." She slammed the door in both of their faces.

Ryan watched helplessly as she limped around the front of the truck and crossed the street, heading for the boardwalk. A car's breaks screeched and the man behind the wheel slammed on the horn. Sophie casually raised her right hand over her head and extended her middle finger. A moment later, she was enveloped by the crowded sidewalk.

Liv squeezed between the two front seats with ease and bounced into the passenger seat beside Ryan. "Well, that could have gone better," she said.

Ryan didn't answer. He was searching the crowd, hoping Sophie might reappear.

"Shit," he said to himself.

14

"Don't beat yourself up about it," Ted had said when Ryan told him about the exchange he'd had with Sophie earlier in the day. Ryan had walked back into the shop with his tail between his legs, ready to be reprimanded. But Ted had simply shaken his head and patted Ryan on the shoulder. "You tried," he said. "We knew it was a long shot. Thanks anyway. It means a lot." Ted's understanding made him feel worse.

After a forlorn rest of the workday, Ryan retired to the loft to consider his next move.

As twilight gave way to darkness, he attempted to read his way out of the despair and guilt that hung low over his head, like the broken moon over the water. But no matter how hard he tried to avoid it, his mind always returned to where she might be. Who she might be with. What she might be doing. Flashes of worst-case scenarios assaulted his thoughts.

At some point between another sip of whiskey and an unfinished chapter, he drifted off into a dreamless sleep, using the open book as a pillow.

***

Sophie awoke to a cold, fluorescent light drilling through her eyelids. Nothingness flooded her mind. Her mouth was so dry it hurt, and her limbs felt like they were tied down to the bed.

She reached for her pocket to make sure she still had her phone. Where she should have felt cotton, her fingers instead grazed against bare skin. Her eyes half open and her head flat against a pillow, Sophie slowly moved her hand over her right hip and felt the lace of her underwear. Ignoring the dizziness and pounding in her head, she bolted upright, eyes wide, searching. The room refused to focus, but her sweatpants were undoubtedly pulled down just below the knee. Her prosthetic was still attached to her thigh.

The mattress moved under her. She glanced over to see a half-naked man rubbing his eyes. "Hey babe," said Geoff, his curly blonde hair unmistakable. He was lying on his side. Too close.

"Where am I?" Sophie demanded.

"You're at Sean's," he said. "What time is it?"

"Why are my pants down?" she asked, trying to control the panic.

Geoff sat up and looked down at Sophie's waist. "Oh, that," he said. "Don't freak out or anything. You passed out downstairs and I brought you up here. Figured you'd want to wake up in a comfortable bed." He seemed proud of himself.

"Why are my pants down?" she said again, her voice rising.

He ran his hands through his hair. "Don't worry," he said. "Nothing happened. I just wanted to see your leg. I was curious." He touched Sophie's thigh as he spoke and grinned playfully.

"Get away from me," Sophie screamed. She pushed his hand away and shoved his chest with every bit of strength she could gather. The force pushed her backwards and she tumbled over the edge of the bed, landing heavily on the cold hardwood with a thud. Geoff stifled a laugh. Squirming on the floor, Sophie pulled her sweatpants up past her waist and scrambled to her feet, using the wall as a crutch.

"What's the big deal?" Geoff asked.

"What's the big deal?" she said. "Are you fucking high?"

He shrugged. "Yeah."

Sophie struggled to keep her balance. Every muscle in her body was sore. "Where's my cane?"

"Probably still on the back porch," he said.

Without another thought, Sophie moved to the door and limped into the hallway.

"Where are you going?" Geoff called behind her. "It's like three in the morning!" he yelled. But his voice was distant, far away already.

She knew he wasn't following, but Sophie hurried as though she were being chased, half-limping and half-hopping as she made her way through the dim hallway. The space was narrow enough that she could use the walls on either side for support as she hustled.

The wall to her left ended abruptly and Sophie nearly fell down the first flight of stairs. She caught herself on the railing just in time. Using only her right leg and the railing for support, she hopped down the steps, taking two at a time. She misjudged the last step and barreled into the wall opposite the landing, a sharp pain firing through her shoulder on impact. Lifting herself to her feet, she descended the second flight more carefully and made it down to the first floor relatively unscathed.

She hurried through the living room, relying on a vague

memory of the floorplan. When she reached the kitchen, a wave of nausea overtook her. She leaned over the sink and vomited onto a pile of unwashed dishes. She hung there over the sink for a moment, unable to move her limbs. Turning on the faucet, she drank like an animal from the stream of water.

The temporary hydration allowed her a slight burst of energy, and with renewed conviction, Sophie pressed on toward the screened door that led outside. When she emerged from the thick, oppressive air of the house, she took a deep breath, savoring the warm, sweet scent of the late night.

She found her cane lying on the floor. Feeling a little more balanced, she limped down the steps and into the open night. Details began to come into focus. A bright, half-moon floated over the glassy bay. Sparks from a dying fire raced into the sky. The wet grass rough against her bare foot. Laughter and conversation.

Sophie rushed over to the three figures encircling the low flames, their faces hidden in shadow.

"Lindsay?" Sophie asked the group.

"Who?" an unfamiliar voice asked, its tone slow and lazy.

The trio burst out in a chorus of laughter as Sophie swayed back and forth just outside the ring of light, her right arm limp and her shoulders slumped. She didn't know these people. All she knew was she had to get away from them, away from this place. She took off in a random direction.

She had no idea how far she had gone when fatigue and nausea finally overcame her. The ground was spinning like a merry-go-round and her chest was beating through her ears when her right leg gave out. Lacking the strength or motivation to fight it, Sophie fell heavily onto the dew-drenched grass.

Lying there on her back, under a canopy of black pine needles and jagged tree limbs, Sophie attempted to slow her breathing. The light of the fire was still visible in her peripherals, so she couldn't have made it very far. She reached into her pocket and found her phone. When she brought it to life, she had to squint through the blinding light of the screen. Searching her contacts, she found Lindsay's number and pressed the screen with her thumb. After four extended rings, she hung up.

As Sophie scrolled, closing her left eye at times to focus the names, she began to cry. She couldn't call anyone. She had alienated everyone that might have been able to help. She'd never felt so alone.

As she scrolled and scrolled, the screen stopped on a contact she didn't even know she had.

Ryan awoke to a buzzing sound. A book containing different carving techniques lay open under his arms, his cheek stuck to the page. A faint glow illuminated the immediate area around him, emanating from a weak desk lamp that created a gloomy, studious atmosphere in the loft.

He was confused at first. Ryan sometimes forgot that he even had a cell phone. Originally, when Ted had offered to buy him one, Ryan had declined. But Ted argued that it would only be for emergencies. In the two months since he had acquired the phone, Ryan remembered using it only a hand full of times. And every time he answered, it was Ted on the other line.

It was a little late for a call, though, he thought as he squinted down at his watch. The phone rang again. Reaching to the edge of the desk, Ryan picked it up and peered into the screen.

Sophie? Ryan looked back at his watch. Three in the morning. *Why would she*—? He answered the phone, cutting off his thoughts.

"Sophie?" he said into the receiver.

"I need help," came the soft reply.

"Where are you?" Ryan asked. He was on his feet, searching the floor for the keys to the Jeep.

Her exhaustive breathing came through the speaker as he waited for Sophie to speak again. Finally, she said, "I'm sorry I yelled at you today." She was crying.

"Sophie, where are you?" Ryan asked again.

"In the Pines," she answered vaguely. "Sean's house, I think." Ryan could barely make out her mumbled words through the tears.

"Do you need a ride home?" he asked hurriedly.

"Yes, please," she answered, as if he'd offered her dessert. "I don't feel well. I don't know what I'm doing. I'm so lost, I just want to go home..." He couldn't make out the rest of what she said.

"Where in the Pines?" Ryan pressed.

"I'm sorry I was so mean to you. I don't know what I'm doing. I don't know who I am anymore."

"Sophie," he said sharply. "Don't worry about that. Where in the Pines are you?"

"Taft, I think. End of the street. Bayside."

"North or south?"

"North."

"I'm on my way," he said. "Don't move."

"Couldn't even if I wanted to," she said.

Ryan hung up the phone, hastily threw on a dirty shirt, and found his car keys on the floor under a pair of jeans. It had been a while since he'd driven the Jeep. He hoped it still ran okay.

He bounded down the steps and hustled across the driveway. The moon was bright, and Ryan could see the world around him as clearly as if it were an overcast day. He jumped into the driver's seat, turned the key, and sped out of the driveway. The tires peeled through the pavement as he pulled onto Coastal Highway.

The road was vacant, and the world was sleeping. But his mind was spinning, his thoughts a symphony of worry. He couldn't get to her fast enough.

His foot to the floor, Ryan pushed the Jeep to its limit as he raced north, forcing his vision to scan each individual road sign faster than his mind was capable of. Garfield. Hayes. Adams. Taft. He slammed on the breaks and spun the wheel to the left, the rear tires sliding against the black-top as though it were ice. His bumper barely missed the road sign, and Ryan slammed on the accelerator as he entered the dark tunnel of pine trees lining the street like sentries. The clear, silvery world grew darker and darker in his rearview.

When he reached the end of the street, Ryan instantly knew which house Sophie had failed to describe. The front porch light was on, naked and bright, its reach illuminating a bicycle and a handful of beach towels thrown carelessly over the railing. Junkie-looking cars spilled out of the driveway onto the road. This had to be the place.

Ryan pulled the Jeep onto the grass and jumped out before it came to a complete stop. He left it running. Clearing the four porch steps in one leap, he strode to the door and tried the knob. The door swung open at his touch, the hinges creaking loudly.

Every light was on, and what he saw infuriated him. Cigarette-stained walls. A passed-out girl lying on top of a half-naked man like a blanket. Two guys playing a videogame, oblivious to the world around them. An overturned table surrounded by red plastic cups. She didn't belong here.

Ryan was about to interrogate the video-gamers when a young man staggered down the staircase in front of him. The guy had long, curly blonde hair and sported a pair of pale green board shorts. Ryan covered the distance between them and sunk his hands into the stranger's shoulders. He threw him up against the side of the staircase.

"Where's Sophie?" Ryan said.

The guy raised his hands in surrender. "Easy, man. Who the hell are you?"

"Her cousin," Ryan answered. "Where is she?"

He pointed toward the kitchen. "I think she went outside. I don't know."

Ryan took off toward the back of the house. "Fuckin' maniac, man," the guy said. Ryan rushed through the landfill that was the kitchen and thrust open the screened door forcefully enough to break a hinge. He didn't break stride as he shuffled down the steps onto the wet grass, realizing for the first time that he'd forgotten to put on shoes.

A trio of late-night burnouts were getting high around a pathetic fire in the backyard. Ryan rushed over.

"Where's Sophie?"

"Who are you?" a girl to his right asked. Her tone was casual, as if she were simply curious, excited at the prospect of a potential addition to the band.

"Where is she?"

"If you're talking about the girl with the limp," a young man spoke up to Ryan's left. "She went that way," he said, pointing north.

Ryan jogged away from the fire.

It wasn't long before he spotted her. The generous moonlight washed over her like a searchlight. He rushed over to where she was lying and dropped to his knees beside her motionless body. The light from the moon cast a mix of blue, white, and gray over her features, as though the stars were sucking the light from her face.

Ryan put his hand on Sophie's cheek. "Sophie? Can you hear me?" he asked. He wasn't sure if he should panic yet.

Slowly, Sophie's eyes opened halfway, and she looked up at him as though he were a puzzle she couldn't figure out. When she realized who he was, she said, "That was quick," and tried a smile.

Ryan smiled back. "Are you alright?" he asked. "Did you take anything tonight?"

"Huh?" she said. "You mean, like, did I steal anything?" Her head was rolling from side to side in Ryan's hands as she struggled to keep her eyes open.

"No. I mean, like, did you take any drugs tonight?"

"I don't think so. I drank a lot, though."

"Good," Ryan said. "Can you walk? Let's try to get you home." He lifted her upright, but as soon as he loosened his grip, she fell back down to the grass.

"You know I can't walk," Sophie answered after her head hit the ground, oblivious to any potential pain. "I don't think I can even move right now. Let's just sleep here tonight," She suggested. She closed her eyes.

"No way," Ryan said. "Come on. Let's get you up." He stood

and straddled Sophie's body. Leaning down, like he was about to do a squat, he slid his hands under her arms and lifted. Sophie was light, and Ryan had little trouble lifting her to her feet. He held her steady as he reached down and collected her cane.

Without warning, Ryan bent down on one knee and scooped Sophie up, throwing her over his shoulder like a fireman. He heard her grunt and giggle as her stomach sunk into his shoulder. Hopefully, as they bounced along the grass, she would be rocked to sleep, and tomorrow the whole experience would be like a bad dream she could forget.

When Ryan came upon the small crowd around the fire again, he passed them by without a word. He could feel them watching in stunned silence, as though they were seeing a ghost, a town legend come to life. He skirted the edge of the house, keeping a safe distance, afraid some invisible force might pull them back in. He made it to the driveway. Her added weight pushed his feet deeper into the gravel as he trudged on, the small rocks like tacks against the underside of his bare feet.

When he reached the Jeep, Ryan maneuvered Sophie into the front seat as carefully as he would a baby into a car seat, reclining it so she could lie back. She was still awake, barely. Hustling around to the other side, Ryan hopped in and backed the car out of the driveway, the tires peeling and kicking up dirt and loose stones. In no time, they were cruising south along Coastal Highway, the haunted house just a rearview memory.

Sophie looked over at Ryan as he drove. "Ryan?" she asked, and he had to look over at her to make sure a small child hadn't said his name, her tone that innocent.

"Yeah?" he answered, his gaze returning to the road.

"I'm sorry I yelled at you today."

He looked over at her. She seemed so weak, so frail; reclined, as if lying on a hospital bed. Only on the outside, he reminded himself. "You never need to apologize to me, Sophie," he said.

"I need to apologize to everyone," Sophie said. She started to cry. "But I can't. I can feel myself changing and I can't do anything about it. It's like I'm tied to a chair, forced to watch myself fall apart." She paused for a moment, her sobs increasing with every breath. "I'm so lost. You were just trying to help. I don't want you to drink yourself to death."

Ryan was quiet as she cried herself to sleep. "We're almost home," he said. He wanted to say so much more. He wanted to tell her she wasn't alone with those feelings, and that he knew *exactly* how she felt. But he was afraid, tied to a chair, forced to watch as he let her face that hell alone.

About a quarter-mile from the house, the car began to slow down without Ryan's foot letting off the pedal. He peered into the green light of the dash. The needle was well below the E on the fuel gauge. "Shit," he said aloud. He pressed the pedal to the floor, but the engine refused to respond, and after a few more feet, the Jeep slowed to a crawl, forcing him to pull into the sandy grass that served as the road's shoulder. "You gotta be kidding me." He looked over at Sophie. She was lost in a drunken slumber, blissfully ignorant of the situation.

The Jeep sputtered to a stop and the engine cut off. Languidly, he shoved the shifter into park. He opened the door and slid out of the seat. In the distance, he could clearly see the gap between two mansions where his destination waited, three hundred yards away.

Ryan took his time as he walked around the front of the car and opened the passenger side door. He unhooked the seat belt, scooped Sophie up in his arms, kicked the door shut, and started walking. It wasn't long before he was already tired. But he trudged on, refusing to slow as the motion rocked Sophie back and forth in his arms. It was strange; his body wanted nothing more than to collapse right there on the side of the road, but his mind was clear, and he realized there was nowhere in the world he would have rather been at that moment. For some inexplicable reason, he felt as though he were exactly where he was meant to be, carrying Sophie home through the dead of the night, away from a deeper darkness she had recklessly stumbled into. And with every step and every breath, he found strength in his reflections, as if they alone moved him forward. Safety and comfort flowed through him as the distance diminished, and the growing sound of crashing waves whispered encouragement, affirming his righteous cause with the aid of a helping breeze. It was comforting, but at the same time, disconcerting. The clarity of thought he was experiencing was undeniable, but the transient nature of it was also unavoidable. Would he recognize similar notions in the morning? Would Sophie remember what happened? Probably not. But for now, he took solace in the knowledge that he was there with her, and she was safe.

When he reached the driveway, rather than feeling elated, he felt a little let down. He could have gone on like that for hours, just walking along the road, Sophie's limp head cupped securely between his arms. He had driven a thousand destructive miles before reaching the town he now called Quicksand Beach, and after a quarter-mile walk, arms heavy and legs sluggish, he had found some semblance of peace of mind that no amount of time behind the wheel could have hoped to unlock. While Sophie's mind fell deeper into a clouded sleep, his breathed to life under uninterrupted moonlight. At least for now.

He walked onto the stone path and made his way to the back deck. He took hold of the door handle with an outstretched index finger and slid it open. And just as he had the previous night, Ryan laid Sophie down to bed.

He hesitated in the lightless room, hovering. He remembered how Ted had unfastened the prosthetic the other night. He'd explained to Ryan that Sophie could develop sores and rashes if it wasn't removed before bed. He flicked on the bedside lamp and leaned over. He hesitated again, afraid he was crossing a serious line. He was about to see something she only allowed her doctors to see, something she kept hidden from the world with the ferocity of a lioness. But it needed to be done, and Ted needed his sleep. With as gentle a touch as he could manage, Ryan rolled up the pant leg of her sweatpants and unfastened the socket attached to her thigh. He slipped it off and rested it gently on the floor, then removed the compression sock. She began to snore. His eyes lingered over the pink scar for only a moment. He pulled up the covers and took one last long look at her sleeping face. "Goodnight, Sophie," Ryan whispered. He switched off the lamp and closed the door.

When Ryan turned around, he jumped back and caught his breath. "Jesus," he whispered aloud. Ted was standing in front of him, like a ghost in the moonlight. "Ted," he said, breathing heavily. "Sorry. You scared me."

Ted stood as if frozen before Ryan. The light of the night highlighted his forlorn features, and the lines across his forehead were like shadowed canyons. For a moment, Ryan thought the man might be sleepwalking, his expression like a sad painting, eyes catatonic. Then Ted blinked and moved his head to the right, as though trying to see through Sophie's door.

Ryan felt he needed to explain the situation. He didn't know how long Ted had been outside the doorway, or how much he'd seen. The whole thing could have easily been taken out of context. "She had a little too much to drink and called me for a ride," Ryan explained. "I—"

"I didn't see your car pull in," Ted said, interrupting him.

"I ran out of gas."

"Where?"

"About a quarter-mile back," Ryan answered, still ignorant of Ted's mood.

"You carried her," Ted stated.

"Yeah," said Ryan. "I figured you needed the sleep."

"I don't sleep anymore."

Ryan was quiet. "I should have called you," he tried.

"No," Ted said, and he rested his arm on Ryan's shoulder, his hand as heavy as a cinderblock. "You brought her home safe. Thank you." Ryan let out an inward sigh of relief. "Get some sleep," Ted finished. He turned and walked across the living room and disappeared through the bedroom door.

Ryan didn't go back to sleep that night.

15

The next day, Ryan was hammering a freshly sanded chair leg into a joint when Ted cried out in pain.

"Shit!" Ted yelled.

"You okay?" Ryan asked. He set the chair aside to dry.

"Yeah, I'm fine," he said. "Just a little cut." With his thumb in his mouth, Ted walked over to the first aid box. He wrapped a band-aid around the cut.

"Gettin' slow, old man?" Ryan asked, trying to vacuum out some of the tension in the room. It had been a quiet morning, the two men lost in similar thoughts.

"I guess," Ted answered, turning back to his work. It wasn't like him to pass on a potential retort.

While the glue was drying, Ryan stepped outside. He leaned against a post and lit a cigarette. The house to the right of Ted and Sophie's was hosting a party of some kind. The mansion's back deck towered over the hedges that separated the two properties, and Ryan could make out a handful of children running around while the adults looked on in amusement. He envied those children; so carefree and ignorant. He tried to remember such a time in his life, but those memories had faded into a transparent mist long ago, spreading out into minutely sized, unrecognizable pieces of a puzzle he'd once thought to be unbreakable. He hoped those children could reach back for these memories when they grew older, when summer represented loss rather than freedom. When they spent more time looking backward than forward.

"I've been thinking," Ted said from behind him. "I was thinking we should get Kevin over here one night, and Laura, and the Palmer's." Then he added, "And maybe a professional. You know, sit down, and have a talk with Sophie. All of us."

Ryan took his time while he thought about how to respond. When he turned around, Ted's eyes were low, as if the older man had said something unthinkable and was waiting to be reprimanded.

"You mean like, an intervention?" Ryan asked, unable to keep the surprise out of his tone.

"I don't know what else to do," Ted answered defensively. "She's going to hurt herself." The desperation in his words was almost tangible; they floated through the space between the two men, hesitating, waiting to be taken back.

Ryan agreed that Sophie was going to hurt herself if she kept this lifestyle up. He was afraid she would go too far and get so lost she wouldn't be able to find her way back. But he wasn't so sure an intervention was the answer. He thought he could feel something from her last night. It was subtle, but a part of him believed she knew she was in over her head.

"I don't know how well that would go over," Ryan offered.

"It would go over horribly," Ted said, as though it were too obvious to even mention aloud. "But she needs someone else to make some decisions for her now. She has to know she can't keep this up. And an outside opinion might do some good." He added, "It's just not who she is."

"Maybe give her a little more time," Ryan said. "I think she may come around soon. She doesn't want this life." He began to gain some confidence in his theory. "I don't think she's to the point where she can't help it. She's close, but she's not lost. I can see it." He didn't know why, but Ryan was suddenly sure of himself. He *knew* he was right.

Ted took a seat on a three-legged chair in the corner and nearly fell over. He stood back up. "You can tell?" he asked. "How?"

"It's just a feeling."

Ted tried a smile. It was a weak smile, like he had been smiling too long for a picture and his facial muscles were faltering. "Well," he said. "I'm going to trust your feeling."

He opened his eyes and caught his breath.

Since his arrival at the house, Ryan's dreams had become increasingly unpredictable. Sometimes the nightmares were as vivid as ever, waking him like a bucket of ice water poured over his face. Other times, he couldn't remember a single detail.

He sat up in bed and ran a hand through his hair. He glanced out the window. Another bright moon hung high in a star-less sky. He stood up and reached for his cigarettes.

The air was warm and the breeze strong off the ocean when he stepped outside. It was impossibly clear, and Ryan could make out every shade of gray painted over the moon. On the landing at the top of the staircase, he ignited his lighter. A tight stream of smoke escaped his lungs a moment later, rising into the night and shading the moon for a moment like a thin cloud.

He leaned over the railing and faced the ocean. The breeze felt refreshing over his shirtless frame. He closed his eyes, allowing the sensation to whisk away any lingering darkness from the nightmare.

Out of the corner of his eye, Ryan noticed a white figure moving along the edge of the pool. It took him a moment to realize it was Sophie.

A long white robe hugged her frame, covering her body from neck to toe. She moved in slow motion, and her head hung low, as if she were following an invisible path she dared not stray from. She skirted the edge of the pool and stepped onto the walkway that led to the beach. He had never seen Sophie move in that direction. She watched sometimes, but never made a move. He hesitated, torn over whether to follow. But his curiosity got the better of him, and Ryan made his way down the steps and toward the beach.

When he reached the beginning of the walkway, Sophie had made it out to the sand, about twenty yards in front of him. The sand was a ruffled silver blanket, and the moon loomed high, resting on a soft bed of clouds now, like a fortune teller's orb on a gray velvet pillow.

Sophie made it to the water and stopped, just out of the surf's reach. She was struggling to stay balanced, even with the crutches, and he wondered if she was wearing her prosthetic. Ryan started walking when she did. By the time he reached the sand, Sophie was immobile, studying the waves like a surfer. A wave rose in front of her, its white tip almost as tall as her. With a deafening crash, the remnants of the wave washed up and kissed her toes.

All other thoughts were erased from his mind as he watched in awe as Sophie slowly undid her robe and let it fall carelessly to the sand. She was wearing a black bathing suit, but not her prosthetic. The two were frozen in time, Sophie watching the ocean, and Ryan watching her. Like the moon, she seemed so close, yet so far away.

She moved toward the breaking waves.

"Sophie," he called. He put his hands to his mouth, hoping that would help his voice carry over the sound of the surf.

Sophie turned her head to the side, allowing him to catch a glimpse of her profile. She continued, as if in a trance.

Ryan started walking toward her. "Sophie!" he called again. "What are you doing?"

Sophie was in knee-deep water now. She turned around and looked at Ryan with a stoic expression, as though her face were still asleep. Turning back to the water, she dropped her crutches and dove straight through an oncoming wave, disappearing as though she'd jumped through a portal into an unknown universe.

Ryan slipped off his sweatpants and took off after her.

Sophie's head surfaced as Ryan dove under an oncoming wave. Before she could swim out any farther, Ryan lunged forward and grabbed hold of her arm.

"What are you doing?" he said. "Are you insane?"

"Let go," she whispered. It was the kind of whisper Ryan heard in his dreams.

"No," he said. "Come on, this is crazy." He pulled on her arm, bringing her closer to an embrace.

"Let go of me!" she shouted. The waves seemed to lose strength at her command. She flashed Ryan a terrifying look and he recoiled for a moment, loosening his grip but refusing to let go. "I'm not afraid," she said, possessed by a frightening determination.

"Well, I am!" Ryan countered, tightening his grip on her arm.

For a moment, Sophie's determination wavered, and she seemed to be considering what she was doing for the first time. But it didn't last. She ripped her arm out of Ryan's grip and attempted to dive back under. He dove after her. Halfway underwater, he wrapped his arms around her waist. Planting his feet on the ocean's floor, Ryan vaulted upwards, lifting Sophie out of the water.

She was kicking her legs, like a child throwing a tantrum. "Let me go! Let me go!"

"No," Ryan said, struggling to keep a firm hold on her wriggling frame. Despite Sophie's exhaustive efforts, Ryan began wading toward shore. Once they were in knee-deep water, a wave crashed and rolled into them like an avalanche, knocking the pair over and washing them onto the sand.

Sophie had fallen on top of him and was shaking against his chest. It took him a moment to realize she was sobbing. He lay back and wrapped his arms around her. Warm tears poured from Sophie's eyes. Ryan held her close, afraid to let go. She rolled off his chest and lay on her back beside him. Her eyes were closed, and her skin glistened in the glow of the moon. Light danced all over her body.

"I've lost my place in the world," she said, her eyes still closed. Ryan listened patiently. "After my Mom died, swimming was all I had. Now I have nothing," she said, like it was a fact not to be disputed.

"You have your father, Sophie," Ryan said.

Sophie was thoughtful. She said, "I know. But I can't be strong for him again. I don't have anything left. I'm so tired."

"I know how you feel."

"What do you know about it?" she said.

Ryan sat up and gazed out over the glistening Atlantic. He

wasn't sure if it was because he thought it might help Sophie, or because he was lonely, or because he thought she of all people would understand. Maybe it was a combination of all three and more. Whatever the reason, he decided to tell her his story. In that moment, they were the same, she and him. Two lost souls on the edge of the world.

"I wasn't always this way," Ryan began. Sophie was still lying on her back, her right leg drawn up. "I used to be motivated. I used to love things." He stopped. This wasn't right. He started over. "My parents didn't love each other," he said. "At least, not when I was a kid. My mother was severely depressed. My father was a businessman, and I only remember them fighting when I was younger. We lived very comfortably, though."

Sophie sat up and hugged her right knee to her chest.

"I wasn't close with either of them," he went on. "I think they resented me because they felt an obligation to stay together because of me. If I hadn't been born, they definitely would have gotten divorced. That's not me feeling guilty, or anything. It's a fact." He felt her breathing change. "I still managed to have a pretty good childhood, though. I had friends, and I was good at sports. So, it could have been worse, I guess." He paused again and glanced at Sophie. She continued to listen patiently.

"Everything changed when Sarah was born," he said. Ryan closed his eyes, remembering the first time he saw her. "I was thirteen at the time. It wouldn't take a genius to figure out that my parents hadn't planned on having another kid. But it turned out to be the best mistake of their lives, and mine." He curled his hand into the sand. "She was born with Down Syndrome," he said. He felt Sophie's head turn. "At first, I was afraid my parents would resent

Sarah, as they had me. But they loved her. I'm sure they loved me too, in their own way. But the love they had for Sarah was different. Somehow, after she was born, my parents fell back in love. I was old enough to understand exactly what had happened."

He smiled. "They called her their miracle baby," he said. "And she really was, in so many ways. I loved her more than life the second I laid eyes on her. She was perfect." He returned his gaze to the sea. Sophie's eyes remained fixed on his.

"We started going on family vacations," he continued. "My dad even bought a lake house. I lived for Sarah; we all did. She was our world. My dad worked a lot, and my mother couldn't always be trusted to stay alert, so I helped raise her. In some ways, she was my sister, my daughter, and my best friend. What else did I need?" He paused, then added, "Through high school, I didn't hang out with friends much. I hung out with Sarah and was more than happy to. I loved her so much." A wave crashed, filling the brief silence.

"The summer after I graduated college, we all went to the lake house," he said. "I brought a couple friends, mostly because it was supposed to be a graduation party. But I didn't care if anyone came. Sarah asked me if I was embarrassed that I didn't have many friends. 'Of course not,' I told her, 'People should be jealous of me because you're my best friend.' She loved when I said things like that."

Ryan sighed. "Believe it or not," he said. "I never used to drink much at all. Or smoke." He laughed. Sophie remained as quiet as a vacant church. "I actually used to consider myself responsible," he went on. "But that weekend, I let loose. I was about to get into the world of finance and start my life, just like the old man. I was good with numbers, and my father had connections. It made sense, I guess." He shrugged and shifted his position in the sand slightly.

"It was overcast that morning, and my friends and I were hungover." He stopped again, trying to gather himself. "We decided to take the boat out. Sarah begged to come with us—she never wanted me to do anything without her." He let out a long breath. "How different everything would be if I hadn't convinced my parents to let her come with us."

Ryan looked out over the water. "If only it had been as calm that day as it is tonight," he said. Sophie's breath filled the air.

"It was a small speed boat, and my friends had snuck on a few beers. I was driving, and Sarah was toward the back. Her life vest was on, and she was having a blast. The longer we were out, though, the windier it got. The water started to get rough, and Sarah loved the feeling of bouncing up and down with the waves." He paused again, recoiling at the memory.

"I was drunk," he said. "I tried to lie to myself for a long time; convince myself that I wasn't. But I was drunk." He stared through the sand, into the past. "At some point, Sarah must have taken off her life vest. I wasn't paying attention. I hit a huge wave." He brought his hands to his face, as if trying to hide. "We never should have been out there. I was going too fast. When I turned around, the others were yelling. It was hard to hear over the wind. Then I noticed that Sarah wasn't on the boat. Her life vest was lying on the floor. I turned around and backtracked. The others weren't sure where she fell in. The waves were so high, and it had started to rain. I couldn't see anything." Ryan's speech was quickening with his breath. Sophie's cold hand fell on his shoulder.

"They found her body an hour later," he said. The memory was a knife. "She was ten."

Sophie caught her breath.

He went on, desperately trying to keep an even tone. "They said she had hit her head and been knocked out before falling into the water. They said she didn't feel any pain. There was no consolation, but that made me feel a little less horrible, I guess. Maybe they just told us that to try and ease the pain. Who knows?" He could hardly hear himself speaking.

"Ryan..."

He wasn't finished. "After the funeral, my father left us, as I knew he would. He couldn't look at me, and I didn't blame him. I couldn't look at myself, still can't. He put thirty thousand dollars in my account before he left. He took a job in New York and I didn't see him for a long time. My mother lost it, as I knew she would, and I didn't care. I didn't care about anything. I had taken away the miracle that saved my family. I was a monster."

"Ryan, you can't—"

He cut her off. He still wasn't finished. "A few weeks after Sarah died, I came home late one night after a long weekend and found my mother on the kitchen floor. She had overdosed on painkillers. She'd been dead for hours." He said it without emotion.

Sophie brought her hands to her mouth. "Oh my God," she whispered.

"I still feel guilty that I didn't cry when I found her," he said. "I just stared, like a deer in the headlights, unable to move, or feel." He paused, then added, "That's when I realized I was just as dead as she was."

His head drooped and his eyes fell to the sand between his legs. No one else existed in that moment. "Even after my mother died, I still felt like I might have been able to squeeze out some kind of life for myself. I was broken; destroyed, sure, but a part of me wanted to be strong, for Sarah. I know she would have wanted me to be happy."

Ryan lifted his head. "So, about a month after my mother's death, I took a job in New York. A friend from college helped me with a gig at an investment company. I was miserable. But so was everyone else. I drank like a fish on the weekends and somehow made it to work on Monday.

"One afternoon, I was walking along the sidewalk and noticed my father up ahead," he said. "He didn't speak to me at my mother's funeral, and it had been a little while. I thought maybe he might be proud that I was following in his footsteps." Ryan could tell Sophie was shaken up, but he went on. He was almost done. "About fifteen feet away from me he stopped. He was with a woman I'd never seen before. They were holding hands. He looked at me, then turned around and walked the other way. I heard him tell the woman he had forgotten something. I stood there for a while, maybe an hour, staring into the empty space. I know I messed up bad, but he was my father. He was the only family I had left."

"I can't imagine how hard that was," Sophie said.

"Something in me snapped after that," he went on. "I couldn't do it. He had started this whole new life within a couple months of everything happening. I guess everyone deals with things their own way. I quit my job, and I've been traveling along the coast ever since. Drinking myself to death, as you said, along the way."

"Ryan, I didn't mean that," Sophie pleaded.

"I know, Sophie," he said. Ryan looked over at her. Her hair was drying quickly in the light breeze and black strands floated around her head like string in the wind. "I've never spoken of it aloud to anyone," he continued. "I haven't felt the need to. I don't know why I'm telling you now. But what I do know is your father wouldn't survive losing you. It would kill him. And I know you think you've lost everything, but you haven't. Not yet."

Sophie was silent, thoughtful. "Sophie," he said. "I know what you think of me, and I don't blame you. I'm not telling you this in hopes that you'll see me differently. I just thought that you might want to hear it. And, so you know that I really do understand, better than most, what you're going through. And I can tell you, if you continue down the road you're on, you'll end up very alone, and you'll lose everything."

Ryan let out a weighted breath, expecting to be struck by a lightning bolt, or dragged underground. Nothing happened, though. The waves continued to crash, and the moon continued to shine. He felt something like relief, but it had been so long, he couldn't be sure.

After a long silence, Sophie said, "Ryan, I—" she stopped, unable to find more words. She surprised him by lightly touching his thigh, her fingers like electricity, and when he looked into her emerald eyes, glowing like green lanterns in the dark, he could feel what she couldn't say. She rested her head on his shoulder, the warmth of her cheek like fire. They stayed like that for a while.

Eventually, he rose to his feet and extended his hand. She looked up at him. "Can I help you inside?" he asked.

She hesitated, regarding his hand as though it were covered in thorns.

Then, finally, she accepted.

16

Ryan awoke the next morning to a little less pain than usual. He rose and pushed himself up off the bed. His shoulders easily moved through the air, and his legs didn't feel quite so heavy.

He made his way down the steps and around the back of the garage. A towel and jeans thrown over his shoulders, Ryan entered the outside shower. It had the look of an outhouse he'd seen in western movies as a kid, with cracks so large in the wood, he felt he could be seen from passersby on the beach. Hot water escaped through the showerhead and covered his pale skin. It burned beautifully. The sun lit up the water, and Ryan felt as though he were showering in light.

When he exited the shower, Ryan chanced a random glance at the pool. He turned away to continue back up to the loft but was forced to stop mid-stride, recalling something out of place. Turning back to the pool, Ryan had to squint to make out the scene before him. Sophie wasn't sitting beside the pool like she so often did. She was *in* the pool, gliding through the water. Her arms stretched out before her, inches under the surface, then parted in a wide arc as her body moved. Her right leg kicked while the left thigh swayed back and forth. He stood still, shocked, as though he had caught sight of a unicorn and dared not move, or even breathe.

Unable to conceal the bewilderment plastered to his face, Ryan continued to watch, arrested as Sophie phased through the crystal-clear water, the morning light piercing through the surface like spears.

Sophie pulled up to the side and rested her forearms on the edge. She rested her cheek against the back of her hand then lifted her head, sensing she wasn't alone. Gradually, she turned in his direction. Her hair was untouched by the tame water, blowing subtly in a light breeze. Her pale skin brilliantly lit. He could see the green of her eyes from twenty feet away. She lifted her hand and waved.

Ryan waved back. He tried a weak smile, a pathetic attempt to mirror Sophie's warm greeting. She held his gaze, and her smile for a moment longer, then went back to her laps.

Ryan rushed up to his room and got dressed in a confused daze.

Later that morning, under the awning, Ryan's attention was stuck on a single blade of grass.

"Okay. What did you do?" Ted asked. Ryan looked over his shoulder. Ted was moving toward him. He helped himself into the chair opposite Ryan and crossed his legs.

"What do you mean?" Ryan asked.

"Well, let's see," Ted began. "I wake up to the smell of eggs and bacon this morning, which my beautiful daughter decided to make for her loving father. Weird, right?" Ted gave Ryan a bewildered look. "But that's not all," he went on. "It gets weirder. She gave me a kiss on the cheek! Can you believe that?" Ryan shrugged. Then Ted added, "I was so stunned, I couldn't even speak. And all this weirdness happens after you cryptically tell me yesterday that she was coming around. Now, all I need to know is, how do you do it?"

"How do I do what?" Ryan asked.

"Tell the future!"

Ryan decided to play along while considering whether to tell Ted what had happened last night. "Look, I didn't ask for this gift, Ted," he said. "It's really more of a curse."

Ted nodded, as if he were afraid that was the case. Then, without warning, the older man burst out laughing. It was a genuine, obnoxiously loud laugh, the kind of laugh that seemed to escape the mouth before the vessel realized how crazy it sounded. Ryan allowed himself a constricted smile. The journey was far from over, Ryan knew, but there was hope. Sophie's father felt that hope in a kiss that morning. Ryan saw it in a graceful stroke.

"Seriously," Ted said after regaining his composure. "What did you do?"

Ryan considered before answering. "I didn't do anything," he said. "I mean, we talked last night. But there's no way that's the reason for her one-eighty behavior."

"Huh," Ted said. "What did you talk about? If you don't mind my asking."

"Well," Ryan replied. "I told her a little bit about myself. About my life before coming here."

Ted relaxed back against the chair and interlocked his fingers behind his head. "Well, that's it, obviously."

"No way," Ryan countered. "There's no way it had that kind of effect overnight."

Ted stared out over the water. "You know," he said. "For someone who reads as much as you do, I think you underestimate the power of a story." He looked at Ryan and raised an eyebrow.

Ryan didn't answer. Instead, he watched the wind move the water; shadows of hovering clouds changed its color from deep blue to murky green, then back to deep blue. Whatever the reason, Ryan was happy that Ted had his daughter back. At least for now.

An hour later, Ted and Ryan were hard at work. The table saw was roaring, and the sander was on full blast. Sawdust swirled around them like a tornado.

The saw ceased and Ryan glanced up to see his instructor watching the open breezeway intently. Ryan followed his gaze. Standing in the doorway, hunched over a pair of crutches, stood Sophie. Everything became still. The dust floating around the room seemed to freeze in place, and Ted looked as though he had been turned to stone. Ryan watched in stunned curiosity.

The sun was high behind her, forcing Ryan to raise a hand against the glare. He turned off the sander and a warm quiet filled the room.

Sophie smiled. "Hi," she said. She was wearing a white buttoned-down shirt and her hair fell untamed over relaxed shoulders. A pair of short, faded jean shorts stopped mid-thigh, leaving her residual limb exposed. No prosthetic or covering of any kind.

A soft breeze helped push Sophie into the room. Ryan and Ted remained where they were. The two men were reacting as if a baby deer had accidentally wandered into the workshop.

Sophie moved closer to the middle of the room, between her father and Ryan. She looked at Ryan and smiled.

"Morning," Ryan said, answering Sophie's greeting two minutes too late.

"Good morning, Sweetheart," Ted said from across the room. "Um. Are you lost?" he joked. Ryan wanted to throw the sander at him. *Don't scare it away!*

"Very funny, Daddy," she replied. Ryan had never heard Sophie refer to her father as Daddy. "Actually, I was wondering if I could help," she said as she moved up beside Ryan and ran her hand over the smooth surface he had just sanded.

"Say that again?" Ted asked. He still hadn't moved a muscle.

"You heard me," she said. "I thought maybe I could paint something. You know, like when I used to help? Or carve. You always said I had a knack for carving." Her tone of voice had changed as well. Ryan was beginning to remember how she was the first time he met her. It had been cruel that he had only been able to witness that side of her for a couple of hours.

"Sweetheart, you can paint and carve me if you want," said Ted. "Ryan, do you mind if she paints you?" he asked. He didn't wait for an answer. "You can paint the house, carve up the truck for all I care."

"Let's call that plan B," Sophie said. "How about that side table?" She pointed to the unfinished piece in the corner.

"That's one of Ryan's side projects he's been working on," Ted explained. "Ryan, do you mind if Sophie paints your table?"

"Of course not," Ryan answered immediately.

"Maybe we could paint it a dark green, with brown trim," Sophie offered. "I bet someone in the pines would eat that up." Ted and Ryan nodded in unison. "Okay," she said through a grin. "Let's get to work, then." But before she moved, she added, "Oh, Dad. Do you think we could make an appointment with the prosthetist soon?"

"Of course," Ted said. "Something wrong?"

"Nothing to worry about," Sophie said. "I just don't have enough socks to balance out the shrinkage in my stump, so I think I need to have the prosthetic adjusted." Ryan had no idea what she was talking about, but he didn't want her to stop.

"Okay, I'll call the doctor right now."

"No," Sophie said. "It can wait. Let's get to work." Ted looked at Ryan, as though he might have something to add. Ryan shrugged and turned back to Sophie. She had set her crutches aside and was kneeling, peering under the counter. She fished out some paint supplies: an old brush, a stirring stick, and a couple different colored paint cans. Right where she left them, apparently.

Ted and Ryan watched her, like a pair of worried parents, waiting for Sophie to ask for help. But the request never came, and soon the two men continued with their work while they strategized individually over how to adjust for the rest of the day.

Sophie laid a white sheet down on the cement floor and easily lifted the small table onto it with one hand, all the while keeping one crutch under her left arm for support. After finding a small stool, she settled in and began priming the wood. Ryan watched all of this transpire out of the corner of his eye. So engrossed by Sophie's movements, he could scarcely concentrate on his own work. She sat on the low stool with her right knee pulled up and her left thigh hanging over the edge. Her right hand gracefully moved up and down as she painted, leaving a trail as green and bright as her eyes. Ryan's head was like a puppet's, following her simple movements as if they were the most enthralling things he'd ever seen. Occasionally, a strong breeze would intrude and blow a piece of the sheet into the wet paint. Sophie simply laughed it off and continued.

Over the next hour, few words were spoken. Sophie painted with care while Ryan and Ted acted as though they were working, instead of watching her every movement.

Around noon Sophie rose. She leaned against the counter, stretched her hands high over her head, and announced she might go for a walk along the beach.

"Ryan," she said. "Wanna come?"

Ryan stared blankly at her then looked to Ted. Ted shrugged. "Don't look at me. You're a big boy."

Ryan turned back to Sophie. "Sure."

"Great. Let me just wash my hands." Her hands and forearms were splashed with white, green, and brown paint, and she was smiling. She hustled out of the shop and into the house.

While he waited at the top of the wooden path, Ryan took the opportunity to gather his thoughts. Apprehension overtook him as he searched in vain for something to lean on. The idea that Sophie's newly rediscovered jovial nature was a result of the previous night's conversation disturbed him. If it was in fact the case, he scolded himself for not telling her earlier. He could have saved Ted more than a few sleepless nights.

"So, did you try to copy me? Or is it just a coincidence," Sophie said from behind. They were both wearing a white shirt and jeans.

"Have you seen me wear anything else since you've known me?"

Sophie tilted her head, thoughtful. "I guess not."

They made their way down the ramp and toward the surf, Sophie a half step in front of Ryan. "It's easier to walk with my crutches on the firm sand," she explained when they were just out of the water's reach.

Ryan looked left then right. "Which way?" he asked.

"Let's go right," Sophie offered, and they started south.

The beach was relatively crowded, and they walked in silence for a while. Blue umbrellas dotted the sand and children threw frisbees and played paddle ball while parents looked on from the shade. A chocolate lab darted out in front of them and chased a tennis ball into the shallow surf.

After about five minutes, Sophie stopped. Using her crutches for support, she lowered herself onto the damp sand. Ryan followed suit. "I never used to sweat like this," Sophie said, pausing to wipe her brow. She extended her right leg and leaned back, her hands catching her weight.

"Me neither," Ryan said. But his mind was somewhere else. Did she know they were in almost the exact same spot where she had been attacked? She had to, he thought.

"It's okay," Sophie said. "I don't mind if you look at it. You've seen worse." He hadn't noticed he was staring at her leg.

It was true, though. Ryan recalled the sight of blood pumping out of her thigh like a hose that morning. He flushed the image from his mind. "You're wearing shorts," he said.

"Yup," she said. "Figured it was time to stop hiding it. It's a part of who I am now. I need to start learning to accept it."

"Quite a change in perspective overnight," Ryan said, unable to hide his skepticism.

Sophie took a deep breath, inhaling the warm breeze. Turning to him, she said, "I've spent all night and all morning trying to figure out what to say, and how to say it."

Ryan watched her in silence as she searched the sand around her toes for the right words.

"The way I've treated you. The things I've said," Sophie began. She paused and dipped her head. "It's unforgiveable."

"I forgive you," Ryan said.

"I've been so selfish," she said. "I'd lost sight of everything that was important, and you helped me remember, even if that wasn't your intention." She turned to face him. "I became the kind of person I despise. I judged you and insulted you. And how did you repay me? By telling me something you've never told anyone. I'm so embarrassed, I can't even put it into words. I didn't consider, even for a second that you had a life, a family; something before all this. All I could see was my own past. My own pain."

"I understand," he said.

"I know you do," Sophie said, leaning towards him. "That's the worst part. All this time, I've had someone who not only understands, but understands in ways that I don't. In ways that no one should ever have to. And I couldn't see it. I couldn't see anything." She shifted her attention out to sea. "But last night I saw you, for the first time. And I felt...I felt so much it hurt."

He envied her. The feeling she was describing was lost to him, a feeling so distant and removed from who he was now.

"All this time I felt so alone," she continued. "I don't even know the meaning of the word compared to you."

"Thanks."

"No, I don't mean it like that," she said. "God, I'm sorry."

"I know what you mean," Ryan said. "And you're right, it has been a lonely road for me. But your father has helped with that, and I'm grateful for it."

"So am I," she said. She chuckled under her breath. "You know, I didn't want to have you stay here at first."

"No?" Ryan said sarcastically, grinning.

"That obvious, huh? But thank God you did. I don't know where I'd be if you'd left."

"You would have managed."

"I'm not so sure."

They were quiet for a few moments. "I know it's a lot to ask," she said. "Probably too much. And I totally understand if you can't, but would you be willing to start over? Like, pretend the last six weeks never happened. I figured this would be a good place to start over." She motioned with her head out to sea, a simple gesture that he knew couldn't have been easy.

"No problem," he answered. "I'm good at pretending."

Sophie turned to him, and Ryan imitated her movement. "I'm Sophie," she said, extending her hand.

"Oh," he said. "We're going that far back?"

"It's a bit cliché, I know, but what the hell?"

"Nothing wrong with clichés," he said. Ryan took Sophie's hand in his. It was warm, and light. He got to his feet and helped her up. "Ready to head back?"

Sophie scanned the umbrellas on the beach, as if searching for something. "Actually, do you mind if we make a stop first?"

"Sure," he said. "Where?"

"Follow me."

Ryan followed Sophie toward a pink umbrella perched in front of the Palmer mansion. Liv was asleep underneath it, her mouth open, a pair of sunglasses crooked over her eyes and nose. She wore a bright red bikini and was lying on a bright yellow beach towel. Her skin was painfully sunburned, almost as red as her bathing suit. An empty beach chair sat just beyond the reach of the shade.

Sophie and Ryan exchanged hesitant glances. Lifting one crutch out of the sand, Sophie poked Liv in the calf. Liv stirred, then swatted the sunglasses off her face and opened her eyes. She raised her hand to shield against the light. Liv considered the two intruders indifferently.

Ryan waved. "Hey, Liv. Lookin' good."

"Ugh, shut up," she said, rising onto her elbows. "I don't want to talk about it." Two seconds later, she said, "Alright, fine. I got hammered yesterday by myself and passed out on the beach without an umbrella. It's boring as fuck around here. I'm not proud of it."

Ryan smiled and Sophie giggled. "Can we sit down?" Sophie asked.

Liv measured her old friend from the ground up. "As long as you don't plan on hitting me with those crutches," she said. She looked to Ryan. He shrugged.

"I promise," Sophie said, and she lowered herself onto the sand beside Liv.

Ryan hesitated beyond the shade. "Do you want me to give you a minute, or…"

"Only if it makes you uncomfortable," Sophie said. Ryan hesitated.

"Woah," Liv said, raising her hand in protest at Ryan. "You're not going anywhere. I need a witness in case she snaps."

Sophie smiled weakly. Ryan inched forward and sat down.

"So, what's going on?" Liv asked after she had decided enough silence had passed.

Unlike when she was with Ryan, Sophie didn't hesitate. "I'm sorry I'm such a bitch," she said.

Liv watched Sophie intently, as though trying to figure out if it was a genuine apology. She looked to Ryan. "Did you guys hook up, or something?" she said. Had Ryan not already experienced the unfiltered mouth that belonged to Liv, he might have been shocked to embarrassment. But he wasn't surprised at all. He shook his head.

Sophie couldn't hide her indignation. "What?" she said, her eyes flashing to Ryan, then Liv. "No! Liv, what are you talking about?"

"Alright, chill," Liv replied, holding up her hands in surrender. "Why the change in mood, then? Did you just have like a six-week period, or something?"

An involuntary laugh exploded from Ryan's mouth, which he quickly snuffed out. Sophie's mouth fell open in astonishment. "Liv!" she exclaimed, her cheeks turning as red as Liv's stomach.

"Oh, please," Liv said. "Don't act like you don't know me. What, you think I'm gonna hold back just cause you suddenly saw the light?" It was turning into one of the more interesting exchanges Ryan had ever witnessed. And as uncomfortable as he felt, he couldn't look away.

Sophie gave in and smiled. "Seriously, Liv," she said. "I'm really sorry. I shouldn't have said the things I said. I don't know what got into me."

"I do," Liv said. "You lost your leg, Soph. I know as well as anyone what that means. And you were angry and sad, and a bitch." Sophie laughed under her breath. "And that's okay." Liv rested her hand on Sophie's left thigh. "It's okay to lose your cool and get pissed, freak out. I know, I do it all the time." Just when Ryan thought he had Liv figured out, she managed to say the perfect thing at the perfect time. "We're best friends, Soph," she went on. "We're gonna be bitches to each other sometimes. Honestly, it's about time you take some of that responsibility. I can only do so much."

Tears brimmed Sophie's eyes. She threw her arms around Liv's shoulders. "Ah!" Liv cried.

Sophie pulled back. "I'm so sorry."

Liv froze, afraid to move. "It's cool," she said through clenched teeth.

"So," Sophie said while Liv rolled a cold, unopened beer can over her arms and shoulders. "We're still friends?"

"Of course, Soph," Liv said. "Love you, girl."

Ryan hadn't moved since the show began. He felt as though he'd been let into a room he wasn't supposed to be in, like he'd stumbled into a slumber party and witnessed things no man should ever see. He felt there was a lesson to be learned from the experience.

17

That evening, Sophie and Ted were sitting in the library. The sun had ducked below the western horizon, leaving behind a masterpiece of colorful clouds that swirled and blended together in a chaotic splash.

Sophie watched the slowly changing painting from one of the upholstered, high-backed chairs. It was one of the more beautiful sunsets she could remember. She recalled one of her co-workers at the bar telling her how badly they had wished they'd lived on the west coast, so they could have watched the sunset every day over the water. He, or she—Sophie couldn't remember who—had claimed that sunrises paled in comparison to sunsets. Neither one was better, she thought, but there was something about a sunrise; something about a new day. It seemed more hopeful, more powerful, like an explosion of possibility. Either way, it was a privilege to witness the start and end of a day, a notion she'd lost sight of for a while. She smiled at the thought.

The identical antique chairs were separated by a small circular coffee table finished in a deep brown stain, like the coat of the chocolate lab she had seen on the beach earlier in the day. A Persian rug lay underneath them, adding to the studious atmosphere of the room.

Never having been much of a reader, Sophie had seldom spent time in the library over the years. She preferred to be outside and the stuffiness of a library made her feel confined. She was like her father in that way. But she had always envied her mother. Reading and relaxing was an art form Sophie never cared to learn, but one that her mother had mastered at a young age. Now that she lacked the ability to run and swim like before, Sophie wished she had taken the time to learn the craft.

Sophie insisted that she and her father spend some time in the library that evening. It seemed a good place for reconciliation. Her father was stretched out in his chair, legs resting casually on a maroon-cushioned ottoman.

She had just finished recounting the events of the previous night, leaving nothing out.

"Goodness," he said when she'd finished. He rubbed his hands over his cheeks as though he were lathering them up with shaving cream. "I knew it was bad, but I didn't know it was that bad," He shook his head. "He really has been dealt a bad hand. Wish I could do more for him," he had said.

But now she was nervous. Sophie had never had a reason to apologize to her father before. Butterflies fluttered around in her stomach, a feeling usually reserved for prior to a swim meet.

Without warning, she said, "Daddy, I'm so sorry." It was all she could manage. Before the words even left her mouth, Sophie started to cry. She tried again, determined to give her father what he deserved. "I'm so sorry," she said. "You must have been so worried." She crushed her palms to her eyes.

He jumped up from his reclined position and moved to Sophie. In a moment, he was on his knees by her chair. He wrapped his arms around her head and pulled her to his chest. "It's okay, Sweetheart," he said, choking back his own tears. "It's okay," he said. He stroked her hair like he used to do when she was a girl.

After a few minutes, Sophie regained her composure. She hadn't realized how badly she needed to cry like that. Relief overtook her as her father pulled away and looked into her pink, bloodshot eyes. He wiped a tear from her cheek. "It's okay," he said again in a whisper.

Sophie sniffled once and peered through her flooded vision into his loving eyes. "No, it's not," she said. "After everything you've been through. After everything, I still pushed you away. I still—"

"Sweetie," her father said, taking her face in his calloused hands. "Listen to me." He lowered his head and looked up into her eyes when she dropped her gaze. "None of that matters now," he said. "So, you were human for once. Join the club." Sophie smiled through her tears and looked up. "Sweetheart," he said. "I'm just happy to have my little girl back."

She threw her arms around him. "I don't know what I would do without you."

"We don't have to worry about that anymore."

Sophie wiped her eyes. "You were right about Ryan," she said. "There is so much more to him than I knew."

He sat back on the ottoman in front of her chair. "He's helped both of us," he said. "More than he knows. Now we need to help him, Soph."

"I know. You've already done so much, Daddy. Let me take over for a little while."

"What are you going to do?" he asked.

She looked out the window. "I'm going to try to be his friend."

That night, Sophie hesitated at the top of the steps that led to Ryan's loft. Her prosthetic was in the house and having left her crutches at the bottom of the steps, she leaned on the railing for support. She hadn't thought much about what she would say to him, and she had no idea what to expect. What did he do up there? Would he be happy to see her, or upset at the intrusion? She shook her head free of the thoughts. She needed to do this and that was it.

She knocked three times. Nothing. She knocked again.

"Come in?" he called. His voice was far away, farther away than she would have thought possible, if she remembered correctly how small the space was. She opened the door and squinted into the dimness. The entire space was cast in shadow. A light emanated from the ground floor of the garage. She looked around the space. T-shirts, underwear, and pants were strewn carelessly on the rug. A couple empty liquor bottles leaned against the railing. Sheets and pillows ruffled atop the narrow twin bed, and a desk pushed up against the slanted underside of the roof below the round window. No surprises, except one. Ryan wasn't anywhere to be seen.

"Hello?" he called.

Sophie hopped into the room and found the railing to her left for support. She peered over. Ryan was sitting on a short stool, eight feet below. He was squinting up at her. On one side of him rested a paint can atop a white sheet that was sprawled out over the cement. On the other side was a bottle of whiskey and a small glass, half full. He had a paintbrush in his hand. Before him, also on the white sheet, was a simply constructed desk, half unfinished and half painted in a bright sky blue. The desk only had three legs and was leaning toward him, unable to support itself. A lamp with no shade stood beside the paint can, creating a circle of honeyed light around the scene. Anything else surrounding him was cast in shadow. It was the last thing Sophie had expected to see.

"Hey," she said, searching for a new game plan.

"Hey," he replied.

"Whatcha doin'?" she asked.

He looked at the paintbrush, then back up to her. "Painting."

"Why?" she asked, stalling.

"Come on down and I'll show you."

Sophie went back outside and shimmied down the staircase, her hands sliding along the wall and railing. She picked up her crutches, and made her way under the staircase, entering through the side door. It opened into the underside of the loft, and when she opened the door, what she saw arrested her. She knew her father used the garage to store his unwanted or broken pieces. What she didn't know was that Ryan had painted nearly all of them.

"Wow" she said as she moved out from under the loft's overhang and into the middle of the floor. Ryan remained seated, watching her carefully.

Against the north wall, a backless chair had been painted seafoam green. Beside it, an armless rocker was covered in a deep ocean blue. A door-less base cabinet was painted a pale yellow. But it wasn't just that they were painted. They looked old and worn out, as though they had been left out in a storm for months. Underneath the green, and blue, and yellow were spots of white or tan. It was a unique effect that left Sophie speechless.

"I think the term they use is 'distressed,'" Ryan explained, following her gaze around the room. "What do you think?"

Sophie took a few moments to answer, still not fully acclimated to the scenery. "I think it's amazing," she finally managed. "Is this what you've been doing up here? Or down here?"

Ryan shifted in his seat and rested the paintbrush on the lid of a nearby can. "For the most part," he said. "Don't need any sharp objects or power tools, so it's a quiet way to kill some time."

"Where did you learn to make them look so…worn?" Sophie asked as she inched closer to where he was. She searched around for somewhere to sit. Her armpits were killing her.

Ryan sensed her distress and jumped up. He jogged to the wall, grabbed the broken rocking chair, and set it down beside his stool. "It's not whole, but it should do the job," he said.

"Thanks," she said, and sat down gratefully.

He sat back down, his bare chest blinding in the naked light of the lamp. His jeans were covered in paint. His feet were bare.

"Actually, I just googled it," he said.

"Huh?"

"That's how I learned," he clarified. "It's actually really easy." She had forgotten what she'd asked him.

She nodded. "I'm sorry. I just wasn't expecting this."

"Why would you?" Ryan asked. He poured more whiskey into his glass and leaned forward.

She realized something; this was his home. He might not see it that way, but in this light, he looked comfortable, as though he belonged there.

"Good point," she said after collecting her thoughts. "So, why are you doing it? I mean, it's incredible. I'm just curious."

He shrugged. "Why not?"

"It's all broken," she said.

He shrugged again. "So?" he replied. She waited for him to elaborate. "I know," he relented. "But honestly it wouldn't take much to make most of this stuff useable. And who knows. Maybe one day it could be sold."

Sophie let that sink in. All this time she had so wrongly, so irresponsibly assumed Ryan just lounged around in the loft, drinking himself stupid every night. The person she saw now, bathed in light, and covered in paint, was beautiful. Rare. The realization made her nervous. "It's all really impressive," she said.

Ryan nodded appreciatively. "I'd offer you a drink, but..."

"I'm good, thanks," she answered. "I've had enough."

"Thought so," he said. He poured more into his glass.

Sophie rocked back and forth. Before she could stop herself, she asked, "Why do you drink so much?"

He wasn't offended. "Isn't it obvious?" he asked.

She'd assumed the obvious answer, but he was proving to be more unpredictable than she'd anticipated. "To numb the pain?" she tried.

"Is that why you started drinking?" he countered.

After a healthy amount of consideration, while allowing her eyes to wander, she said, "I don't know, honestly. I really never liked it. I used to say I didn't drink because I didn't like the feeling of losing control. But honestly, I think I just hated the hangovers too much. It wasn't worth it."

"Maybe you wanted to lose control for a while," Ryan offered.

"You think so, Doc?" Sophie said, flashing him a wry smile.

He laughed softly, then became serious, his expression

changing on command. "I don't drink to numb the pain," he said, as if she had passed a test and was worthy of hearing the truth. "Actually, it's the opposite. I drink to enhance it," Ryan explained. He was thoughtful. "To feel," he finished. "Anything."

Sophie's features softened as she considered the weight of his words. He stared into the half-painted, three-legged desk before him, seeing something she couldn't. Changing the subject, Sophie said, "Does it get lonely in here?"

"I've known lonelier," he said. "This is actually crowded compared to what I'm used to." She laughed but cut it short when she realized he was completely serious. Silence filled the space around them, and the ambience made Sophie feel like they were waiting out a storm by candlelight. It was oddly romantic. "So," he said, waking her. "What did you want to talk about?"

Sophie had completely forgotten why she had even made the climb in the first place. "Oh," she said. "Well, I…" She paused. "I don't think I properly thanked you. I'd spent all last night and all day trying to figure out the perfect thing to say to you today, and I forgot the most important part."

"Thank me for what?" he asked. Genuine confusion radiated from him.

"For saving my life," she said. "I don't think I've ever actually thanked you for what you did." She laughed mockingly at herself. "It's so embarrassing, I almost didn't believe it myself."

Ryan frowned. "I guess you didn't," he said. "I didn't realize."

"Well," she said. "Thank you. For saving my life."

He smiled. "You're welcome."

"Twice," she added.

"Debatable," he said. "But you're welcome, again."

Sophie rocked, unsure if she was satisfied with how the exchange had transpired. Ryan seemed amused, when suddenly he jumped up. "I almost forgot," he said, and he stormed out of the garage. She could hear his heavy footfall against the steps outside, and a moment later, he was rummaging through a stack of books above her. When he'd found what he was looking for he darted back outside, and an instant later, he was seated beside her again. She couldn't help but be impressed. He was fast. He was holding two different-sized sheets of paper in his hand.

He offered them to her, his hand hovering over the open paint can between them. "Sorry I didn't give these to you earlier," he said. "I found them a couple days ago. I was afraid they might upset you."

Perplexed, Sophie took the two sheets. She turned the smaller one over in her hand. She instantly recognized her mother's handwriting as she began scanning the handwritten note, her pace slowing as she realized what she was reading. Tears brimmed her eyes, and her hands began to shake as the words flowed through her like warm water. She was unprepared for the wave of emotion that assailed her in those extended seconds. She sat, frozen to the seat, staring into her past. In an instant, all of her childhood memories, the most vivid and euphoric she could remember, ran through her like lightning.

Misinterpreting her emotion, Ryan said, "I'm sorry. I hope it isn't—"

"Where did you find this?" Sophie asked.

"In one of the books I read from her library."

"I don't know what to say," she said, wiping a tear away from her cheek. "It's the best gift I've ever been given." His face was blurry through her obscured vision.

He shrugged nervously. "Well, it's yours," he said.

She placed the note in her lap and flipped over the larger sheet. She knew what it was right away.

"Your mother was an incredible artist," Ryan said.

Sophie looked up at him. "It's not me," she said. "It's her."

Ryan frowned. "What?"

"It's my mother. She's beautiful, isn't she?" Sophie turned the heavy piece of paper toward Ryan.

"Absolutely," Ryan agreed. He squinted. "Then who drew it?" he asked, leaning back.

"My dad," she answered. "We thought we'd lost it."

"No kidding," Ryan responded. He was shocked. "I had no idea he was such a talented artist."

Sophie laughed under her breath. "He would never call himself that. But yeah, he is," she said. She stared through the floor for a moment, recalling a memory. She looked up. "Well, I think that's enough crying for tonight," she said, smiling. "And I thought I'd used up all my tears." She rose to go. "I'm gonna go to bed. Do you mind if I take these?"

"They're yours," he said, opening his hands.

She looked down at the sketch again. "We might never have found these without you," she said. He smiled. "Goodnight," Sophie said over her shoulder as she made for the door.

"Goodnight, Sophie."

She stopped before reaching the door.

"Everything alright?" Ryan asked.

She turned around. "Say that again," she said.

"Say what?"

"Goodnight, Sophie."

"Goodnight, Sophie," he obeyed.

She smiled, her gaze knowing.

"What?" he asked.

"Nothing," she said. "I'll see you tomorrow?"

"See you tomorrow," he said.

Part Three

18

Over the next two weeks, Ryan and Sophie got to know one another. Apprehensive early on, Ryan had insisted Sophie already knew everything she needed to know about him. She wasn't convinced, pressing the issue whenever she could. It still took some time for him to open up, but eventually, he found himself confiding in her in a way he never thought possible. Time spent with Sophie had made him realize just how alone he had been.

Ryan's daily routine changed with hers. In the mornings, he drank his coffee beside the pool while he watched Sophie swim faster and faster every day. When exhaustion finally overtook her, she would rest her arms on the edge, plant her chin on her hands, and look up at him lounging on the edge of a chair.

One morning, he was forced to pause mid-sip, hypnotized as Sophie's obscured form emerged from below the water's surface. Bubbles exploded over the clear water as she broke free into the cool morning air, her eyes fluttering open. Her hair, sleek and shining in the sun's early light, combed itself straight down her back. She glided to the edge and assumed her normal position. She wore a bikini for the first time since Ryan had known her.

"So," she said, her chin atop her interlocked fingers. "Where have you been?"

He briefly told her about his travels. How he'd moved often, never staying in a city or town for more than a few months at a time. They were dark times, memories he preferred to forget. But discussing them with Sophie somehow made them seem a little less depressing. "I spent a winter in the Poconos. That wasn't so bad," he said, offering a rare detail.

"Must have been cold up there," she said.

It wasn't too bad. She would be amazed at how quickly he could warm himself up splitting wood. He told her about the man he lived with. "At first he seemed normal," he said. "But he drank more than I did. And one night, in a drunken rage, he accused me of stealing his change. He pulled his shotgun out and told me to get the hell out of his house. It was the middle of the night, halfway through a brutal winter. But still, he didn't need to ask twice."

"Oh my gosh," she gasped. She didn't know the half of it.

"I didn't touch his damn change," he said. She giggled.

He spent some time in Philadelphia, mostly washing dishes. "That didn't last long," he told her. "I've never been one for big cities. And it was too expensive, anyway."

She told him that she hadn't traveled much, and she envied him. "You're really not missing much," he said. "Anyway, I didn't see anything. I just wandered, keeping my head down most of the time."

He told her of the spring he spent in Montauk cleaning boats at a marina.

She asked him if he wanted to join her in the water. "It's not cold," she said.

"No, thanks. I can't stand the water."

She nodded. "But you worked on boats."

"It was a job," he said, shrugging. "I considered setting them on fire every day." She smiled, but he was serious.

They were quiet. "Okay, now you ask me a question," she said. I think that's how this works."

He narrowed his eyes. "And what exactly is *this*?"

She shrugged, her shoulders peeking over the edge then disappearing. "I don't know," she hummed.

Ryan peered into his coffee mug. "Okay," he said. "What does it feel like?"

"What? My leg?" He nodded. "Excellent question," she praised. "It's kind of hard to explain. Some days I can feel my whole leg. Like my calf, my foot, my toes. I swear they're there, and they hurt," she explained. Ryan frowned. "It's weird, I know," she went on. "They call it phantom pain. Supposedly it happens to everyone."

Ryan nodded. "What about the prosthetic?" he asked. "What's that like?"

"Hmm," she hummed again, pursing her lips, and twisting her mouth. "That's even harder to explain. I guess it's like walking on stilts. But I've never walked on stilts so I can't say for sure. But I would imagine that's what it's like." She was thoughtful. "And I can feel the ground under the fake foot, almost like I can with the real one, when I have a shoe on. So, it's really not as weird as I thought it would be." She shook her head. "I don't know, something like that," she finished.

Ryan was silent, unable to think of any more questions.

"My turn," she said. "What's the necklace all about?" She pointed at the black string around his neck. He hadn't realized the white beads had fallen out of his shirt.

Ryan traced the letters with his index finger. They were like hot coals. "Sarah made it for me," he said.

Sophie rose over the edge and leaned forward, hugging herself for protection against the cold deck. "R. I. A. N," she said, squinting as she spelled out the letters.

Ryan chuckled under his breath as he looked down at the misspelled name. "She was four when she made it." He smiled at the memory. "Weird," he said. "I just realized I never made anything for her."

"Never too late," said Sophie.

Ryan smiled. "I haven't taken it off once. Never will."

In the afternoons, they took long walks along the beach, Sophie becoming stronger with every step. Each day they walked a little farther, and each day her limp became a little less glaring.

"She was so smart," Sophie said one overcast afternoon, referring to her mother. She looked out over the water. In the distance, under a blanket of gray cloud, a cargo ship inched along at a snail's pace atop the obscured horizon line, threatening to spill over the edge. From her vantage point, it was no larger than her index finger. A handful of infant seagulls darted out in front of her and Ryan, searching beneath the surf for a snack until the foamy remnants of a wave rushed onto shore, forcing them to flee back into the softer sand.

"So I've heard," Ryan said from beside her. His hands were tucked into the pockets of his jeans and his arms were tight to his sides.

"She was always reading," Sophie went on. "She would read

anything, and I mean anything. I caught her reading a book about the history of Irish kings one time. She said it interested her." Sophie shrugged as she finished. "She was so smart." Ryan nodded as he tucked a strand of hair behind his ear. After a few quiet steps, Sophie said, "Okay, tell me something about yourself. Something weird. Something nobody else knows." Ryan squinted, an expression she had come to learn meant that he was deep in thought.

Sophie hadn't realized just how hard it was going to be to get Ryan to open up. She felt she needed to tread lightly and choose her words carefully, lest she scare him back into his shell. But as the days progressed, and the nervous tension of conversation dissipated, she began to peel away the seemingly impenetrable exterior he had spent so much time fortifying. It had taken time, caution, and patience, like peeling a stubborn orange. But once she'd found a soft spot, the pieces began to fall away with less resistance.

After about a minute, Ryan said, "I used to love Disney movies." He turned to her; his jet-black eyes unreadable.

"What?" Sophie said incredulously. "That's the best you've got? Everybody used to love Disney movies." She flashed him a disappointed grin.

He sighed. "When I say used to, I mean, like, last year," he admitted. "Not just when I was a kid." Sophie raised her eyebrows and waited for him to continue. "Sarah used to make me watch them all the time when she was younger," he went on. Sophie lowered her head and lifted her eyes. "Okay, fine," he said. "I made her watch them. I couldn't help it, they're just so damn magical."

Sophie laughed. "Okay, that's a little weird I guess," she said. "I never would have guessed it coming from you, so you passed."

They were coming up on a bend in the beach, signifying they

were about a mile north of the house. Sophie was tired but refused to let Ryan know. During their first walk together, she had realized right away he was slowing his pace on her account. She had told him not to, that it would be better for her if she tried to keep up. He'd listened, and although her prosthetist had adjusted her socket and it was much more comfortable now, she was regretting her stubbornness as she thought about the long trek home.

"Ready to head back?" Ryan said, reading her mind.

Sophie nodded. They turned around and began the long journey back.

"Your turn," Ryan said after a few quiet strides.

Sophie pursed her lips and twisted her mouth. "Oh!" she said. "I have a really annoying, obnoxious laugh."

Ryan tilted his head toward her and frowned. "I've heard you laugh plenty of times, and it isn't annoying, or obnoxious."

"No," she corrected. "You've heard me giggle and chuckle. I mean, like, laugh out loud, uncontrollable, and rolling on the floor. When I was younger, people made fun of me, so I tried to hide it. Now I hardly ever *really* laugh in front of people."

"We have that in common," he said. The sound of the surf filled the silence between them.

"Well now I'm curious," Ryan said.

Sophie smiled wryly. "You're just gonna have to make me laugh," she said.

"Don't hold your breath," he replied with a grin.

Another gust tore off the water, and another strand of hair tumbled loose of Ryan's weakly tied ponytail. "Here," Sophie said, stopping. Ryan stopped with her. "Hold this," she handed him her cane. He grasped it gently, confused. "Turn around," she commanded. He obeyed without protest. She tore off the rubber band he had used to tie his hair back. Straddling his neck with her hands, she reached around his head and made a visor with her hands over his forehead. Slowly, with more care than she would use on her own hair, Sophie pulled the hair back. It curled around her fingers as they ran over his scalp. Ryan was as motionless as a stop sign, but she could hear his breath quickening over the sound of the waves. When she had a handful of hair secured at the back of his head, she reached forward with her other hand and cleaned up any loose strands she may have missed. When she was satisfied, Sophie pulled a hair tie from her wrist and quickly tied a tight bun. "There," she said. He turned around. "A tornado won't mess that thing up."

Ryan reached behind his head and felt the finished product. "Thanks," he said.

"Any time," she said. They're eyes remained connected longer than necessary.

In the evenings, after dinner, Sophie and Ryan continued their conversations on the back deck. Ted often joined them, but only for a little while. "I'm gonna finish up some things in the shop," he would say. Ryan thought Ted did this intentionally, like it was all a part of his master plan and things were finally progressing well.

Ryan wouldn't have minded either way. But it was true that some things he and Sophie said to one another may have been omitted in Ted's presence. Not that the pair spoke of anything Ted shouldn't hear, it was just something younger people did. Ryan thought Ted understood this and was more than happy to leave them alone. He could have been wrong.

One night, almost two weeks after Ryan had confided his past in Sophie, the pair relaxed outside after a paralyzing Italian dinner. Ryan sat at the round table with his legs propped up on a vacant chair while Sophie lay back on a lounge chair a foot away. The floodlight drizzled down on them like yellow mist while the surrounding darkness circled quietly.

"You sure you don't mind the smoke?" Ryan said.

"How many times do I have to tell you?" Sophie answered in a playfully scolding tone. "It doesn't bother me at all. I actually kind of like the smell."

"Oh," he said. "Well, you're welcome then."

"I wouldn't go that far," she said, tilting her head to the side. Her hair rolled over her shoulders onto her chest. She looked as relaxed as Ryan had ever seen her.

He still couldn't believe how much she had changed over the past two weeks. She had pulled a Dr. Jekyll and Mr. Hyde on him. He'd told her as much. "But wasn't that guy a monster?" she'd asked.

"Exactly," he had said, and Sophie had punched his arm as she laughed. It seemed unimportant, and to most people it wouldn't have been worth remembering. But Ryan remembered it as vividly as his nightmares.

The question of whether they were flirting or just being friendly had crossed Ryan's mind. But he quickly dismissed the idea. It was completely out of the question to even think such thoughts. Yet he couldn't help wondering what might be going on in Sophie's mind. Did she think about it the way he had? Or did she forget it instantly, as any reasonable person would? He may have been out of the loop and not in tune with the world, but Ryan innately understood that trying to figure out what was going on in a woman's mind would be enough to drive him even crazier than he already was.

"It's funny," Sophie said, waking him up. Her hands were up over her head, grasping the back of the chair while her eyes were fixed on the dark wall of night beyond the deck.

Ryan leaned over and tapped on the cigarette. The dark gray ash fell as slowly as snow into the tray. "What is?" he asked.

"I always felt more comfortable in the water, for as long as I can remember," she said. "Swimming just felt more natural to me than walking or running. And I loved the water. It was so simple. Nothing to analyze or figure out." Ryan waited for the funny part he knew wasn't coming. "And I didn't take it for granted," she said. "Not once. And it was still ripped from me, as if I didn't understand and needed something horrible to happen in order to learn. I was a good person. I helped people when they needed it. I worked hard, I…" she trailed off. Ryan was holding his breath as he listened. Sophie sighed. "I don't think I ever said goodbye to my mom," she said. She shifted in place and her eyes fell to the floor. "Not really. I was waiting to do something incredible, something she would be proud of. Then I could say goodbye." She paused for a moment. "Then I could move on with my life. Every day I swam, I felt close to her out there. It was like she was with me. I felt safe in the water." Her features darkened. "Now it terrifies me."

Ryan crushed out his cigarette and leaned forward, elbows on knees. "I know it might not be my place, Sophie," he said. "But from what I've heard about your mom, she was proud of you, in or out of the water."

Sophie looked into his eyes. "It is your place," she said softly.

221

19

The next afternoon, Ryan was helping Ted unload a stack of old barn wood from the truck. He tossed two thick pieces over his shoulder, careful to avoid the multitude of rusty nails, and passed them through the massive west window to Ted waiting in the workshop.

"You should have seen this guy," Ted said as he pulled the wood inside and stacked it neatly in a corner. "I mean, full Santa Clause beard down to his fat belly. Guy looked like he was ninety-five." It was a small load, and Ted had assured Ryan he could handle the pickup on his own. "Seemed like a nice guy on the phone," Ted went on as Ryan made the short trip back to the truck. "But when I got there, he tried to jack the price up on me," he said. Ryan was only half listening to Ted's hilarious account of the overweight farmer. The other half of his attention was fixed on Sophie. She was in the driveway, about ten feet away, standing beside her mountain bike, inspecting it as though it was a horse she had no idea how to ride. "I mean, who does that?" Ted went on. Gripping the handlebars, Sophie tossed her right leg over the seat, struggling for balance. "I told him to forget it, then," he continued. Her prosthetic wobbled on the pavement as she held on for dear life. Ryan froze with the last of the wood in his hands. Before he could stop himself, he was moving around the truck, leaving the wood hanging halfway off the bed, swaying up and down like a seesaw. "He came back down after that," Ryan heard Ted finish. With her back to him, Sophie pushed the pedal down and tried to accelerate the bike enough for the wheels to make a full revolution. Her balance wavered, and she was forced to stop after only a foot or two, barely catching herself before falling over.

Ryan rushed to her side and rested his hand over hers on the handlebar. He placed his other hand on her back for support. She turned to face him and tried a weak smile. "Not as easy as it used to be," she said. She looked heartbroken.

"Just like riding a bike, right?" Ryan joked.

"I wish," she answered. His hand remained on the small of her back.

Ryan looked out onto Coastal Highway, and before his mind got in the way, he said, "Want to go for a ride?"

She looked up at him skeptically. "How?" she asked.

"Yes or no," he answered, grinning. She considered him for a moment then seemed to make up her mind. She nodded.

Sophie sat atop the handlebars, her right leg dangling beside the front wheel while her prosthetic jutted out stiffly. Her hands gripped his like vices. Ryan walked the bike toward the driveway's opening to the road, his forearms tight against her waist for support.

"You sure about this?" he asked from behind her.

"Are you?" she challenged over her shoulder. She was nervous, but not because she felt unsafe. She could feel his breath on the back of her neck. Butterflies materialized inside her stomach, their wings beating furiously.

Ryan pushed the bike past the threshold and steered it left, crossing the yellow lines. She felt like she was floating above water, the feeling reminiscent of when she went parasailing as a kid. "Just lean back against me if you start to get unsteady," he instructed.

"Are we gonna do this, or not?" she said playfully. He chuckled and quickened his pace. "Wait," she said, and he pulled on the break. Sophie reached behind her head and tore off the constricting hair tie. She was going to get the full effect. "Okay," she said and returned her grip to the handlebars.

He started at a slow walk that quickly turned into a trot. She felt his feet leave the ground, and they were coasting along the pavement, the double lines passing faster and faster. But not fast enough.

"Faster," she called over her shoulder. Responding with his legs, Ryan pushed the pedals harder. There were no cars in sight.

With every rotation of the tires, they picked up speed, and Sophie felt her hair begin to blow behind her in the wind. "Can you see alright?" she asked, raising her voice against the wind.

"Don't worry about me," he answered. "I've got you."

She relaxed, her tight muscles loosening, giving in completely to the euphoria. Sophie closed her eyes and allowed the sensation to course through her like liquid fire. Her heart pounded like thunder.

The wind screamed in her ears and she laughed out loud, taunting it, begging for more. "Come on, you can do better than that!" she wailed. "Come on!" She craned her neck back and fell into Ryan's shoulder as he pedaled faster.

A red sports car zoomed around them, honking as it passed. "Screw you!" Sophie yelled after it with a smile. She lifted her left hand to flash the car her middle finger. The slight movement threw off Ryan's balance for an instant and the handlebars wobbled.

"Shit," he said. He eased on the breaks and brought the bike to a slow stop. "You okay?" he asked.

Sophie turned around in her seat, twisting her torso. "Never better," she said, out of breath. "Let's go again."

Ryan was exhausted when he finally turned back into the driveway. But he would have gladly kept going for Sophie's sake; the light and excitement in her face reminded him of his sister's the first time she saw Disneyworld. Sophie must have picked up on his elevated breathing patterns, though, and mercifully told him she was ready to head back home.

He steered around toward the workshop and stopped the bike on the edge of the grass. He was just happy they hadn't wiped out. But as the bike came to a complete stop and he planted his foot on the grass, the bike started to tilt to the left and Sophie tilted with it. He tried to keep it steady, but her momentum quickly became unmanageable. He gave up on the bike and decided to fall with her, keeping his body between hers and the ground. Sophie let out a yelp as she crashed down on top of him, her shoulder crushing into his chest.

"Are you alright?" he asked, lifting his head off the grass, searching for her face. Her cheek was planted against his chest, and her body was convulsing against his. She was making a strange sound he'd never heard from her before. She rolled off him and into the small shadow on the grass created by the Japanese maple tree. Only when he was able to see her face did Ryan realize she was laughing. It was unlike any laugh he had ever heard. It started with long, drawn-out ha, ha's. As the laughter built, however, it turned into faster and faster ha, ha's, as though she were vibrating. It repeated every few breaths.

"Oh my God," he said in mock shock. "What is that noise? Turn it off, turn it off." Sophie turned towards him and lay on her side, the fit increasing with her every breath. "Is that a laugh? It's terrifying."

Sophie punched his arm. "Shut up," she said. "I told you it's embarrassing." She continued to laugh uncontrollably.

"Good Lord, it's awful. Please stop." Ryan cupped his hands around his ears.

"Shut up," she cried. "I can't help it." She leaned over and shoved him.

Without thinking, Ryan took hold of her hands and pulled her on top of him. He laughed with her, having absolutely no idea what was so funny. As they both realized the position they were in, the laughter gave way to a deafening silence. Her head was blocking the early afternoon sun and the sharp yellow rays spread out around her like a halo. Her hair fell around his face like dark curtains, the flowery smell intoxicating. Her hands straddled his head as she held her chest an inch above his. His hands were on her waist, and he could feel her breath quicken.

"Thank you," she said after a few seconds. "I wasn't sure I would ever have that much fun again."

"Any time," he said. Her face was only a few inches from his, and he suddenly felt the urge to rise and kiss her.

"I think I might vomit," came an intrusive voice. Ryan moved his head to the side. Liv was standing behind Sophie, her arms crossed, a look of disgust sketched over her features. Sophie slid off Ryan and sat up. Ryan rose as well. "That might have been the cutest damn thing I've ever seen in my life," Liv continued.

"Shut up," Sophie said, still smiling. "We just fell off the bike. It was hilarious." Ryan stood up and offered Sophie his hands. She grasped them and he pulled her up with ease.

"Yeah, I could tell," said Liv. "I could hear your weird laugh from Grandma and Gramps's house."

"No, you couldn't," Sophie challenged, as if she were afraid it might actually be true. She looked at Ryan for support. He shrugged helplessly. "Screw you guys," Sophie said. "I'm proud of my laugh."

"Good for you," Liv said. She was wearing a blue t-shirt ripped at the neck and a pair of faded jeans. The red streak in her blonde hair was now blue. She looked at Ryan and grinned.

"Hey," Ted called out of the shop's window. "These nails aren't going to pull themselves out." He was leaning against the sill, leaving Ryan to wonder how long he'd been there and how much he'd seen.

Ryan and the two girls made their way into the shop. Ted was scanning the newly acquired pile of lumber. "I don't know if we should cut it or burn it," he said, apparently to himself. Liv hopped up on one of the worktables and crossed her legs, swinging them back and forth and looking around the room as if for the first time. Sophie remained by Ryan's side just inside the door. She seemed to be deep in thought.

"I have an idea," she said. "I think we should have dinner."

Ted looked at Ryan, Ryan looked at Liv, and Liv looked at Ted. Liv looked back at Sophie and said, "You thought of that all by yourself?" Ryan and Ted laughed under their breath.

"Yes, as a matter of fact, I did," Sophie said proudly. "What I meant was we should have everyone over for dinner." She looked at her father. "Uncle Kev, Mrs. Ginny, and Mr. John." She added, "Maybe Laura," with a smirk, and Ryan wondered what that was all about. "Liv, I guess you can come too."

"You're so funny," Liv said.

"I think that's a great idea, Sweetie," said Ted. "When?"

"Tomorrow night?" Sophie asked. Her eyes shuffled from Liv to Ryan.

"I'll have to check my schedule," said Ryan. "But I think tomorrow works."

"I'll help you cook," said Liv. "And what I mean by help is I'll watch and offer emotional support. You're welcome."

"Tomorrow night, then," Ted confirmed.

"Speaking of food," said Liv as she hopped down from the table. "I'm starving. Want to get some lunch?" She looked from Sophie to Ryan.

Sophie said, "Yeah, we could go into town and see Laura."

Liv made a check mark with her thumb and forefinger under her chin. "Hmm," she said. "Didn't we already try that?"

"I'll behave this time, I promise," said Sophie.

Ted fished in his pockets and tossed his keys to Ryan. Ryan caught them and said, "You sure you don't need me to stay?"

"The nails will be here when you get back," Ted answered. "Besides, I don't trust her alone with Liv."

"Hey," Liv said in mock protest. She bounced over to where

Ted was standing, stood on her tiptoes, and kissed his cheek. "You know I'm an angel."

Ted smiled graciously down at Liv. "So was Satan," he said with a wink.

"How were the tacos?" Liv asked Ryan after wiping her mouth free of some persistent guacamole.

They were finishing up their meal at a local taco joint that was conveniently located a few doors down from Laura's shop on the Avenue. Sophie and Liv used to ride their bikes into town twice a day to eat there. The restaurant was called The Taco Shack, but the interior décor suggested something very different. Checkered black and white tiles covered the floors like a chessboard. Booths lined three walls while vinyl-covered stools stood guard before a low bar. An open window behind the bar left little to the imagination as to the goings-on in the kitchen. It was the kind of place one expected to serve burgers and shakes. Sophie assumed the Taco Shack's owner had decided to save a few bucks on renovations and keep the fifties diner theme. She didn't care, the tacos were so good she often forgot where she was. But not today. Today she was sitting on the inside of the booth, and Ryan was beside her—Liv had made sure of it.

Sophie gazed out the window and watched in amusement as vacationers struggled to navigate through each other, rushing as though afraid the ocean wouldn't be there tomorrow. Her right leg was pulled onto the seat. Under the table, her prosthetic was propped up on the opposite seat beside Liv.

"Eh," said Ryan, smirking. "I've had better."

Liv threw her napkin down. "Bull," she paused, "shit," she finished. "These are the best tacos on the east coast, and you know it."

Ryan leaned back. "I'm just saying," he said. "I wouldn't bike two miles for them."

"I would crawl two miles for them," Liv said. "Hands and knees and everything. I would do literally anything for one of these things."

"Anything?" Sophie said.

"Literally anything," Liv said. "And so would you, you know it." Sophie looked at Ryan and nodded, conceding the fact. They all laughed.

Everything was going so well until Sophie glanced over Liv's shoulder and saw someone she hoped she would never see again, strutting down the narrow aisle between tables and booths. She looked away, hoping he wouldn't see her.

"Hey, Soph," said Geoff. He stopped in front of the table, inches from Ryan. A kid she had never seen before was behind Geoff, wearing a loose black shirt, baggy jeans, and an arrogant smirk. She couldn't believe he still had the audacity to call her Soph. "Haven't seen you around," he went on after Sophie refused to respond. "Lindsay says you aren't answering her calls."

Liv looked from Geoff to Sophie and frowned, as if to say, "Who the hell is this guy?"

"I wonder why," Sophie said without meeting his eye. She wanted nothing more than to punch that smirk off his face, but she restrained herself, knowing it wouldn't do any good.

"Hey man," Geoff said to Ryan. He extended his hand. "Sophie's cousin, right?"

"Cousin?" Liv said.

Sophie glanced at Ryan. He was staring up at Geoff, silent, refusing to shake hands. After a few awkward seconds, Geoff turned back to Sophie, seemingly unperturbed by Ryan's denial. "Well, it's good to see you," he said. "Hopefully, we'll see you around the house," and he and his silent follower headed toward the back of the restaurant.

"Who was that loser?" Liv asked Sophie.

"It doesn't matter," Sophie replied. She wanted to put that recent past as far behind her as possible.

Ryan rose from his seat. "I'm gonna hit the bathroom," he said.

"Okay," said Sophie. "We'll get the check."

"Cousin?" Liv asked again. Sophie shrugged.

Ryan was washing his hands when he heard the familiar voice of the curly blonde-headed guy.

"I know, man," he was saying to his buddy. "I was so close." The sink and mirror were on the opposite side of a wall that hid the urinals and stalls from Ryan's view; he couldn't see them, and they couldn't see him. "You should have seen her," the blonde one went on. "She fell off the bed and almost fell down the stairs. It was hilarious." The pair laughed like hyenas and Ryan stopped moving his hands under the faucet. He looked up into the mirror. The water was getting hotter and hotter, but he didn't feel it.

"Damn," said his friend. "That would have been awesome if you'd hit that, though."

"I know, right? I almost banged a one-legged girl! Could have checked that one off the bucket list." They laughed again.

Ryan's reflection stared back at him. He calmly turned off the faucet, wiped his hands dry, and turned around.

Liv was signing the check when Ryan emerged from the hallway at the end of the bar. He was walking faster than usual, but his expression didn't betray haste. He appeared as calm as ever.

"Thank you, Gramps," Liv said as she finished signing the check with an exaggerated flick of her wrist.

Sophie's concentration remained fixed on Ryan as he wove through the scattered tables. He approached their table, extended his hand to Sophie, and said, "Ready? We should probably get out of here." Now that he was closer, she detected a hint of urgency emanating from his eyes and posture.

"Everything alright?" Sophie asked.

"Everything's fine," he said. He stretched his hand closer to her.

"Okay," Sophie said, taking his hand. He helped her out of the booth patiently.

Ryan led Sophie through the front door first, followed by Liv. Ryan exited last. Before the door shut, Sophie heard footsteps scurrying along the interior tile and the familiar voice of Geoff shout, "Where do you think you're going, you son of a bitch." Ryan pulled the door closed and ushered the girls along the sidewalk toward Laura's shop.

"What the hell's going on?" Sophie asked.

"Keep walking," Ryan answered, his hand on the small of her back. She could only walk so fast and struggled to keep up.

Ten feet behind them, the restaurant door flew open, and

Sophie turned her head to see Geoff and his friend searching the now dwindling crowd on the sidewalk. When their eyes fell upon her, Ryan, and Liv, they darted after them. Ryan sighed beside Sophie and turned around. He gently placed his hand on Sophie's waist and pushed her behind him. Geoff's nose was bleeding badly, blood pouring over his lips, along his chin, and down his neck, and he was squinting against apparent pain in his eyes. Behind him, his friend had a bad cut along his right eyebrow, a string of blood framing that side of his face. She was nervous, tense, and excited at the same time. But she wasn't scared, not even a little bit.

"We are gonna fuck you up," said Geoff as he came within five feet of Ryan. Sophie looked down at Ryan's clenched fist by his side.

But before they closed the gap, Liv stepped in front of Ryan. "Back off asshole," she said.

Geoff grabbed Liv's shoulder and shoved her to the side. Liv tripped over an uneven block of sidewalk and fell to the cement. Before Sophie could protest, or even move an inch, Ryan's fist shot out quicker than her eyes could follow and collided with Geoff's nose. Geoff screamed out in pain and stumbled backwards. His back-up stepped forward and took a heavy, belligerent swing at Ryan's face. Ryan ducked with time to spare and landed a hard right hook to the guy's exposed ribcage. While the sidekick searched the sidewalk for a breath, Ryan's left fist came down hard onto his temple, and Sophie watched in horror as another gruesome cut was opened on the poor guy's eyebrow. Ryan pushed him to the ground, and he doubled over.

Geoff rushed at Ryan again. "I'm gonna kill you, man," he cried, arms wide as if to tackle Ryan like a football player. As Ryan prepared himself—he hadn't moved more than a few inches from his original spot, the entire time keeping Sophie safely behind him—another figure joined the party out of the corner of her eye. Sophie's Uncle Kevin, dressed in full uniform, rushed out of nowhere and tackled Geoff to the ground.

"Get off of me!" Geoff cried. Uncle Kevin lifted him off the ground with practiced ease and slammed him up against the brick wall of the antique store that occupied the space between The Taco Shack and Laura's shop.

"You gonna relax?" Uncle Kevin asked, his forearm tight against the small of Geoff's back. Geoff's friend was still curled up on the cement, unwilling to participate in round two.

The entire exchange of blows and threats happened within seconds, and only now did Sophie realize that a sizeable crowd had gathered around the participants, some looking on in disgust, and others wide-eyed, digging for their phones to snap a few pictures. A few eyes were locked on Sophie, followed by hushed whispers. Liv picked herself up, dusted her clothes off, and moved to Sophie's side. On instinct, Sophie curled her fingers around Ryan's. His hand was shaking. She held it tighter.

"Let me go," Geoff protested again.

"You gonna relax?"

"Yeah, I'm cool."

Uncle Kevin loosened his grip. He looked at Sophie. "Are you alright?" he asked. Sophie nodded.

"Is she alright? Look at me!" Geoff complained.

"Shut up," Uncle Kevin ordered. Uncle Kevin turned to the crowd. "Okay, that's enough," he said. "Show's over, please move along." Few followed his orders, but enough went on with their day, allowing a little more privacy. Uncle Kevin turned Geoff around and released his grip. His hands down at his sides and eyes as alert as a hawk's, Uncle Kevin stood between Geoff and Ryan. "What happened?" he asked.

"This asshole just blind-sided me and Kyle in the bathroom for no reason," Geoff spat, pointing his finger at Ryan. Kyle had picked himself up and limped to his friend's side.

"You were looking right at me," Ryan said. His stare was confident and calculated, and Sophie didn't know whether to be proud or scared.

Geoff lunged toward Ryan, but Uncle Kevin held him back. He looked from Geoff to Kyle. "Do you two need an ambulance?" he asked. Both of their faces were covered in blood.

"I'm fine," Geoff said, more confidently than he looked. His eyes were watering, and he brushed away a tear with the back of his hand. Kyle shook his head, mute for now.

"Then get out of here," Uncle Kevin ordered.

Sophie wasn't sure what protocol demanded in this kind of situation, but she was confident an order like that wasn't part of it.

"What?" Geoff said angrily. "You're not gonna arrest this piece of shit?"

Uncle Kevin looked closely at Geoff, as if studying his wounds. "Geoff Crowley, right?" he asked. Geoff appraised the officer and nodded. "You have a DUI hearing coming up, don't you?" Geoff's eyes betrayed fear. He nodded again. "Assault probably wouldn't look good on your record going in, would it?"

Geoff's fearful gaze shot from Ryan, then to Sophie, and finally to Liv. He looked at his friend. Kyle's gaze burned through the sidewalk. "This is bullshit," he said defiantly. He nudged Kyle's shoulder and said, "Come on." The two backed away and disappeared through the crowd.

Sophie relaxed and felt the tremors throughout Ryan's body subside. Uncle Kevin ushered them over to a wooden bench shaded by a thin tree on the edge of the sidewalk. Sophie sat down beside Liv while Ryan and Uncle Kevin remained standing.

Once the crowd's movement returned to normal, Kevin turned to Ryan. "What the hell was that all about?" he said.

Ryan looked away and shrugged.

Uncle Kevin narrowed his eyes. "I think you better tell me," he said. "I'm risking something here. I don't think it could have been more obvious which side I took. People don't like to see that."

Sophie and Liv looked to Ryan expectantly. Ryan lowered his voice and moved closer to Kevin, as if to tell a secret, but Sophie and Liv could still hear him clearly. "I overheard them talking about Sophie in the bathroom," he said.

"What did they say?" Sophie said.

"It doesn't matter," Ryan answered.

Sophie stood up and gripped Ryan's arm. "What did they say?" she repeated.

"Soph," Uncle Kevin tried. She shot him a disquieting look and he stopped short.

She looked back to Ryan. Liv was by her side now, the four creating a tight circle. Ryan sighed and recounted the conversation he'd overheard, omitting any offensive language. It didn't matter, the point was made.

"Those mother—," said Liv, and she stepped forward, making a move to chase the two young men down. Uncle Kevin rested a cautionary hand on her shoulder, and she relented.

Sophie dropped her gaze. She had never experienced the feeling of something so horrible being said about her. It hurt. But her anger subsided rapidly as she realized it was her fault as well. "It's okay," she said. All three pairs of eyes looked at her uncomprehendingly. She went on. "It's my fault," she said. "I never should have put myself in that position." Admiration flashed in Uncle Kevin's eyes. Liv frowned. Ryan was unreadable. "Forget it," she finished.

"Forget it?" said Liv indignantly. "If I see those assholes again—"

"What did I miss?" said a familiar voice. Sophie instantly recognized Laura's feathery voice as the older woman approached the group. Laura slid in between Sophie and Liv, fitting into the circle like a missing puzzle piece. She was wearing a flowy white and blue summer dress. She looked as stunning as ever.

"Oh, nothing," Liv answered. "Just a world-class beat-down, courtesy of Ryan." Laura raised her eyebrows at Ryan. "Don't worry," Liv assured. "They deserved it."

Another officer was approaching. Uncle Kevin said, "I need to take care of this." He turned to Ryan. "I can't guarantee they won't press charges. But I doubt it."

"Thanks," said Ryan. "Again."

Uncle Kevin smiled. "Ice that hand." He turned to go.

"Oh," Sophie said, remembering why they were there. "Uncle Kevin," she called. He turned around. "We're having dinner tomorrow night. Want to—"

"Your dad told me," he said. "I'll be there." He moved to intercept the approaching officer.

Sophie turned to Laura. "Can you make it?"

Laura threw her arms around Sophie and hugged her tight. "It's about time," she said. "Wouldn't miss it."

20

Sophie stood in front of her bathroom mirror early the next evening. She balanced on one leg, her hands firmly gripping the edge of the sink for support. Her reflection stopped short of the end of her left thigh, creating the cruel illusion that there was more skin, muscle, and bone extending down to the bathmat. She could even feel her left foot on the floor, her toes curling into the fabric. Before, when she was lost in despair with seemingly no way out, she would often stare at herself like this, with dead eyes glazed over in transparent stone. She would convince herself there was something there, something more, when she was afraid to look down at the truth, the unfair reality that had become her life. Now, as she hopped back a step and the reflection revealed nothing but empty space beneath her residual limb, she didn't feel scared. Her stomach didn't feel quite as empty. She felt hopeful.

Her mind drifted to Ryan. She thought about the conversations they enjoyed on the back deck, as evening turned to night, bringing with it blindingly illuminating knowledge of someone she had come to care about more deeply than she'd ever thought possible. She thought about her hand in his and his secure embrace as they rolled around in the grass. Those thoughts over-powered the destructive, forlorn, and melancholy ones she had become so accustomed to, washing them away like a strong wave. She thought about what she saw when she looked at him now. It was as though she were walking along a sidewalk, on a street lined with brilliantly lit, luxurious homes. She could see inside every house, through every hallway, and into every room; little left to the imagination. Sandwiched in between these transparent structures, was an old house fallen into disrepair. Every window was boarded up, and vines constricted the life out of the chipped and faded wood. Other passersby continued, unwilling to look harder or search for an opening, only offering the occasional pitiful glance. But she could see through the barriers, past the overgrown shrubs and weeds. He had allowed her a glimpse through the seemingly impenetrable façade. In this world, she could walk unhindered, and she climbed the rickety steps and glided through the crumbling entranceway. Carefully, she began to flip on the lights, patiently drifting from one room to the next. She pulled back furniture covers, and dust swirled around like snow. She opened curtains, allowing in a thick evening glow. She dusted tables and straightened works of art along the walls. It was a process, but one she was willing to spend as much time as necessary on. She would pull the weeds, repaint the walls, and sweep the floors. Whatever it took. Because in time, she knew the world would see what she saw; they would see strength, warmth, and love. They would see Ryan, whether he liked it or not. She smiled and her reflection smiled back.

She touched up her make-up, taking far more care than she was used to, then sat down on the toilet and slid into her leg. Using the sink for support, Sophie rose to her feet and reached for the dress that hung from the shower rod. She slipped the navy-blue cotton dress over her head and studied herself in the mirror again. The garment fell just below the knee, and she didn't care that it failed to cover up the prosthetic. Pulling back her hair, she tied it in a loose bun. Satisfied, Sophie cleared the make-up off the sink.

"Soph?" came the sharp voice of Liv. Before Sophie could respond, Liv let herself in as if it were her own bathroom. Liv stopped in the doorway and took a step back. "Damn," she said, raising her eyebrows. "Who you tryin' to impress?"

Sophie smiled shyly. "No one," she lied.

"Sure," said Liv, lengthening the U.

"Shut up," Sophie said. "Come on, let's get dinner ready."

"Ugh, fine," Liv complained. "But I already started drinking, and I'm not gonna stop."

Ryan felt like he was on a wooden raft, bobbing up and down, at the will of the rhythm of the waves. He could clearly make out everyone on shore: Sophie, Ted, Liv, Laura, Kevin, John, and Ginny. They were jumping up and down on the sand, waving, begging him to just paddle. All he had to do was paddle a little bit. A favorable wind and generous current urged him on. But he couldn't do it. He turned around. The black clouds and blinding lightning he had, without knowing, somehow escaped for the time being, were still so close. A part of him desperately wanted to make it to shore, to ride a wave in like a surfer and embrace each one of them, begin the new life that spread out before him like a search party. But Sarah was still out there, somewhere in the middle of that perpetual storm, all alone and scared. He couldn't leave her. So, he stayed where he was, somewhere in between, unwilling to commit.

These troubling thoughts plagued his mind as he and Ted labored in the sun-filled and wind-swept workshop while Sophie and Liv prepared dinner. Ted was cutting some lumber down to size with the table saw while Ryan measured and marked. After the unfortunate events of the previous day, Ted had ordered Ryan to take the rest of the day off so he could ice his swollen hand. As a result—he felt guilty for allowing Ted to de-nail the barn wood all by himself—he awoke earlier than normal and got a head start on the day's work.

But that wasn't the only reason he had awoken early, or that he'd started working before the sun came up. A gentle dawn had met him that morning, with a sun's eye he could meet without squinting. He should have been hopeful or taken a picture. Instead, he felt guilty; he hadn't dreamt about Sarah. He hadn't dreamed about her in over a week. He had become comfortably accustomed to the nightmares, and until recently hadn't needed to reflect on how important they were to his life, no matter how terrifying. They were a part of him, like another organ. They used to be the only part of him, maybe the only thing keeping him alive. But that was changing. He had allowed himself to care for the family he now lived with, and everything that came with it.

He thought about the things those two punks had said about Sophie. Anger swelled inside him, the pencil marks on the wood growing darker and darker as the disgusting words snaked through his mind. He could have killed those guys for what they'd said. He thought about Sophie's hand in his. He thought about what he could lose. His life had suddenly become very complicated.

Ryan failed to hear the audible quiet that fell over the room when Ted turned off the table saw. When Ted's hand fell on his shoulder, Ryan flinched reflexively, as if a snake had crawled under the table.

"You okay?" Ted said, his soft voice climbing over Ryan's shoulder.

"Yeah. Fine," Ryan answered loudly, not quite adjusted to the quiet yet.

"Call it a day?"

Ryan nodded. "Sure." The guests would be arriving soon. He needed to get his act together. Tonight was for Sophie.

Slumping into the patio chair, Ryan lit a cigarette and exhaled louder than necessary, as if he could blow the thoughts out of his head. It was another cool evening and the sun had begun its descent on the opposite side of the workshop. A mountain range of sharp clouds loomed in the distance. A four-piece family was gathering up its chairs, umbrella, and shovels from the sand.

Ted leaned against a post to Ryan's right that supported the awning overhead. The older man was watching the water, lost in thought. He said, "How's the hand holding up?"

Ryan looked down at the back of his right hand. It was still red and a little swollen, but it didn't hurt. "It's fine," he answered.

Ted nodded. There wasn't much more to say on the matter. Ted had heard about what happened, patted Ryan on the shoulder, and asked if Sophie was alright. End of story. And Ryan was grateful for it.

"You and Sophie seem to have hit it off. Who would have thought?" Ted said casually.

"Yeah," said Ryan. "She seems to be back to her old self."

"Almost," Ted responded, his tone betraying a hint of

skepticism. But only a small hint. "I think tonight means a lot to her," he went on. "It's almost like a coming out party of sorts, you know?" There was no question how much tonight's dinner meant to Sophie.

Ryan nodded.

"You sure you're alright?" Ted asked again.

"Yeah," Ryan answered. "Really."

Ted wasn't convinced, but he let it go. Changing the subject, he said, "Sophie said you were thinking about working through 'til the end of the summer, then planning on heading out." It wasn't a question and Ryan was slow to respond.

"It was a thought," Ryan replied. "Honestly, I haven't thought much about it." That may have been true yesterday.

Ted walked over and settled into the chair opposite Ryan. He leaned forward. "Would you just promise me something?" he asked. "If you decide to leave, tell us first? I think it's obvious by now that neither Sophie nor I want that at all. But if you do, don't leave in the middle of the night, or something." Ted's voice lowered. "It was hard not knowing where Sophie was all those nights. If I didn't know where you were, my sleep would be no less restless."

Ryan turned his head and looked up at Ted. Ted's gaze was transfixed on the shore, as if he needed time to consider his own words. Ryan considered them quickly.

"I promise," he said. And he meant it.

Ted lay his hand on Ryan's back and allowed it to linger there for a moment. "Now," he said. "Help an old man with a picnic table."

***

Sophie opened the oven and took a final look at the dish she had prepared: manicotti with garlic bread. Her and her mother's favorite. It had been a long time since Sophie had attempted to cook, but she would never forget how to make this dish.

"I have to say," Liv said from the opposite side of the island, a tall glass of wine dangling between her fingers. "You do look damn cute in that apron."

"Tell me something I don't know," Sophie answered jokingly.

"I made out with a girl last semester," Liv said, too drunk to notice the rhetorical nature of Sophie's question. Sophie didn't respond right away. "And you know what?" Liv went on. She looked behind both shoulders, making sure the coast was clear. "I liked it," she whispered.

Sophie burst out laughing, mainly because of the confused look on Liv's face because of the revelation. "Good to know," Sophie said.

A ding sounded from behind her and Sophie turned around. She pulled the dish from the oven and rested it on the counter, taking care to focus on her balance as she did so. She glanced outside for a moment to see Ryan and Ted throw a red tablecloth over the aging surface of the picnic table. It made her happy to see them together.

Lost in thought, Sophie accidentally touched the hot dish with her bare hand. "Shit!" she yelped, jumping backwards, nearly losing her footing.

Liv perched up on her stool to get a better view. "Ouch, must've hurt."

"Seriously?" Sophie scolded. "You're just gonna sit there?"

Liv appeared genuinely hurt. "You think this is easy?" she said, lifting her eyebrows with the glass. "I have to like, keep my arm steady so I don't spill."

"You gotta be kidding me," she said. As Sophie ran her finger under some cold water, she heard a knock at the door. Quickly drying her hands, she made her way to the front of the house, without the aid of her cane. The limp was noticeable, but she didn't feel unsteady.

Her finger still tingling with lingering pain, Sophie opened the door to her first guest. As she had predicted by the innocuous knock, it was Laura. And as she had also guessed, Laura looked as stunning as ever. The older woman—who could have passed as Sophie's sister—was draped in a flowing seafoam green dress that drizzled from her narrow shoulders straight down to the floor, teasing the surface below like a bird's wings skimming the ocean. Laura's lush auburn hair framed her immaculately proportioned face and tumbled down around her shoulders, the setting sun adding a luminescence to the already pristine portrait.

"Hey, beautiful girl," Laura said in her distinctive tone that could lull a lion to sleep. Laura's posture resembled Sophie's; she stood with one side a little slumped, as if she always had her hand on one hip. It added to her allure, Sophie knew.

"Me?" Sophie answered. "You look radiant. Literally."

Laura smiled. "What, this? I just woke up." She crossed the threshold and hugged Sophie tight.

"Thanks for coming," Sophie said as she led Laura through the hall and into the kitchen.

"Wouldn't miss it."

"Although," Sophie went on. "I have to say, I always thought you were the fashionably late type. You're the first one here."

"Not when it comes to you, Soph," she said. "I think I've waited long enough." Laura floated into the kitchen. She put the bowl of salad and bottle of wine on the counter. "Hey, Liv," she said. "Smells amazing in here,"

"Thanks," said Liv, raising her glass toward Laura.

Sophie noticed Laura glance outside. Ted and Ryan were finishing up setting the table. White plates on a blood-red cloth. "He has been such a huge help to your dad," said Laura.

"He's been a huge help to everyone," Sophie responded.

"He's handsome, too," Laura observed. Sophie shrugged. She cut a few pieces of garlic bread.

"A good kisser, too," offered Liv.

"What!" said Sophie, nearly cutting her thumb as she looked up at Liv, eyes wide.

Laura looked at Liv in amusement. "Why am I not surprised?" she said.

Sophie tried to collect herself. "When?" she asked.

"Relax," Liv said. "Nothing happened, except for the kiss, of course. He didn't want to go any farther, and the only logical conclusion I could come to was that he was in love with you."

"Or maybe he just wasn't into *you*. Ever think of that?" Laura said.

"Ha," Liv snorted. "That's hilarious."

"When?" Sophie repeated.

"When I first got into town. How was I supposed to know you two were in love?"

"What are you talking about?" Sophie said, her eyes shifting back down to the cutting board.

"Oh, please," Liv said. "You two go on long walks on the beach, stay up late talking about your feelings, roll around in the grass like a couple of cute little puppies. Seriously, it makes me sick." She drained her glass and reached for the bottle.

"I guess I've missed more than I thought," said Laura.

"She doesn't know what she's talking about," Sophie said. But her façade was crumbling.

"It is literally written all over your face, Sophie," Liv went on. She was relentless.

"I don't know what you're talking about," Sophie continued stubbornly. She was re-cutting the slices into thinner slices.

Liv raised herself up off the stool and leaned over the island. "Keep telling yourself that," she said. "But one thing is for sure." She leaned closer as if to whisper a secret. "He's not going to make a move. He's too scared. Plus, he may have forgotten how to, you know, use it," She winked at Sophie.

"Liv!" Sophie said. She threw one of the pieces of bread at her friend.

Liv raised her hands in surrender and slid off the stool. "Just sayin'." She turned around and shuffled toward the sliding glass door. "I need a cigarette," she said over her shoulder.

After Liv closed the door, Laura turned to Sophie. "I hate to say it, Soph, but she might be right," Laura said. Sophie looked outside and sighed. The thought had crossed her mind dozens of times already. "You know he feels the same way, right?" Laura added.

Sophie stopped cutting and turned to Laura. "How could you possibly know that?"

Laura shrugged. "He's still here." Sophie didn't know what to say to that. "Looks like the Palmer's just got here."

Sophie ingested Laura's logic for a moment. She had assumed Ryan was still there because of her father. But when she thought about it, it didn't seem so outrageous.

Mrs. Ginny and Mr. John entered the picture from the right side of the deck. They must have taken the scenic route along the shore. She watched as hugs were exchanged. Mrs. Ginny opened the glass door and joined the girls.

Uncle Kevin was the last to arrive, a case of beer fastened securely under his arm. He handed the beer off to Ryan, who placed it on the floor of the deck. Ryan had traded in his white V-neck for a white button-down. She wondered where he got it. Her father wore his go-to salmon polo and khaki shorts. Uncle Kevin sported a sandy polo and jeans. And Mr. John donned a navy-blue button-down with khaki pants. All wore flip-flops. The four men made an interesting sight. Three different generations. Such similar demeanors.

With Sophie's massive portion of manicotti, a couple dozen pieces of garlic bread, Laura's verdant Caesar salad, and two bottles of red wine, the table was set, and the guests were eager to dig in.

Sophie felt the need to say something.

Everyone had drinks before them, and when Sophie rose from her seat, conversation stopped, and the table's attention turned to her. Ryan was on her left.

She was nervous. Sophie had hated her public speaking class in college and felt similar butterflies now. Swallowing her pride, though, she spoke honestly. "I know it's been a while since we've all been together like this," she said. "And I'm mostly to blame."

Mrs. Ginny looked as though she would protest, but her husband rested a gentle hand on her arm, anticipating such a response from his wife. "I lost sight of what was important, of who I am," she continued. She glanced down at Ryan, then at her father on the opposite side of the table. "But I'm starting to find my way back. And it's nights like these that remind me of how lucky I am." Sophie scanned the table as she spoke. Laura looked up at Sophie with a warm grin. Mrs. Ginny and Mr. Palmer looked at her as if they were seeing her all grown up for the first time. Uncle Kevin smiled at his niece with an uncle's unconditional love. As always, Ryan's expression was difficult to read. And her father looked up at his daughter with pride. "Thank you so much for coming. It means the world. And I hope you like the food," she finished.

"Cheers," said Laura. And the rest of the company repeated it.

Sophie sat down, satisfied.

Uncle Kevin, Ryan, and Mr. John drank beer with their meal. The ladies and Sophie's father enjoyed red wine. Uncle Kevin pointed this fact out early on, setting the playful tone for the evening. "Hey," her father snapped defensively. "I'm going to enjoy a nice glass of wine with my nice Italian dinner that my beautiful daughter made." He eyed Kevin and Ryan. "You're the weird ones," he added after a short sip. That got a laugh from the table, and soon after, everyone dug in and conversation weaved through the table without prejudice.

Ryan leaned over, stealing Sophie's ear for a moment. "Moving speech," he said. She couldn't tell if he was making fun of her or if he was genuinely moved. Sophie nudged him with her left arm under the table, assuming the former. He smiled and continued eating.

The evening's temperature was as cool and comfortable as the conversation. An occasional light breeze swam through the party of eight, rustling the tablecloth but never threatening. The pale blue evening sky was dotted with small clouds that looked like marshmallows. Contentment filled Sophie as she watched Laura and Uncle Kevin reminisce about high school. Mr. John and her father spoke about the furniture business, which her dad insisted wasn't a business at all. Mr. John wasn't convinced.

Mrs. Ginny pressed Ryan on what his plans for the future were. How could she know that was the one question to be avoided when speaking with him? Sophie was quick to come to his defense, and Mrs. Ginny picked up on the subtleness of Sophie's interference. "Ryan mentioned he was considering taking some wood-working classes," Sophie said.

Ryan picked up where Sophie left off. "Yeah," he said. "You know, explore all my options."

Mrs. Ginny just smiled, amused at the game. "Well, if you ask me that would be a waste of money. You have the best instructor on the coast right here." She glanced over at Sophie's father. "For free," she added.

At this, her father joined the conversation. "You kiddin' me?" he said, the wine already influencing his tone. "I'll be taking lessons from him soon. The guy's a natural." Her father took another healthy sip from his oversized wine glass and added, "And he reads. A powerful combination of intelligence and common sense."

At this, the table went quiet for a moment. Ryan's face bled embarrassment, and the guests looked at him with a mixture of amusement and confusion. Maybe they had underestimated this young man from…They didn't even know where he was from,

Sophie remembered. In fact, they knew almost nothing about Ryan. They knew that he saved Sophie's life, and like her father, that was enough for them. It hadn't been enough for Sophie. Not at first. She realized that Ryan commanded a lot of respect at this table, and he had no idea.

"I may just have to steal him away from you, then, Ted," Laura said. "Maybe this town's furniture trade needs a little competition. What do you say, Ryan?"

Ryan opened his mouth, but no words came out. "Don't listen to her, Ryan," said Sophie's father. "Don't let that beautiful exterior fool you. She runs a sweatshop over there." Laura tried to respond, but he continued. "And," her father said, pointing his glass at Laura as if it were a finger, "don't think I don't know you sold that table to these nice old folks." He shifted his accusation to Mr. John and Mrs. Ginny now. "Traitors."

"Who you callin' old?" Mr. John put in.

"Hey, some of us have to make a living around here," Laura responded defensively. Then she added, "And I sold them two nightstands last week too."

"And I bought a rocking chair," Liv put in, not having spoken in five minutes and simply needing to say something.

Sophie's father put his free hand to his chest and leaned back as if he had been stabbed in the heart. Laughter exploded, circulating the table like a lit fuse. The fact that anyone at the table would pay for anything her father made was unacceptable. Sophie fought back tears of joy.

Late evening transitioned into early night, and as twilight gave way to darkness, the meal moved from manicotti to Mrs. Ginny's homemade cheesecake. Only a fork full of manicotti remained when the slices of cake were cut, and Sophie concluded it had been a hit.

After all present were sufficiently stuffed, the men insisted on cleaning up the table while the women enjoyed the last of the wine. Mrs. Ginny and Mr. John were the first to take their leave, citing fatigue. Not long after the elderly couples' exit, Laura and Uncle Kevin called it a night as well. Sophie's father walked them out.

Liv—easily the drunkest one there—stood and said, "I'm outta here." She snatched a wine bottle from the table and headed for the sand.

"You want some company?" Sophie called after her, afraid Liv might start walking the wrong way along the beach.

Liv raised her hand over her head and gave a thumbs up. "I'm good," she slurred.

Once again, Sophie and Ryan found themselves alone on the back deck, on opposite sides of the picnic table now. The table had been cleared, but the space between them was still very much crowded. Tension, satisfaction, and expectant quiet had replaced the silverware, plates, and laughter on the table. The weak light from the surrounding torches created an orange glow on Ryan's face, making it difficult for Sophie to judge his mood. He had been quiet during dinner. Even quieter than normal. She reminded herself that the experience could have been overwhelming for him, but it was just as much for him as it was for her; she wanted him to see first-hand the result of everything he'd done for her.

Sophie imagined her mood was much easier to judge. It was written all over her face with firelight. His face was a shadow, his dark eyes low.

"So, what did you think?" Sophie asked. "Not a bad night, right?" She wished he would give her something, anything to let her know he was as happy as she was.

"It was great, Sophie," he said, refusing to look up from his glass. "You have a beautiful family here."

Sophie became more alert. There was something about the way he said it. "Thanks to you," she said.

Abruptly, Ryan stood. "God," he snapped, shaking his head. "I wish everyone would stop saying that." He moved to go.

"What's wrong?" she said, frozen in place.

He ran his hands through his hair and turned to face her. He was standing over her now. "I'm not this person you all think I am," he said. He began to pace back and forth. "This," he motioned to the empty table. "I don't know how to do this, Sophie. I feel—" he cut himself off, unable to find the words to continue.

"What?" she tried. "You feel what? Help me try to understand."

He rubbed his eyes with his palms and turned to go.

"Where are you going?" Sophie asked.

"To bed. I'm beat," Ryan replied. He disappeared into the night, beyond the reach of the torches.

Sophie sat alone at the table. Less than fifteen minutes ago she had been in the clouds, the wooden bench beneath her like a pillow. Now it felt hard and cold. She sat there, alone with her thoughts, desperately trying to relive every detail of the night. Had she said something? What was she missing? After a while, she rose and blew out the weakening flames, leaving her alone in the dark. When her father came outside, she stepped by him.

"Everything alright, Sweetie?" he asked.

"Yeah. I'm tired," she answered. "I'm gonna go to bed."

Thunder rumbled in the distance as she closed the door.

21

He was in the open ocean. Arms and legs like rubber. The water was rough, and horizon surrounded him on all sides. "Sarah!" he yelled into the thick air. His lungs were as weak as his limbs, his voice carrying only a few feet in any direction. Where was she?

The water hit him like ice.

A lone rock not far from where he struggled to stay afloat bobbed with the waves; a massive boulder floating in the water, the size of a truck. Ryan began what should have been a simple swim to his salvation, no more than a few strokes.

A girl clung to the edge, her back to him.

"Sarah! I'm coming," he screamed. "Hold on!"

She didn't turn her head to acknowledge her big brother's presence, but she knew he was there. "Help. I'm slipping," she cried. She was so scared.

Ryan powered two long strokes through the water, but as he moved, so did the rock. Every stroke he made, it moved exactly that much farther away. He was only a few feet from her. But he would always be a few feet from her. The water wasn't going to give her back. He pushed on for what could have been hours, or days.

Then, without warning, he was sinking. No matter how hard he tried, he couldn't resurface. He was dying. A few more seconds and he would suffocate.

The scene changed and he found himself in a cemetery. It was raining, and he was alone. A single tree stood before him, looming in the gloom of a sunless day, the leaves hovering over his dejected body like an awning. He looked down at the gravestone. "Here Lies Sarah Marguerite Monroe." But the grave was empty. A perfectly dug hole with no body or coffin, only wet earth, with small, pale brown puddles.

"It should be you in that grave," a voice from behind him spoke with malice. Ryan turned to see his mother and father standing side by side. He didn't know which had spoken the words that he had himself thought so many times before. "She was innocent," the couple said in unison.

"I would trade places in a second," he responded. He was a little boy again as his parents gazed down at him with contempt and hatred.

Slowly, methodically, Ryan's mother extended her arm and shoved him into the grave. He was powerless to stop her. He tried to scream as he fell but nothing escaped his lips. He braced for an impact that never came. He continued to fall, fall, fall...

He awoke in a cold sweat, gasping for air. Absolute darkness surrounded him like a heavy blanket. He attempted to peer through the night, but all he saw was his mother's face, following him like the eyes of a painting. Hard as he tried, breath refused to come. He was suffocating. Throwing the sheets over the edge, Ryan leaned forward and crawled off the bed and onto the floor. Straining for breath, still half in a nightmare that refused to let go, Ryan stood and moved forward, his arms outstretched, searching the wall of black before him for a way out.

His limbs felt heavy, as if he were being held back by the shadows around him. He reached a wall and scanned it with his hands as though reading braille until they fell upon what had to be a doorknob. Ryan twisted the knob and opened the door. A gust of wind backed by piercing rain met his tortured face and bare chest. The rain was like ice and the wind sought to push him back into the nightmare. Squinting against the assault with what little strength he could gather, Ryan moved through the threshold.

The steps were treacherously slippery as he fought to keep his footing. Using the railing as a crutch, he managed to make it to the bottom. He saw no darkness; he felt no rain. His parent's faces continued to follow his half-closed eyes wherever they went. He wanted to run, run as far and as fast as he could from this place. But he couldn't. He could barely walk.

Wet grass beneath his bare feet, Ryan limped around to the back of the garage. He didn't notice the motion-sensing floodlight blink to life, and the aggressive smacking of rain against the roof of the house was inaudible to his ears. The sound should have been deafening, but all he could hear was his mother's voice. "It should be you in that grave." It was on repeat, the volume being turned up with his every step. He clamped his hands over his ears, but it only got louder.

Lifting his head to the sky, Ryan opened his mouth and breathed in the wind and water. It rushed over his face, along his slumped shoulders, and down his hunched back. His legs gave out beneath him, as if an unseen force had pushed the backs of his knees forward, and falling to the softened ground, he extended his hands at the last moment before crashing face first into the earth. He stayed there, staring into the ground, the rain pounding his back like a thousand whips. Water rolled along his pained face, onto his nose, and down to the earth.

The ground had become so soft, he felt as though his hands and knees were sinking. As if he were in quicksand. The nightmare was still so vivid and fresh in his mind, he couldn't distinguish the earth underneath his soaking wet frame from the empty grave of his dreams. He began to weep, which quickly transitioned into an uncontrollable sob, his tears mingling with the rain. Unable to hold himself up anymore, the weight of the shadow proving too strong, Ryan allowed his arms to give way, and he fell to the ground. Wet sand and grass met his body, and he lay there motionless, like a corpse.

Sophie couldn't sleep that night. She was frantically searching the closet of her memories for an answer she knew wasn't there. What had she done wrong? What could she have done differently? She tried to remind herself how selfish such lines of thought were. Why should his mood be affected by her actions? Sophie knew better than anyone that Ryan was fighting a perpetual battle within, just as she was. Maybe he just had a bad day. Then, like a vicious cycle of insecurity, she would allow the previous worries to crowd her conscience once more, keeping any chance of sleep at arms-length.

She thought of the attack, something she had so successfully avoided of late. It was as if the memory had been crouched in the corner all this time, patiently awaiting the opportune time to strike. A sinking feeling in her stomach that made it seem as though she were being swallowed up by her bed, the sheets wrapping her up like a cocoon. Sophie shook her head in an attempt to physically dispel the intruding thoughts. *No.* She wasn't going back there. If she had to run, she would run, no matter how bad it hurt. Anything was better than where she had emerged from.

As she made preparations for her defense—erecting barriers of pleasant thoughts and indestructible memories—Sophie noticed a line of light creep around her curtains. So deep in thought, she hadn't noticed it was raining outside. Focusing, Sophie could now distinctly hear the soft tapping against the windows throughout the house, like fingernails on a chalkboard.

Sophie arose and swung her leg over the edge of the bed. She stood up on one leg, balancing her weight easily, and hopped to the window. The house was warm, and she needed no more than a tank top and underwear to stay comfortable. When she reached the window, Sophie's mind needed a moment to catch up with her eyes.

What she saw terrified her at first. Ryan was on his knees, sitting back on his heels. He was half-naked with his arms around himself, as if hugging his body for warmth. The light from the garage painted his back. The front of his body cast in shadow. It was as if a spotlight were on him while he was acting out a heartbreaking scene on stage. The light offered the effect that it was only raining on him. From her angle, he might have been praying. Sophie cracked the window, and the sound of down-pouring rain flooded her bedroom. It was so loud, she was afraid it might wake her father. But he slept like a bear in hibernation, she reminded herself, and she lifted the window all the way up. The screen allowed a gentle mist through the barrier that felt refreshing.

"Ryan!" Sophie called. No response. "Ryan!" she tried again.

"What are you doing?" No acknowledgement. Instead, he began to rock back and forth. An image of a patient in an asylum wearing a straitjacket came to her mind. She was scared now. She had no idea how long he had been out there.

As quickly as she could manage, Sophie hopped to the bed, sat down, and slipped into her prosthetic. She hustled out of the bedroom, snatching up her cane on the way out. The living room was covered in total darkness, and Sophie considered grabbing a flashlight before going any further. But she was in a hurry, and the back door was only a few feet away. She wished now more than ever that she could run. Ryan may really need her help, and the best she could do was limp to the rescue.

Sophie made it to the door and slid it open. She took one step onto the deck and her valiant rescue attempt was almost cut short before it had even started. Her right foot met what felt like a sheet of ice and slid out from under her in an instant. Sophie managed to catch herself on the side of the door before falling to the cold surface of the deck. She pulled herself upright and continued on.

It was about fifteen feet from the sliding door to the steps leading to Ryan, and Sophie treated it as if it were fifteen feet of ice, choosing to slide her feet along the deck, as if she were ice skating. Already drenched, and shivering, Sophie made it to the top of the shallow staircase. She scolded herself for not putting on a raincoat, or at least pants. But more accustomed to the terrain now, Sophie managed to scale the steps with relative ease.

When she reached the bottom, she looked up for the first time. He was still on his knees, but the rocking had ceased. She remained motionless herself for a moment.

"Ryan," she said, continuing forward. No movement. She was

now only a few feet away from him. She wanted to rush to him, but something about the entire scene kept her from moving too quickly. She felt as though she shouldn't be here, as if she were disturbing some kind of ritualistic meditation of his. Did this happen every night? Did he even sleep?

She tensed against the relentless onslaught and quickened her pace. When she approached the scene, she fell to the ground. She rested her arm softly on Ryan's back. "Ryan? Can you hear me?" Sophie asked. "Are you alright?" She was able to perceive a slight movement in his eyelids. "Ryan, come on. We have to get you inside. It's pouring, you're gonna catch a cold." Still no answer. There was no way she could hope to physically move him, but she tried anyway. With her free hand, Sophie scooped her arm under his and lifted. He scarcely budged. However, he seemed to have finally acknowledged Sophie's presence. At least, his body seemed to. He looked up at her, and his expression changed twice, quickly. First, it flashed fear, as if the very sight of her terrified him. But his features quickly re-formed into what she believed was recognition. For a moment, they just looked at each other, the wind ceasing to roar and the rain freezing in mid-air. If it were possible, his eyes seemed darker.

Then, the cold and wet returning and time beginning to tick, Sophie attempted to lift Ryan again. "Come on," she said. "We need to get you back to bed." His eyes opened a fraction more and he slowly began to rise. Sophie rose with him, her hand never leaving his back. "Come on," she said, turning him around to face the steps. She led him as though he were blindfolded. "This way." At least he was alright, she assured herself. He didn't seem to be injured.

Ryan followed her without a word, his head drooped and his

eyes on the ground. Cane in one hand and Ryan in the other, she led the way through the rain toward the steps. Without hesitation at the bottom, Sophie began to climb the staircase with her disoriented patient.

Eventually, they reached the landing. Sophie opened the door and ushered him inside and out of the storm. When she closed the door, the sound from outside became muffled, lowered to a whisper instead of the screams she had become accustomed to. The floodlight outside remained alit long enough for Sophie to scout the short road ahead. But after she and Ryan took their first step, the light went out, and they were draped in total darkness. Sophie limped to where she believed Ryan's desk to be and found the switch under the lampshade. A honeyed glow filled the room, instantly warming Sophie.

She glanced back to find Ryan unmoved, shivering. He stood there in front of the door, blank-faced, as if he had drunkenly stumbled into someone else's home. Sophie covered the short distance between them and pulled a dry towel from a hook on the wall. Tossing it around his shoulders like a cape, she led him toward the bed. She could feel him trembling under her hands. She was trembling also, but the vibrations sprinting through his body were different. They came in spurts, and every time he exhaled, his body shook uncontrollably. She needed to get him into bed and under a warm blanket.

He lay down obediently and curled up on his side. Sophie reached down and pulled the blanket over his glistening body. In the faint light, she could see that his eyes were closed again, but she couldn't tell if he was sleeping. His breaths were light.

Like a mother watching over her newborn baby with a cold,

Sophie lingered, hovering over the twin bed anxiously. Ryan's fragile state arrested her movement. She had helped him out of the rain, and now she should go back to her bed. But she couldn't leave him like this. It pained Sophie to think that this was how Ryan spent his nights.

As soon as the thought crept into her mind, Sophie knew she was going to go through with it. Still soaking wet, she bent down onto the mattress. She unfastened her leg and shuffled up to the head of the bed. It was soft and low to the ground and Sophie's exhausted body fell lazily onto the damp white sheets. Ryan's shivering created a tremor throughout the bed as Sophie settled into a comfortable position behind him. For a few minutes, she just watched the back of his head and the rise and fall of his shoulders, lost in the staggering rhythm. She shifted her body forward so she could feel the warmth of his back against her chest. Her arm was loose around his waist and rose and fell as he struggled to breathe steadily.

After a few minutes, Sophie felt the vibrations weakening. And not long after that, they subsided altogether. Once it was clear Ryan had fallen asleep, Sophie considered sneaking out of the bed and going back to the house.

But no. She wasn't leaving tonight.

"Good night, Ryan," she whispered. She prayed that she awoke first, and before long, she fell into a dreamless sleep.

Ryan awoke first. The storm had passed, and the sun was on the rise. Early morning light filled the room. He rubbed his eyes and stretched his neck. Images from the previous night flashed in his mind's eye, but he struggled to put the pieces together. It only took a moment for him to realize he wasn't alone.

He turned his head while keeping the rest of his body still, allowing the movement to take far longer than necessary, afraid of what he would find. Peering over his shoulder, Ryan's worried eyes fell on Sophie's sunlit face. She was asleep. Her left arm was curled against her chest as if she were hugging herself. The other arm was fastened securely around his waist. He stopped breathing, and the sound of her soft breaths filled the room.

He remembered being out in the rain. He couldn't breathe. It was cold, but he was unable to fully comprehend the feeling, half-awake, convinced he was still dreaming. Then she came to him. She looked like an angel against the light. He remembered thinking she *was* an angel; some heavenly creature come to take him out of the rain and back to bed; reassure him that everything was going to be okay. He remembered her touch. It was like fire, an innocuous flame that only warmed and couldn't burn. He followed her back up to the loft. He would have followed her anywhere.

Then it dawned on him. She must have slipped into bed with him, afraid to leave him the way he was. She must have been terrified.

His eyes remained fixed on her slumbering form while he attempted to recall details. Her hair was still a little damp from the rain, and the sun highlighted her porcelain skin. Her breath warmed his back. Her scent filled the room, overpowering the smell of cheap whiskey and unwashed clothes. He wanted to touch her cheek and watch her sleep all day. But this couldn't be real. He had to be dreaming. But he didn't have these kinds of dreams, of love and warmth, and safety. Dreams like these had been taken from him, replaced with nightmares of a rough ocean and a faceless sister. Underneath the illusion of contentment was the nagging fear. Always the nagging fear.

As if from an alarm sounding, Ryan awoke from his ruminations. He had no idea what time it was, and for all he knew, Ted was walking up the steps right now to come check on him. Reluctantly, Ryan turned away from Sophie's face and cautiously lifted her arm so he could slide out from under it. She didn't wake. He lifted one leg, then the next onto the floor, and sat up on the side of the bed. With luck, he might be able to sneak down to the shower without her stirring.

Ryan felt Sophie's body twitch. He turned to see her eyelids open a fraction. She stretched her arms high over her head and arched her back. A subtle smile crawled up her cheek. Her eyes opened and she stared at Ryan for a moment, blinking away the sleep. She shot up, awake and alert. It took her a fraction of a second to inhale her surroundings. "Oh my gosh," she said.

"Good morning," Ryan said casually, showing her his profile. He waved.

"I'm sorry," she rushed. "We didn't—I mean, nothing happened last night." She started to shuffle around in the bed, searching for a way out.

Ryan twisted his torso. "I know," he answered softly.

Her expression assumed a friendlier mold and she stopped moving. "You remember what happened?" she asked. She sat up.

"Vaguely," he said. "I'm a little fuzzy on the details." He paused. "But I would remember that."

Sophie nodded, then tried to hide a smile. He wondered what she was thinking. "I'm embarrassed," she said. "I know it was a massive invasion of your privacy. But I—"

"I'm happy you did," Ryan said, cutting her misplaced apology short. "There are worse ways to wake up. Trust me."

"Oh," she said. "Well. You're welcome."

For the first time, Ryan noticed that Sophie's shirt was white, and she wasn't wearing a bra. "Um," he said. "Your shirt is kind of, um." He turned away.

"Oh," she said, and quickly covered herself with the blanket.

He reached for his phone. "Shit," he said. "It's nine o'clock."

"We slept that long?"

"I should jump in the shower," Ryan said, offering to go out first.

"Okay," Sophie said. "I'll go make some coffee." And, to his bewilderment, she swung her legs over the edge of the bed, slipped into her prosthetic, reached for her cane, and made for the door before he could stand up.

He watched her go.

After an unusually long shower, Ryan got dressed and walked out to the pool deck. The sun was halfway up the sky by now, and he wondered what Ted was doing. Sophie's father had drunk more wine than anyone the previous night.

He took a seat on the edge of a lounge chair and lit a cigarette.

He smelled the coffee in her hands before he heard her. She descended the stairs with ease and strode towards him.

"Here you go," Sophie said brightly, handing him an oversized coffee mug.

"Thanks," he said.

Sophie took a seat beside him and they sat in silence for a few moments while both wrestled inwardly with how to begin. Sophie dove in first. "I understand if you don't want to talk about it," she said.

"I have nightmares," he said, staring into the coffee mug, the images of the previous night's dream materializing in the black circle. Until that moment he hadn't decided how honest he wanted to be with Sophie. But he couldn't help himself. It wasn't only that she deserved to know. A part of him wanted her to know so that maybe she would spend that night with him, and the next night. And maybe the next.

Sophie didn't respond, and after a moment, Ryan continued. "They started after I lost Sarah. It's always the same dream. I'm swimming towards her. She's crying for help. I can't even see her face." He stopped, hiding his hesitation with another drag off the cigarette. "I can never catch her," he went on. "I can never save her." He decided to tell her what he assumed was obvious. "Your screams woke me out of one that morning I pulled you from the water."

He could feel Sophie watching him as he spoke, his eyes never leaving the black circle inside the mug.

"Is it always that bad?" she asked. "I mean, are you always like that when it happens?"

"No," he said. "Usually, I just wake up. It hurts for a while, but the pain lessens as the day goes on. But last night was different. I was over her grave, and my parents were there. They told me it should've been me in the ground." He was emotionless as he spoke. But he didn't mind repeating the experience to her. She had been there with him, and he believed she wanted to understand.

"Ryan," Sophie said. "I can only imagine." She rested her hand on his hunched back. It felt as warm as it did last night. "Do the nightmares come every night?" she asked, genuine care attached to every syllable.

"They used to," he answered. "But recently they've become less frequent." He paused. "Since I've been spending time with you," he finished. He looked up for the first time and met Sophie's eyes, and there was nothing forced about the way they looked at each other. Neither felt the urge to look away. "I'm sorry I was so short with you after dinner," he said. "You seemed so happy."

"It's alright," Sophie said. "I was afraid I had done something wrong."

"You didn't do anything wrong," he reassured. "You've done everything right. I know it's still hard for you, but you're making a difference." He took a deep breath. "Yesterday wasn't a good day. But the messed-up thing is, I was down because I hadn't been having nightmares. I've had more dreamless sleeps in the past two weeks than I have in the past two years. And I was scared. I'd become so accustomed to them. It's like they're a part of me. I'm afraid to let them go. And I'm afraid to keep them." He trailed off, aware of his rambling. He never used to ramble. Sophie was staring through the water, searching for what to say next. What could she say?

"Why did you stay with me last night?" Ryan asked.

Sophie leaned back on her hands and crossed her right leg over her left and breathed out. She turned to him. "Why did you put me to bed those two nights," she said. "After I was so horrible to you?"

He frowned, trying to remember if he'd told her about that. "I thought you were asleep?"

"I remember," she answered. Her expression evinced gratitude and something else he couldn't place.

He set the coffee mug on the stone and reached for his necklace nervously. "I guess I wanted you to have a more comfortable sleep."

"I guess I wanted the same thing for you," she answered. She suddenly seemed so much older to him in that moment, so much more mature, and the strength and confidence he'd known was there, emanated from her like an intoxicating fragrance.

They were quiet after that, alternating sips of coffee.

"Anyway," Sophie eventually said. "Cheer up." She stood and offered him her hand. "You have a wedding to take me to."

22

"I can't believe I let you talk me into this," Ryan said to Laura through the bathroom mirror.

"What you mean to say," she replied, "is you can't believe how lucky you are to have such a beautiful and talented woman cutting your hair."

He looked at himself. He was staring at a stranger's reflection.

"Admit it," Laura went on. "It's nice to finally be able to see your whole face." She had insisted on shaving his face as well. "I mean, it was a crime to hide that jawline."

It was true the shave had felt amazing. Laura was a pro. And he had to admit, he was getting tired of scratching the damn thing every few seconds.

Laura had the lightest touch, and every time her feathery fingers fell on his neck a chill ran down his spine. The experience reminded him of when Sophie tied his hair back that day on the beach.

"Well," Laura said after using the clippers one final time. "All done. What do you think?"

He stared hard at himself, unsure what to think. "I hardly recognize myself."

Ryan was sitting on a stool, and Laura leaned in, opposite his left ear so he could feel her breath. "You can thank me later," she said. "I'll let you get dressed. We don't want to be late." Laura turned back and allowed herself one more look at her masterpiece through the mirror. "Sophie won't know what hit her," she said.

"Thanks," he said as she closed the door. He took one more look at himself, shook his head, and got dressed for the wedding.

Sophie and her father were waiting in the living room. She could barely conceal her anxiety. The last week, since she spent that night with Ryan, had been uneventful. She had felt so good about what had happened and what might happen as a result. However, they hadn't talked about it at all after that morning. Sophie knew she was in love with him. She lay awake every night since that storm, wanting so badly to go to him, to make sure he was okay. It killed her to think he might be having another nightmare, trembling alone in bed.

But she restrained herself. She told herself that if he wanted any help or comfort, he would ask. But he never did. He acted as if it had never happened. Was he scared? Nervous? Was she completely misjudging the situation? She had felt so close to him, and she believed he felt the same way.

Well, she had decided, if he wasn't going to address it then she would. She thought about what Liv would do if she were in her position. It didn't take long to come to the obvious conclusion. She was going to have to take control.

Sophie spent more time getting ready for today than she ever had for anything. She wore an emerald green dress that flowed down to the floor. Her hair fell around her face like smooth, steep slopes on a mountain. After dusting it off, she wrapped a white pearl necklace around her neck and fastened a pair of her mother's diamond studs to her naked ears. Laura had given her the okay.

"You okay, Sweetie?" her father asked. He was dressed casually in a white button-down and sun-tanned slacks. It was a beach wedding, after all.

"Yeah, fine," she answered immediately. "Why?"

"You just seem a little on edge."

"Nope."

"If you say so."

Laura emerged from the hallway. Finally, Sophie thought. "It's about time," her father said. "What did you do to him?"

"Just styled him up a bit," Laura responded coolly as she glided across the floor.

A few minutes later, Ryan emerged from the bathroom. When he entered the living room, everyone went quiet. Laura smiled.

Sophie's father spoke first. "Well, I'll be damned," he said. "Look who cleans up nicely."

Sophie was at a loss for words. It wasn't Ryan who emerged from the hallway, but someone else, someone with short dark hair, swept carelessly to one side. Someone whose smooth face revealed a sharp jaw which ran down to a pointed chin that might prick Sophie's finger. It was as if Ryan had unzipped himself from the top of his forehead all the way down to his toes and emerged from the packaging a new man. He actually looked his age. Small ears that hadn't seen daylight in months listened to the stillness around them. A clean, white button-down clung to his upper body and angled down to his waist, tucked in neatly. His straight, light brown pants fit perfectly. The only missing piece of the ensemble was confidence. Embarrassment gripped his features, replacing the hair that had so recently been shaved off. He was unsure of himself. Did he see what she saw? She had tried to envision him like this before, but her wildest imagination could never have created such a perfect incarnation of what she knew was always there. Under the surface, beneath the murky top layer, was a man. She was still waiting for Ryan to walk into the living room behind this ethereal figure.

"I think it's safe to say Laura's a magician," Ted said, filling the extended silence.

Sophie only nodded, still unable to pluck any vocal cords.

"All right, that's enough fuss," said Laura. "I'm a miracle worker, and Ryan looks great. Are we ready? We're going to be late." She hooked her arm around Sophie's father's.

Ryan moved toward Sophie, his bare feet quiet against the hardwood floor. "What do you think?" he asked, spreading his arms as he closed in.

Finding her voice finally, Sophie answered, "I think everyone is going to wonder if we pulled you out of a magazine."

He was inches from her face. He seemed taller, his chin in line with her nose. She could smell the aftershave on his face.

"I was thinking the same thing about you," he answered. He became more comfortable the closer he got to her.

Sophie smiled. "This should be fun."

Late afternoon shined down on the four of them as they walked the short distance along the beach to the Palmer's mansion. High above, a few stray clouds kept the sun honest, unwilling to allow too much of a glare. The water was as calm as the breeze, and a more perfect day for a wedding would have been hard to come by.

Sophie's eyes couldn't help but stray toward the clean-cut young man walking beside her. She had hoped that perhaps the make-over would illuminate what she hadn't been able to see; that maybe his feelings were somewhere under those locks and that beard, and now she would be able to read them like text. But the expression hadn't changed, and the eyes continued to hold their pain like a tightly sealed jar.

Intentionally allowing themselves to lag behind the older couple, Ryan and Sophie stayed safely out of earshot. "So," Ryan said. "Your dad and Laura, huh?"

Sophie turned her attention to the pair up ahead. "He says they're just friends," Sophie answered. "We'll see about that."

"We can hear you," Laura called back.

Sophie and Ryan suppressed a laugh.

"Don't leave me alone today," Ryan said abruptly, his tone serious. "I'm not exactly going to be in my element."

Sophie looked up at him. "Not for a second," she said. She knew how uncomfortable he would be in such a large crowd. Sophie had anticipated this. She'd considered everything.

When they came upon the portion of the beach reserved for the wedding, Liv rushed over to meet them. "Who the hell are you?" she asked accusingly of Ryan. Before he could answer, Liv went on, clearly not in search of a response. "Damn. Well, I guess that's it for us." She frowned like a puppy, feigning sadness. "I liked the beard."

"Thanks?" Ryan said. There was a certain way to talk to people like Liv, Sophie knew. She was grateful Ryan hadn't cared to learn the craft.

Liv wore a loose-fitting yellow dress that stopped just short of mid-thigh. A translucent white shawl hung around her shoulders. Sophie thought she looked pretty, while still managing to pull off sexy. "But," Liv continued. "I have to admit. You two look great together." She winked at Ryan and hugged Sophie. "I have to get back," she said. "My cousin is *actually* Bridezilla today. She's freaking out about her hair and make-up. So, naturally, I have to come to the rescue." And she was gone as quickly as she'd arrived. Sophie thought she was like a hummingbird, eager to swoop in, check out what was going on, then take off without warning. But everyone always remembered seeing her, even if only for an instant.

Sophie took a moment to look up at the mansion she had spent so much time in as a child, running around and getting lost in. She was still convinced she hadn't explored every room, even after twenty years. Weathered cedar shingles covered the exterior. She remembered it being browner when she was a child. Now, however, a gray hue had settled in, offering the effect that the house physically aged, like a person. Three full floors rose up the east side, dozens of windows sprinkled throughout. Two sunrooms straddled the back deck, leaving the space enclosed on three sides, with nowhere to go but east, toward the water. The roofs of the sunrooms' supported separate decks, each with enviable views. Now that she thought about it, the place seemed tailor-made for hosting weddings.

Laura and Sophie's father had already taken their seats. They waved Sophie and Ryan over. Before they reached their destination, though, they were intercepted by the Palmers.

"Is that Ryan?" Mrs. Ginny said, bewildered.

"Believe it or not," Ryan responded.

"Wow. Look at that baby face," she gushed. She ran her hand along his cheek.

Ryan stood still, like a puppy being pet by a stranger. Mr. John only nodded and smiled. There was a knowingness to Mr. John's smile, as though he weren't surprised at all to see Ryan's transformation. Sophie would never understand the older man; his cryptic glares and knowing smiles.

After Mr. John and Mrs. Ginny took their seats, Sophie and Ryan managed to squeeze through the other guests toward Laura and her dad. It wasn't the first Palmer beach wedding that Sophie had attended. Liv had dozens of cousins sprinkled throughout the country, and they all came here to get married.

It wasn't a pretentiously decorated scene. A white arbor intertwined with green leaves presiding over white chairs occupied by casually dressed guests on the sand. Copy and pasted from the last wedding.

Sophie and company sat toward the back right of the crowd. They had no trouble seeing the bride and groom. The ceremony was short and sweet. Sophie noticed a tear fall down Laura's cheek, and a moment later, her father rested his hand over Laura's.

Ryan was alone at one of the dozens of tables strewn throughout the back deck that would serve as the reception venue. Sophie had held true to her word and watched over Ryan like a lioness.

Although he only recognized a few people at the event, Sophie knew just about everyone, and she was the center of attention. They all wanted to know how she was doing and offered their condolences about the accident. She handled the endless line of guests like a gracious hostess, deflecting what needed deflecting and offering just enough information as needed. Ryan hardly had to speak at all. Anytime someone asked Ryan anything about his past or something he might struggle to answer, Sophie would swoop in, casually redirecting the conversation toward a more comfortable subject.

But the use of the bathroom was an unforeseen obstacle that could not be avoided. Sophie promised to be right back, leaving Ryan alone at the table he shared with Laura, Ted, Sophie, and a small family he had no interest in getting to know.

His gaze surfed through the throng of guests as he waited. He enjoyed a long sip of the best bourbon he'd had the pleasure of drinking in a long time. The open bar was like an old friend come to settle his nerves among a multitude of strangers. While the wedding party was down on the beach having photographs taken of them jumping up and down and smiling until it hurt, many of the guests took the opportunity to explore the house. Ryan could see clearly through the glass walls as guests wandered aimlessly from room to room as if they were spending the day at a museum; the place had enough priceless artwork. Groups gathered high above on either of the second-floor balconies, no doubt enjoying the views before retreating inland. All around him, on the main stage, clutters of smiling guests caught up and reminisced as if they were attending a family reunion instead of a wedding; the event doubled as such, as most of the guests were related. Sophie told him that John and Ginny had almost forty grandchildren.

He could only people watch for so long, though, and after a few more minutes, he began to feel stuck. He rose from the small white chair and made his escape down to the sand.

The wedding party was just finishing up with their pictures and sneaking around to the front of the house so they could make a dramatic entrance. Ryan made his way down the flights of steps, hoping to go unnoticed.

The fading light rested over the tired ocean, as if whispering its child to sleep before turning in itself. The conversation from the party sounded like the waves crashing before him. He enjoyed another long sip of bourbon, inhaled deeply, and let out a stream of smoke, an ugly addition to the serene atmosphere.

"I guess I shouldn't be surprised to find you out here," someone said. Ryan turned to see John Palmer shuffling toward him, having broken off from the wedding group. The older man, casually dressed in a white button-down and pants the same color as the sand, came up beside Ryan and sat down, Native American style. Ryan remained standing, unsure what to do. "It's more comfortable from this view," John said.

Ryan accepted the invitation and sat down. "Do you mind if I smoke?" Ryan asked, holding up the half-smoked cigarette.

John waved his hand dismissively. "You kidding me?" he said. "I grew up in a time when it was weird if you didn't smoke." For a few minutes, the two men, separated by sixty years, sat in silence, watching the waves come and go while seagulls searched for scraps and a few guests snapped pictures of the view.

"Did I ever tell you I was sitting right here, that morning you saved Sophie?" John said. Ryan stopped, frozen, the rim of his rocks glass an inch from his lips. He turned to John and shook his head.

"Yup," said John. "It was early, before the sun came up. You were passed out right over there." He pointed to a spot twenty feet away. Ryan was surprised, but also confused.

"You just let me stay there?" he asked. It was a private beach, after all, and it was hard to believe even the impossibly gracious Palmers would allow a drunk to use their sand as a bed.

John considered the scene before him. "I almost kicked you awake," he answered. "But when I got close, I noticed you were talking to yourself. In your sleep, of course." John looked over at Ryan and raised his eyebrows.

"What was I saying?" Ryan asked.

"I think you know," John answered. And all at once, it became clear; why every time John had looked at Ryan, he seemed to know him, know what he was thinking. His deepest secrets. "So, I let you sleep," said John. "And thank God I did, right?" Ryan wasn't sure what to say. "I watched Sophie pass by, as I always do, and then I went back into the house to make breakfast. You know what happened after that."

Ryan took another sip. "Why are you telling me this now?"

John traced a half circle in the sand with his ancient finger. "I had a brother," he said. "A twin brother. Years ago. We went to war together. He died saving my life." John was pensive, allowing a memory to run its course. "I come out here every morning and watch the sun rise. Been doing it for as long as I've had the place. Strange that I found you out here on the anniversary of his death." He looked out over the water. "Makes me wonder," he said. Understanding washed over Ryan as he listened, unaware now that there were a couple hundred people celebrating a wedding not far away. In that moment, the two men were alone in the world.

"How did you get past it?" Ryan asked.

John looked over at Ryan and narrowed his eyes. "Past?" he asked. "You don't get past something like that, Ryan." He paused. "You find someone to share it with."

Ryan wanted to hear more. He wanted John to continue, to tell him everything; the secrets to life he was sure this old wizard had. But instead, the older man rose to his feet and said, "Well, I should get back," and he made his way back up to the party, leaving Ryan in the sand, confused, and yet more aware than he'd ever been.

"Hey."

Sophie's voice carried down the last flight of stairs like a calm wind come to cleanse the air around him. She quietly descended the final few steps and limped to his side.

"Hey," he replied.

"I thought I'd lost you," she said. "Sorry I was so long. Too many Palmers. I couldn't escape," She was breathing heavily.

"Hey, you're a popular girl. I can't expect to have you all to myself."

"Why not?" she countered.

He wasn't prepared to answer that question. "Because it wouldn't be fair?"

"Fair?" she replied. Her tone wasn't indignant, but patient, as if Ryan had yet to learn that life isn't fair and that she would be glad to explain the matter. She was about to go on when she stopped herself short. Sophie had been inspecting Ryan's eyes during the exchange, as if searching for something, something behind his words she couldn't grasp. "Been enjoying the view?" she asked, changing the subject.

"Yeah," he said. "I had a little chat with John. Got me thinking."

"Really?" she said. "What did you talk about?"

"I'm still trying to figure that out."

She nodded knowingly. "You want to get out of here?" she said, surprising him.

"Now?"

"Yeah, now," she said. Her confidence was intimidating.

"What about the wedding? They're about to serve dinner. And dance and stuff." He was stalling.

"I'm not hungry. But if you want to stay and dance…"

Ryan rolled that idea around in his head for half a second. "Yeah. Let's get out of here."

The walk back to the house was speechless. The ocean was quiet and the wind calm, but a storm was raging inside him, a force of emotions that spun in his mind like a tornado.

Sophie had slipped her arm through his, a maneuver that might pass as friendly. But it felt different now. For some reason, Ryan's thoughts returned to a memory of the first time he'd kissed a girl. He was in middle school and he and the young girl had walked behind the gymnasium. The part that stood out to him was the quiet which had fallen between them during that walk, as if they were both only capable of thinking about what was going to happen, instead of talking about it. This walk felt similar. He was equally nervous now as he had been all those years ago.

He wondered if Sophie was experiencing similar feelings.

***

She was terrified. Sophie had never been so nervous in her life. Butterflies tickled her insides so much it hurt. She would have welcomed the adrenaline-fueled nervousness that twisted her stomach before a swim meet. But like her competitions, she desperately tried to evince an air of casual confidence as she matched Ryan's stride along the surf. She had slipped her arm under his, and she could feel his pulse quicken. She couldn't help reciting the lines she had rehearsed over and over, and images of how she wanted the next twenty minutes to transpire projected in her mind's eye. The time for rehearsal was over, though, and a certain calm fell over her, the kind of calm that accompanies a confident decision. She knew what she wanted. And he had spent enough time alone.

When they arrived back at the house, Sophie moved to the edge of the pool. Ryan hung back and took a seat on the edge of a lounge chair. He fished around in his pockets and found the half-empty pack of cigarettes.

"So," he said, slipping a cigarette into his mouth. "What now?"

He was looking down at the blue stone around his feet as he spoke. When he lifted his head to light the cigarette, Sophie was standing before him, looming over his hunched figure, smirking. Only a few seconds ago she had been five feet away, studying the water in the pool. He hadn't heard her move.

Gently, Sophie reached out and pulled the cigarette from his mouth. The small flame from the lighter lit up her features. Her eyes were now level with his. They were on fire. But there was no danger.

Ryan's mouth remained open after she had removed the cigarette and tossed it aside. He dared not move, or protest, the light touch of her slender fingers having turned him to stone. Her eyes lingered on his for a moment. He remained hypnotized. If she said speak, he would have spoken.

Without a word, Sophie rose to her full height, towering over Ryan like a queen among her subjects. She turned and glided back to the edge of the pool. If she limped, he didn't see.

Perilously close to the edge, Sophie turned her head to the side, allowing Ryan a glimpse of her profile. Then, in a movement as serene as he had ever witnessed, Sophie reached her left arm over her right shoulder and slipped the strap of her dress off, so it lay loose on her arm. She repeated the process unhurried on the other side. When gravity took over, the emerald garment fell to the ground, as if Sophie's body had vanished from underneath it. It lay at her feet like a small puddle of liquid green among the blue stone. She unfastened her prosthetic and let it fall to the surface beside her. She balanced herself with ease, showing no signs of wavering. What remained was a white strapless bra and white underwear. Her brown hair covered most of her back.

Sophie hesitated on the edge for a few seconds. She bent down, and using her arms for support against the stone, slowly lowered herself into the water. She waded into the middle of the pool and turned around.

"Well?" she said softly. "What are you waiting for?"

Ryan stood up. He unbuttoned his shirt and slid off his pants. His performance was clumsy and rushed compared to hers. Stepping to the edge of the pool, he hesitated. She wasn't in trouble. She didn't need saving. The water looked cold.

"It's just us, Ryan," Sophie said, her voice a calming siren. "Trust me."

He took a slow breath and lowered himself into the water. Eyes glued to hers, he moved to meet her.

Within seconds only inches separated them, and Sophie's warmth controlled the water's temperature.

He was unsure what to do next, so he waited; she seemed to know the script much better than him. Sophie's hands gradually emerged from beneath the surface and wrapped themselves around his neck. Instinctively, he slid his hands under the water and found her waist. It was smooth, like touching marble. She leaned a little closer. He felt her rise as she easily lifted her body to meet his eye.

"I'm nervous," Ryan whispered.

"Feels good, doesn't it?" Sophie asked.

"What?"

"To feel," Sophie answered. And she leaned in and kissed him.

Nothing he had ever touched or experienced in his short life compared to the delicacy of Sophie's kiss. It was like something he hadn't even known to dream of, his imagination incapable of conjuring such perfect designs. Her body pressed into his as her arms tightened around his neck. He hugged her close. The world was quiet, the ocean silent, and the wind was still. It lasted forever.

Together, they broke the embrace, and the world was turned back on. They looked at each other.

Tears rose in Sophie's eyes. Ryan held her gaze. "I don't know what I can give you," he said. "I'm broken."

She smiled and leaned into his ear. "So am I," she whispered.

23

Sophie awoke early the next morning in Ryan's bed. The sun fed through the window like water through a showerhead. She watched him breathe, mimicking his breaths, staying in sync with his every inhale and exhale.

The memory of her night with him played in her mind like a broken record. As she studied his every feature like an artist, Sophie relived every second of the experience.

Ryan had carried her up to the loft from the pool so effortlessly, never taking his eyes off hers. She trusted him completely.

The loft had been cast in a blue glow, as the sun had just recently fallen out of sight. She thought about how gentle he was with her, lowering her onto the bed as if she were a priceless sculpture. He fell with her, hovering inches above her face before they kissed. His lips and face were so soft. She could feel the lingering moisture from the pool as she pulled him closer.

She remembered him kissing her scar. At first, she'd been hesitant, embarrassed even. It had been the one thing she was worried about. Would it bother him? Would he hesitate at the touch? She'd stopped his hand reflexively when it moved over her hips and toward her thigh. He gently put her hand back in its proper position on the pillow beside her head and continued without a word. She remembered wishing she could kiss his scars too. But his were hidden below the surface.

As twilight succumbed to the inevitable darkness, they made love.

She thought about how—

A door opened from below, tearing her away from the memory. Heavy footsteps punished the cement floor beneath them. She knew that walk.

"Hello?" her father called from below, his tone curious. "Anyone home?" Ryan's eyes shot open. Terror gripped him as realization spread over his features.

Sophie couldn't help but smile. She would have preferred he awoke to more pleasant thoughts, but the look on his face made her suppress a laugh. He appeared as though he had just been caught in his girlfriend's bedroom by her intimidating father. She guessed he had, in a way.

Ryan put his finger to his lips and widened his eyes, silently begging Sophie to be quiet. Sophie rolled over and swung her legs over the edge of the bed. She slipped on a pair of Ryan's underwear and threw one of his white shirts over her head.

"What are you doing?" Ryan hissed. He propped himself up on his side.

Sophie turned around, leaned over, and kissed him lightly on the lips, then raised her finger to her lips. She turned away. Using the railing for support, she stood up and looked over the ledge. Sophie spied her father standing with his hands in his pockets. He was wearing the same clothes he had on from last night. "Hi,

Daddy," she said brightly. She glanced over her shoulder and watched in amusement as Ryan crushed his hands to his face and crashed back down to the mattress. He rolled over into the fetal position.

"Good morning, Sweetheart," her father said. "Just checking in. We missed you last night." He walked out from under the loft.

"Yeah," Sophie answered. "Sorry about that."

Her father tilted his chin and looked through the railing. "Sure you are," he said. "You, um, left your clothes out on the pool deck. I just wanted to make sure you two didn't, you know, vanish or something."

"Did we?" Sophie asked. She turned back to the bed, as if Ryan might offer some clarity. He looked like he was ready to jump out the window.

"Yeah, well…" her father said. "Anyway. There's fresh coffee made whenever you're ready." Then he added, "You can have some too, Ryan."

"Thanks, Daddy," Sophie said. She turned back to Ryan. The back door opened and closed.

"Well," Ryan said. He sat up, clasped his hands together, and let out a long breath. "I guess I'll pack my things."

Sophie jumped onto the bed and pinned him back down, straddling his waist. "You can try," she said. She pushed his hands behind his head. "I have a strong grip."

"Don't I know it," Ryan said. He lifted his head to kiss her. "But seriously," he said. "What the hell?"

"What?" Sophie frowned. "Oh, come on," she said, sitting back on his stomach. "What were we going to do, hide it?"

"No, but—"

"Don't worry. He would throw me out before you. He loves you."

"We'll see."

"We should probably get up, though," Sophie said.

"Yeah," Ryan answered. He rose onto his elbows. Sophie pushed him back down against the bed and kissed him again. "Or not," he said.

Ryan stood with his hands on the railing. He didn't realize his nails were digging into the wood. Every few seconds, he took a sip of coffee. Sophie and Ted were inside, leaving him to gather his thoughts before having to explain himself. He considered making a run for it. It would only take a minute to pack his things. He could be out of town before they even knew he was gone. But that wasn't going to happen. He was in deep now, and there was no getting out.

He didn't want to get out either. The quicksand he'd unknowingly stumbled across wasn't dangerous or life-threatening. And Sophie was there with him. He needed her as much as he needed the cool ocean air to breathe. He also realized, the more he thought about it, that he wasn't worried about what Ted would say or think. Any amount of scolding or yelling or disappointment from Ted was nothing compared to the night he had just spent with Sophie. If he had to wake up every morning from here on out to be reprimanded by Ted, he would do it gladly, if he were able to wake up with Sophie beside him the next day.

What was there to fear when he had that to look forward to? What was there to be angry about or sad about when he had that to wake up to?

As quickly as that comfortable realization put him at ease, a darker, more terrifying one made itself known. What if he lost her? Ryan took a sip of the hot coffee and looked out over the ocean. The waves were bigger than normal this morning, crashing onto the sand with purpose, as if they had something to prove. The sky was the same shade of blue in every direction, the clouds having decided to take the day off. He wished he could just enjoy the feeling of being in love, enjoy the morning with the knowledge that she loved him as much as he loved her. But he couldn't shake the feeling that he had just made a fatal mistake. The truth was this town wasn't made of quicksand. He was. And he had just invited Sophie in.

The sliding door opened, and Ryan braced himself. The fear of confronting the father quickly returned. His stomach was twisted in a tight knot. But the older man didn't seem upset. Ted came up beside him and rested his hands on the railing. He didn't say anything, and Ryan watched him out of the corner of his eye.

"Well," Ted finally began. He stretched his arms wide as if to hug the new day. He let his hand fall to rest on Ryan's shoulder. Ryan suppressed a flinch. "Why don't you and Sophie take the day, huh?" And with that, he turned and made his way toward the workshop.

Ryan watched him go, too stunned to respond.

Ryan had moved down to the pool deck to wait for Sophie. Take the day? What did that mean? Were they supposed to put up an umbrella and lounge on the beach? That didn't sound too bad, he supposed.

As he had so many times before, Ryan heard Sophie coming

down the steps before he saw her. She was wearing a loose-fitting white top that fell below her waist. A black bathing suit was clearly discernable beneath the garment. As she moved by him, Ryan reached into his pocket and pulled out the pack of cigarettes. He hadn't smoked yet this morning. He put one to his lips and was about to light it when Sophie turned and snatched it out of his mouth. She didn't say anything, just like before. With one hand, she broke it in half and continued walking.

Ryan looked down at the tobacco spilling out of the white paper on the ground. He smiled. "Is this gonna be a thing now?" he asked. "Because I don't know if I can afford it."

"I don't know what you're talking about," Sophie said with her back to him. As she spoke, she crossed her arms around her waist and pulled the loose top over her head. Ryan forgot about the cigarette.

She removed the prosthetic and lowered herself into the water. She turned around and rested her elbows on the blue stone. "So," she said. An alluring grin climbed up her cheek.

"So," he answered. She was so perfect right there, where she belonged. He hated that he couldn't shake the sinking feeling.

"What are you thinking about?" Sophie asked. The way she said it was so innocent, so simple. He wished he had a simple answer.

"How beautiful you look," he lied.

"Liar," she said, her eyes penetrating. He should have known better.

He considered how to articulate his scrambled thoughts.

"Where the hell did you two sneak off to last night?" Liv yelled as she hustled up the boardwalk. She was still wearing her dress from the wedding, as well as the make-up she forgot to take off. She walked around the pool and sat down heavily next to Ryan. She looked from Sophie to him, twice, and understanding quickly sketched itself on her exhausted features. She said, "Well it's about damn time. It's been painful watching you two dance around like a couple of elementary school kids."

"Morning, Liv," Sophie said.

"Shut up."

Ryan smiled at Liv. "Rough night?" he asked.

"You have no idea," she said as she sunk back into the lounge chair. After a moment of silence, she added, "You will be happy to know you aren't the only ones who got laid last night."

"Well, don't keep us in suspense," Sophie said. "What happened?"

"Gimme a cigarette, Ryan," Liv demanded, ignoring Sophie's question.

He tossed the pack to Liv. She completely missed the catch and grunted as she reached down to pick it up. "Oh, no. You first," she said to Sophie. She lit the cigarette. "Take a hike, dude," she said to Ryan, tossing her head in the direction of the workshop. "Me and Soph need to talk."

"Liv," Sophie said.

"Come on," replied Liv. "You guys can stand to be apart for two minutes."

"It's alright," Ryan said. He stood up. "I'll see if your dad wants any help."

"Don't get lost," Sophie said, smiling.

"Ugh, gross," Liv muttered.

She tossed the pack of cigarettes to Ryan. He caught it,

considered for a moment, and tossed it back. "Keep 'em."

Liv frowned. "Who are you?"

Ryan walked through the open doorway of the workshop. A strong breeze nudged him forward just in case he thought better of the idea. It was strange; he felt as though it had been months since he'd been there. A sensation of nostalgia rolled through him as he made his way toward Ted. It had only been a day. But a lot had happened in that day. He looked around with new eyes. Everything was where it was supposed to be: the drill press, the table saw, and the worktables. Maybe he had changed.

Ryan had been so caught up in his relationship with Sophie, he hadn't allowed much time to think about his work with Ted. Somewhere between working in the shop and working on his relationship with Sophie, Ryan had created what might pass as a normal life, if only for a little while. It felt good to be back among the lumber and natural light that furnished the shop.

Ted was deep in thought as he measured a piece of old barn wood and marked his spots.

"Hey, man," Ryan started. "Need any help?

Ted looked up from the table. "It's your shop too, Ryan," he said. "If you want to work, you know what to do. Where's Sophie?"

"She's in the pool talking to Liv," Ryan answered. He walked over to a three-legged chair he had been working on.

"Ah," said Ted, and he continued with his measurements.

Ryan picked up a sander, then put it down when he realized he didn't need it. He faced Ted. "Look, Ted," he said. "I don't know if there's anything to be said, but I just want you to know I didn't plan on anything happening between Sophie and me. I mean, it wasn't like I've been planning it all this time, or anything." He felt he owed an explanation to the man.

Ted stopped what he was doing and put down the tape measurer with the same care he would with a saw. He stood up straight and leaned back against a table. For a moment he only looked at Ryan, measuring. After enough time had passed to make Ryan sufficiently uncomfortable, Ted said, "I know that Ryan. You don't need to explain anything. Actually, I think you're the only one who's surprised by what's happened." Ryan was beginning to believe that was the case.

"But there is something you need to know," Ted went on. "And this is important." *Here it comes,* Ryan thought. "I don't only want what's best for Sophie. I want what's best for you." Confusion took hold of Ryan like a riptide. It pulled him out as he attempted to swim sideways toward understanding. Ted began to clarify what should have been obvious. "I've seen you two over the last few weeks and I can't say I didn't see this coming. And I think it's a good thing, for both of you. I really do. You've both been through so much at too young of an age. And only through each other can you learn to live with it. I truly believe that." He stopped, looked outside, and smiled. "You've come so far since you've been here. You might not be able to see it. But to me, it's night and day."

Ryan remained silent as Ted searched for what to say next. A sense of déjà vu swam through Ryan. He remembered the first time he had been in the shop with Ted. They had almost been standing in the exact same places. The atmosphere had felt similar as well, as though raw emotion resided within the walls.

"I hope you've found what you've been looking for," Ted

continued. "It's been right in front of you all this time. I just hop
you're ready to accept it," he said. Ted had no interest in scoldin
Ryan or giving him a talk about how he'd better treat his daughte
right. Ryan leaned back against a sawhorse. "It's not so much tha
I'm worried about what would happen to her if she lost you, bu
rather what might happen to you if you lost her," he went on. "
want you to know that I understand that feeling better than mos
And we're all in this together. You're not alone."

Ryan took in the older man. "Thank you, Ted," he said softl
He wished he could have said more, but he needed time to proces
He looked around at the various pieces of furniture scattere
throughout the floor. He hadn't been looking for anything when Te
happened to be driving by that night. At least he hadn't thought so
But despite Ryan's efforts, he'd found something, someon
Someone like him. Someone to love.

For the first time in a long time, Ryan felt like he was a part o
something. For the first time, he allowed himself to consid
permanence. He looked around the shop. Could he make this plac
his home? He need only say the word. But the word was stuc
somewhere deep down, unable to free itself from the oppressiv
walls of his heart. Those same walls were weakening, though. H
could feel it.

Late that night, Ryan awoke from a deep sleep. He shot up. It wa
dark, he couldn't see an inch in front of him. Uncertain of where h
was, he felt the panic coming on and the breaths quickening. H
brought his hands to his face, hoping to blur the vividness of th
nightmare.

A warm hand fell upon his back. At the touch, Ryan enjoyed a deep inhale, as if the warmth had loosened his lungs.

"It's alright, Ryan." Sophie's soft voice carried the short distance between them through the darkness. He relaxed. Her words provided every bit of illumination he needed. He turned his head toward her voice. He couldn't make out her face, but he didn't need to. She was close. "It's okay. It was just a dream. I'm here."

Sophie sat up to meet him. She wrapped her arms around his neck and rested her head on his shoulder. Sophie waited patiently for Ryan's breathing to return to a normal pace. After a few minutes, his breath slowed.

"Come on," Sophie said. "Lie down."

Ryan obeyed and, with Sophie's help, he eased back into the bed. His eyes were wide as he lay his head back into the pillow. Sophie threw an arm over his chest and rested the upper half of her body on his. He slipped his arm around her shoulders and pulled her close. He couldn't hug her hard enough. He couldn't pull her close enough.

"I love you, Sophie." It was the middle of the night. He was tired and had just awakened from a nightmare. In the past, he might have said that he wasn't thinking clearly and that he didn't know what he was saying. But he meant every single one of those four words. There was nothing else to say in that moment.

He felt Sophie's head rise from his chest. The room became even quieter. "I love you too, Ryan." She kissed his chest and lay her head back down.

Ryan smiled in the dark and fell back into a dreamless sleep.

24

Over the next week, Ryan and Sophie spent as little time apart as possible, enjoying a honeymoon of their own, of sorts. They slept together every night in the loft. The outside shower was large enough for two, and they took full advantage of the space every morning.

Ryan was smoking less as a result of Sophie's knack for intercepting his cigarettes. His drinking habit began to falter as well. He didn't feel the urge to drink as much around Sophie anymore.

He was in love, there was no doubt about it, and he was going to try to enjoy it, for both their sakes. He found it difficult to dwell on the past when the alternative was so enticing. Every time he was in danger of losing himself in sorrow, she was there. She simply wouldn't allow it. She was so much stronger than him, to have endured what she had, and to still make subduing his suffering her priority.

A few days after the wedding, Liv announced that she was leaving to go back to New York. "I know, I know," she'd said. "But you two will be alright without me. Back to the real world." It was a bittersweet parting. He liked Liv, and Sophie had successfully rekindled a failing friendship. The girls promised to stay in touch and never allow the distance to come between them again. Liv's absence was noticeable, and the quiet that lingered took some getting used to.

Ted kept his distance, willing to watch with a smile as Sophie and Ryan attempted to navigate the first steps of a relationship. He was like a gardener patiently watching his plants grow.

It was almost unfair, Ryan thought one day, just how happy he was when he was with Sophie. The idea that life could be like this was unfathomable. And the idea that he could experience this kind of bliss was somehow an injustice. He didn't deserve it, but he wasn't going to allow that doubt to ruin the dream he had stumbled into.

"You sure you want to do this?" Ryan asked. His arm was secured firmly around her waist while she balanced on one leg. The surf tickled her toes invitingly, and she gazed out over the water with a sense of nervous excitement.

"Are you?" Sophie said.

He peered down at her, then looked over his shoulder at her father and Laura. They were sitting comfortably in identical beach chairs. Laura seemed happy to be there. Sophie's dad looked anxious. He hadn't been overly excited about the idea.

"Absolutely not," Ryan said, turning back to Sophie.

She smiled. "Come on, before we lose our nerve." She hopped forward. The water level rose quickly to her ankle, calf, knee, and finally her waist. Ryan's grip tightened the farther out they went. The water was colder than she remembered. The night Ryan had pulled her out, she had been in a dream, a dark tailspin in which all her senses had been curbed. Now she felt everything. The gentle breeze was accompanied by a swarm of affectionate sunlight. The wet sand curled under her toe, the sensation shooting up her leg and swirling around in her head like a sandstorm. The waves climbed up her chest as she lifted herself above them, forcing her to catch a breath. Everything she loved about the water. Everything she missed. It all crashed into her in those few moments. A barrage of memories seeping into those dark places inside of her. Like water through a crack in a submarine; there was no stopping them.

"Ready to go under?" Ryan asked.

Sophie nodded, and together they let their legs fall out from under them, allowing their heads to be swallowed up by the water. Sophie held tight to Ryan's arm. Her grip sunk deep into his skin. All sound was dispelled in an instant, and her eyes were closed. She let the underwater world swirl around her. She couldn't see, but she felt everything.

The eyes of her mind opened. A terrifying pair of black eyes were staring into hers, and the shark's mouth was wide open. Sophie pushed off the ocean floor, releasing her grip on Ryan, and shot up through the surface. Gasping for air, her eyes were wild and horrified. She was screaming in terror.

Before she could make for the shore, Ryan's gentle, yet unavoidable grip fastened itself around her waist once more and he pulled her to him. Within seconds, her face was an inch from his.

"Hey, hey," he said, trying to calm her down. Her eyes were glued shut and she was breathing heavily. "Hey, Soph. Look, look at me." He cupped her chin in his hand. Slowly, willing her breathing to return to normal, Sophie opened her eyes. "See," he said. "It's just us out here." He pulled her closer.

She wrapped her arms around his neck and breathed a sigh of relief. "This might take longer than I thought," she said into his shoulder. Only now did she realize he had been moving her toward shore the whole time, and he was supporting all her weight in the knee-high surf.

He let her down. "We have all the time in the world," he said.

On a Saturday night, exactly one week after the wedding, Ryan and Sophie were tangled in bed together in the loft. Ryan lay propped up against a pillow as he leafed through a book on the history of French furniture. He was amazed at how intricate the design and execution of the various pieces were. Perhaps he might become capable of such artistry someday. As it stood, he would lose his mind attempting to recreate such masterpieces. Maybe he didn't have to recreate anything, though. Maybe he could just create. Now that was a terrifying thought.

Sophie lay half on top of him as he read, her right leg sprawled over the lower half of his body like a primate clinging to a tree branch. Her head rose and fell to the beat of his chest. Occasionally her hair would tickle his cheek. She was wearing one of his white shirts that he insisted looked much better on her.

The bedside lamp shared barely enough light for him to make out the small words on the pages. Sophie insisted that he would need glasses soon. It was like reading by candlelight, she'd said. Terrible for the eyes. Fortunately for him, Ryan was more interested in the pictures.

"You know what I just realized?" Sophie said.

"Hm?" Ryan muttered as he turned the page.

"We haven't been on a date."

Ryan looked down at the top of Sophie's head, her expression hidden. He thought a moment, then replied, "Sure we have. What about all those walks, and conversations by the pool? People would kill for that kind of date. We learned everything about each other."

Sophie wasn't convinced. "Yeah, but we didn't know we were on a date," she said. "We were just friends. I mean, like, dinner and a movie. Or something."

"I didn't take you for a dinner and a movie kind of girl," Ryan said.

Sophie lifted her head and rested her chin on his chest. "Well," she said, grinning wryly. "I guess we didn't learn *everything* about each other, did we?"

"Okay," he said, defeated. "Dinner and a movie it is."

She smiled, leaned forward to kiss him, and returned to her preferred position.

"Oh," Sophie said abruptly. "My dad's birthday is coming up. I want to do something nice for him."

A jolt ran through Ryan as she said the words. He immediately stopped reading and stared forward, as if an intruder had burst through the door. Birthday?

"What's today?" he asked urgently. He couldn't hide his alarm.

"The fourteenth," Sophie replied. "Why?"

Ryan's face fell, every muscle turning off like a light. How could he have forgotten?

"What's wrong?" Sophie asked. She turned around to search his eyes.

"Nothing," Ryan lied, attempting to collect himself. "Sorry, I just got distracted. Your dad's birthday. Yeah, we should do something nice," he said. He tried a smile.

"Liar," she said.

"Really," he said. "I'm fine." Before she had a chance to reply, Ryan said, "I'm beat," and he reached over and turned off the light.

He could feel Sophie staring through the dark at him. And he could feel the disappointment from her as she rested her head back on his chest. "Goodnight," she said.

"Goodnight, Sophie."

25

Sophie was in the kitchen with her father. She poured herself another cup of coffee. She was nervous. Something was wrong. Ryan's mood had noticeably shifted the previous night. To anyone else, it might have been imperceptible, but to her, it was like an earthquake.

"So, I'm going to head out in a few minutes, Sweetheart," her father said from beside her. Sophie had almost forgotten he was there.

She turned to him. "Okay."

"Is everything alright?" he asked. He was watching her closely.

"Yeah," she lied.

"Come on, Soph," he said. "It's obvious Ryan's been in another world this morning. What's up?"

Sophie hesitated. But she needed to talk out her thoughts. "I honestly don't know, Dad. Everything has been so good lately. And last night he just went away for some reason, as if a switch had flipped off. I don't know what to do."

He wrapped his arm around Sophie's shoulder. "Soph, this is going to happen," he said. You and Ryan didn't exactly meet under normal circumstances. He's still trying to work through all this. And so are you. You have to be patient."

"I know," she said. "I just want everything to be perfect. It's too much to ask for I guess."

"It's not too much to ask for," he said. "But nothing is ever perfect for long. You know that, Sweetie. He's not going to be okay overnight. It'll be a lifelong struggle for him, and you're going to have to accept that if you plan on being with him. He'll need you now more than ever."

Sophie looked up into her father's eyes. "I know," she said. "Thanks, Daddy."

He leaned down and kissed her forehead. "Do you want me to stay home today?" he asked, pulling away.

"No. Go ahead. We'll be fine."

"You sure?"

"Yeah."

"Okay," he said. "I won't be long. They say a storm may hit a little later. Nothing too bad, but if it gets nasty, I'll call. It looks like it's going to stay offshore."

"Yeah, I heard," she said. "We'll be fine. I'll see you later."

"Okay," he said, and he kissed her again before turning to go.

Ryan leaned forward and looked out over the ocean. The water was rough today and becoming rougher before his eyes.

He raised the bottle to his lips. It wasn't yet noon and he was already drunk.

Sophie's footfall on the boardwalk interrupted his thoughts. She wasn't wearing her prosthetic. The difference between the sound of the prosthetic against the wood and the crutch was easily distinguishable. He knew when her right foot touched the ground, and when the crutch touched an extended second later. He had come to know her many different walks well.

But he didn't want to talk to her today. Any other day, he thought. Just let him get through this nightmare alone. He knew it went against everything they had agreed upon. They were supposed to talk through these things, together. No exceptions. And he had agreed with everything. He swore. That thought made him scold himself even more. He knew it, and yet he felt like he couldn't do anything about it.

Sophie made her way to where he was seated on the sand and settled in next to him. He was ashamed to meet her eye.

After a long moment of quiet during which Ryan defiantly indulged in another sip of whiskey, Sophie said, "A little early, isn't it? Even for you."

Ryan nodded. His eyes remained glued to the ocean. The wind picked up, waking the tall grass on the dunes behind them.

Sophie exhaled audibly. "Are you going to tell me what's wrong?" she said. She sounded frustrated.

"I'm fine, Soph," he lied. He took another sip.

"You're not fine. So stop saying it. We can rule that out completely. But I can't help if you won't talk to me. I thought we had a deal?"

Ryan turned his head halfway toward Sophie. Her face was an empathetic mural, her emerald eyes pleading. He retreated, unable to hold her gaze.

She rested her hand on his shoulder. "Please," she said.

Ryan hung his head. "I forgot Sarah's birthday," he said. The words were like poison in his mouth.

"Oh, Ryan," Sophie said. "I'm so sorry." She squeezed his shoulder. "I wish you would have told me last night."

"I was embarrassed," he said. His head remained limp.

"Come on," said Sophie. She put her hand on the small of his back. "Come inside. We can talk about it. It's starting to get dark over the water."

Ryan shot up, as if the sand had instantly become scalding hot. "Jesus, Sophie. You don't get it," he snapped. It was the first time Ryan had raised his voice to her. He couldn't remember the last time he had spoken so harshly to anyone.

Sophie opened her hands and frowned. "What do you mean?"

Ryan began to pace back and forth. "I'm running around here in this perfect place, like nothing ever happened," he said. "I've forgotten what I've done. I've allowed myself to be happy."

"It's okay to be happy," Sophie said.

"No, it's not!" he yelled. "Not for me."

A bolt of lightning burst across the sky over the ocean.

"Ryan," Sophie said. "Don't you think Sarah would have wanted you to be happy?"

Ryan stopped and looked down at Sophie. "You know nothing of what she would want," he said. "You know nothing about her. You don't even know me."

Empathy and a yearning to understand turned to shock and anger on Sophie's features. She stood up as well, easily balancing on one leg. The clouds seemed to have darkened even more at Sophie's command, as if her mood controlled the weather. "I don't know you?" she asked. "I'm the only one who knows you." She leaned down, picked up the crutches, and turned to go. Turning back, she said, "I thought you understood that." She made her way back up to the house.

Ryan settled back into the sand. The bottle hadn't left his hands during the argument. He allowed himself to fall back. He stared up into the gray sky. Leave it to him to screw up the best thing that had happened to him in twelve years.

His mind returned to the task of kicking himself while he was down. He hadn't even gotten Sarah a present.

A thought leaked into his head. It was as though he had just remembered where he had left his keys. He *could* do something right, he realized. He wasn't completely worthless. It seemed so obvious now that he'd thought about it. He could make her a toy, or a chair, or anything! A kind of insane joy rushed through him. He'd figured it out. Sarah couldn't stay mad at him if he made her something beautiful.

Bottle still in hand, Ryan arose with conviction, determined to make up for his unforgiveable mistake. He stumbled toward the workshop as heavy raindrops began to fall.

Sophie was in the kitchen making a sandwich. She used the countertop for balance, having left her prosthetic over by the couch. The big screen above the fireplace was turned on to the local news network covering the weather. It looked like part of the storm was going to hit land. The skies had become noticeably darker and she could hear the strengthening wind howling against the house. With only the oven light and a couch side lamp for light, the kitchen and connecting living room betrayed a studious atmosphere.

She was angry. She shouldn't be, she knew. Sophie was well

aware of how easy it was to retreat inside. It wasn't long ago that she had done the exact same thing. But she thought they were moving through that. And his reluctance to confide in her was frustrating. What was even more frustrating was that she didn't know what to do now. Should she keep trying, no matter what he said or did? Or should she give him time to cool off, in hopes he would come around in time?

They would get through this, she thought. They had been through so much together already. This was nothing.

A particularly angry gust of wind wailed against the house. She put down the knife and considered whether to go check on Ryan. She could say it was a safety thing. Just making sure he was okay. But when she looked up, she noticed him walking slowly along the deck toward the door, bracing himself against the wind.

Sophie slipped on her disappointed face and prepared for the confrontation. She dropped her eyes back down to the counter and continued slicing the tomato.

The door screamed and whistled as it opened. The wind flooded through as if seeking shelter. Sophie refused to look up, awaiting the apology she was certain she deserved. Heavy bare feet smacked against the wood floor. It sounded different from his normally quiet and casual stride.

"Sophie," he said. A long pause followed. "Sophie, I'm sorry." His voice was low, almost too low to hear.

She kept her head down. "Ryan, we need to talk about these things. I—"

"I wanted to make Sarah something for her birthday," he said faintly, interrupting her. The right half of his body was hidden by an unlit lamp beside the couch. His voice was failing him. Deep breaths in between words. He was soaking wet. And he looked tired.

"What?" Sophie asked. "Ryan, what's wrong?"

Panic took hold of her.

It happened in an instant.

His legs buckled and Ryan fell lifelessly to the floor on the opposite side of the counter.

"Ryan!" Sophie yelled. She turned and attempted to take a step. Before falling to the floor, Sophie caught herself on the corner of the counter. Lifting herself back up, she hustled around to the other side of the island.

Every thought and every feeling she was capable of having was replaced by a wave of fear. Ryan lay face down on the cold hardwood, a pool of blood expanding by the second around his right arm. "Ryan!" Sophie yelled again as she rushed to where he lay. She fell to the floor beside him. She searched for the source of the blood. On the outside of his right forearm, a cut led from the wrist all the way up to the elbow. It was deep—Sophie thought she could see his bone—and blood poured from the wound as if from a fountain.

She tried to remain calm, but panic swelled inside.

With all of her strength, Sophie rolled Ryan over, so he was lying on his back. He was still breathing. His eyes were half-closed.

"I'm sorry," Ryan whispered. His face was covered in sweat and as white as a cloud.

Sophie slid her hand under his neck and lifted, searching his eyes for any sign of recognition. "It's going to be okay," she said. "Hold on." She ripped off her shirt and wrapped it around the wound as tightly as possible. The shirt was instantly drenched, and her hands looked as though she had dipped them in red paint. Sophie lifted herself off the floor and vaulted over the couch. She reached for the telephone. A deafening crack of thunder exploded overhead. The TV and lights went out simultaneously, stripping her world of color, and help.

"No, no, no," she said hysterically. She grabbed the phone and punched in 911. No dial tone. "Shit." She reached for her cell phone on the coffee table and dialed 911 again. Call failed. No service. "Shit!"

Sophie reached for her prosthetic and fastened it as fast as she could. It was dark inside, but not pitch black. She was able to make out the shapes of the furniture scattered around the room as she hurried toward the bathroom. She passed under the archway and through the hallway. The bathroom was as dark as night. Sophie ripped open the cabinet beneath the sink and grabbed a handful of towels. Her hand fumbled upon a small box and she pulled that out as well. When she exited the bathroom, the weakening light from the front windows allowed her to see that she had grabbed a first aid kit.

"Ryan!" she said as she rushed back through the hallway. "Can you hear me?" she called. No response. The wind continued to increase. It sounded like a tornado was spinning around the house.

Ryan lay where she had left him, unmoving and struggling for consciousness. Sophie dropped the first aid kit and towels beside his arm and fell to the floor. She unwrapped the shirt she had tied around Ryan's arm.

"Sophie," Ryan whispered.

"It's okay," Sophie said as she pressed her palm to his cheek. "It's going to be okay."

In the twilit living room, Sophie hesitated. She didn't know what to do. She had no medical experience. She couldn't call for help. Panic came on heavily, mercilessly. But she dispelled the hesitation immediately. She was his only chance. They were alone together.

She wrapped the blood-soaked shirt around Ryan's right bicep, attempting to hinder the flow of blood. She squeezed it as tight as she could. Opening the first aid kit, she found a roll of gauze. She lifted his arm and wrapped the gauze around it, starting from the wrist and ending just below the elbow.

She worked as though someone was holding a gun to her head. They might as well have been, her movements fast and erratic. "Ryan?" she said. "Ryan, can you hear me?" She repeated the question over and over as she worked to stem the blood flow. Sophie could hear Ryan's faint breathing, even as a heavy rain sang against the siding.

She needed to get him to a hospital. He was bleeding out and every second counted. She picked up one of the towels and wrapped it over the gauze around Ryan's arm. It was as secure as she had time to make it. With an effort, Sophie rose to her feet, bent over as if she were trying to touch her toes, and hooked her arms under Ryan's shoulders. With all her strength, Sophie pushed off the floor and took a step backwards. He was so heavy.

"Come on, Ryan. Come on," she said as she pulled his seemingly lifeless body across the floor. Ryan's cheek fell against his shoulder and his limbs were limp as Sophie struggled. "Come on," she repeated. Eventually, Sophie made it to the hallway. The front door was only a few feet away.

"We're almost there, Ryan. We're almost there." But they weren't almost there. She needed more strength, more endurance.

Her body sagged with her confidence and she stopped struggling. Out of breath and panting as though she had run a marathon, Sophie felt a wave of nausea overcome her. Ryan lay curled in her lap. She couldn't do this. She couldn't save him.

Then something awoke inside of her. One after another, flashes of arms and legs pumping through a relentless ocean breathed to life in her mind's eye. Sophie remembered when she could swim miles before the world woke up. She remembered pushing herself beyond her limit every day. She remembered doing things people wondered at, things she had been told were impossible. She remembered her mother. "Your strength doesn't come from your arms and legs, Sweetheart," her mother had said. "It comes from here," and she'd touched Sophie's heart. And there, in that darkened hallway, a spark, fanned by the breath of a memory ignited the smoldering flame in her heart. She wasn't hysterical. She was focused. She wasn't afraid. She was angry.

"Come on," Sophie wailed. "Come on, Ryan." Suddenly he wasn't so heavy. The adrenaline was flowing through Sophie's veins like lightning. Her grip was a vice under his arms. She dragged and dragged until they made it to the door. Letting go of Ryan for a moment, she grabbed the keys to the Jeep and flung the front door open. An angry gust of wind accompanied by a thick spray of rain greeted them as Sophie pulled him through the threshold.

Sophie lost her footing and fell backwards toward the steps. She bounced back up and towed Ryan across the porch to the top of the staircase.

"I'll be right back," she said. "I promise."

Aided by the railing, she hustled down the steps and ran to the vehicle. She had never attempted to run with the prosthetic before. It should have felt awkward. She should have fallen to the pavement after the first stride. But she didn't. It felt natural. She could run like this for days. But that wasn't needed. Only a few more feet.

She reached the car and ripped open the driver's side door. She leapt into the front seat, turned the ignition, and jammed it into reverse.

It was the first time she had driven in months. The tires peeled and screeched on the slick pavement as Sophie steered toward the steps, her right arm draped over the passenger seat. Her vision was obscured to near blindness as she peered through the back window. Unsure if she had gone far enough, Sophie slammed on the breaks. The tires screeched and a moment later the bumper smashed into the railing at the bottom of the steps. Unfazed, Sophie threw the car in park and hustled out, back into the strengthening storm.

When she reached Ryan, he was unconscious. "Ryan?" she yelled. "Ryan, come on. We have to go." She pressed her ear to his mouth and tried to listen. He was still breathing, barely.

Sophie leaned down and reached under Ryan's arms. She dragged him down the steps, his body thumping along the way. On the last step, she slipped and fell backwards onto the blacktop. Ryan's limp body tumbled down on top of her.

Her head throbbing, Sophie struggled to her feet and opened the back passenger side door. She shuffled herself onto the floor behind the passenger seat then pivoted onto her knees. With every ounce of strength she had, Sophie reached down and lifted Ryan up off the ground. She inched backwards to allow more room and lifted again, digging deep down for the reserves she knew were there, somewhere. "Come on," she said as she repeated the process again and again. Somehow, she managed to pull Ryan three-quarters of the way into the back of the Jeep, the upper half of his body lying on her lower half as if she were cradling him.

She could have stayed like that forever. Every muscle in her body was on fire. Never in all her years of swimming had she been this tired. But the adrenaline wasn't spent yet. Sophie slid out from under Ryan, reached over and tucked his feet inside, then slammed the back door shut.

Sophie hurdled over the center console, threw the car into drive, and slammed on the gas. She didn't know how to turn the windshield wipers on, and before she knew it, Sophie had crashed through the bushes that hid her house from the street. She yanked the wheel to the left and steadied the car, barely avoiding crashing into a telephone pole on the opposite side of the road.

Finally, she found the switch and turned the wipers on maximum strength. Even with the aid of the windshield wipers, it was impossible to make out the yellow lines.

"Ryan," she said, keeping her eyes on what she hoped was the right side of the road. "It's going to be okay. We're almost there." Sophie's eyes were determined, panicked, wide, and a little crazy. She wasn't even sure how to get to the hospital.

She chanced a glance behind her. Ryan lay curled on the floor. His right arm was on his stomach, a blood-soaked towel hiding the hideous gash.

She felt a vibration on her right thigh. With one hand on the wheel, she reached into her pocket and pulled out her cell phone. She hadn't realized she'd put it in her pocket. She glanced at the screen and pressed the green button.

"Dad?" she yelled into the speaker. "Dad!"

"Sophie, I'm here," came his panicked voice on the other end. "It's me. What's wrong?"

"Dad, I'm scared," she said. "Ryan cut himself. It's bad, it's really bad. He's unconscious. I have to get him to a hospital." She couldn't stop talking, her voice strengthening in hysteria with every word.

"Sophie, slow down," he said. "Where are you?"

"I'm in the Jeep," she said. "Ryan's in the back seat. I think he's still breathing but I don't know. Dad I'm scared."

"Sophie, listen to me," her father said. "You need to stop driving. It's too dangerous. You could kill both of you. Do you understand? You need to stop the car."

"No," she answered immediately. "I need to get him to a hospital, Dad. I can't wait."

"Where are you?" he said. "Please stop the car."

"No!" she yelled. "I'm not stopping."

"Sophie, where are you?"

"Coastal highway, I think."

"Okay, listen to me," he pleaded. "Go to the firehouse. The hospital is too far away. Go to the firehouse. You aren't far. They'll have an ambulance and paramedics." Sophie was silent a moment, struggling to comprehend the simple directions. "Sophie, do you hear me? Go to the firehouse."

"Okay," she finally answered. "Daddy, I'm so scared. We got in a fight earlier. He—"

"Sophie, it's not your fault," he said. "Everything is going to be okay. I promise. Now you have to hang up and concentrate on the road. Okay? I'll meet you at the firehouse." Silence again. Sophie was second guessing herself. Should she have waited for help? Had she made things worse? "Sophie!" her father's voice exploded out of the speaker.

"Yeah, I'm here."

"Hang up the phone, Sweetie."

"Okay."

"I love—" Sophie pressed end and her father's reassuring tone cut out.

Sophie tossed the phone onto the passenger seat and sped on. The wheel shook under her grip. She sat on the edge of the seat, her back straight and her eyes wide, as if the windshield were a television screen and she was watching a thrilling movie.

She passed a stop sign. She had made it to the Avenue. She jerked the wheel to the right. The car slid sideways. Another car honked its horn and a moment later, Sophie was rocked back and forth in her seat as the two vehicles collided. The impact straightened the Jeep out and Sophie slammed on the gas, leaving the scene behind.

Peering through the windshield, she was able to make out the sign for the firehouse. Sophie yanked the wheel again, jumping the curb and taking out a No Parking sign in the process. She slammed on the breaks and skid into one of the massive garage doors. On impact, her body sprung forward, and her forehead smashed into the windshield.

A warm liquid ran down her forehead, down her nose and into her mouth. She touched her fingers to her head and brought them away. Her blood, not his.

Sophie opened the driver's side door and limped down to the cement. Immediately, strong hands took hold of Sophie's shoulders. The blood from her forehead had trickled into her eyes and she couldn't make out any specific features on the woman's face. "Are you alright? Can you hear me?" the woman was saying.

"Ryan," she said to the woman. "He's in the backseat. He needs help. Please."

The woman said something to a man behind her and within seconds, a team of paramedics and firemen were carrying Ryan out of the back seat toward a parked ambulance inside the firehouse. Sophie attempted to follow them, but the woman's firm grip held her in place with ease. "Calm down, Sweetheart," the woman said. Tears, rain, and blood ran down Sophie's face as she tried to calm her breathing.

"I'm fine. I'm fine," said Sophie. "He has to be okay. Please, let me go."

"You've done all you can, Sophia," the woman said. "You've been so strong. He'll be alright." The woman knew her name? And Sophie knew that voice. "We need to look at the cut on your head. Come on. Come on inside," she said. The woman led Sophie through a side door. Sophie turned as she heard the sirens ring and watched as the ambulance tore out of the garage and sped out of sight, heading west away from the storm.

Florescent light blinded Sophie as she entered the firehouse. She was led to a bench. She sat down heavily. A cool rag wiped at her face and her vision cleared. Confusion took hold as the form before her took shape. "It's not too bad," the deep voice said. "Just a scratch, really. You're lucky."

It was a man's voice. A bearded man with kind eyes. "Where's the woman?" Sophie asked, squinting.

"It's just me," the man said. "You're safe."

The last thing Sophie remembered was her mother's face before she fell forward into the man's arms, her adrenaline finally spent.

26

He was surrounded by color, and his bare feet were planted on what seemed to be glass. But it could have been water. Whatever he was standing on reflected the sky. He couldn't move his feet, only turn his head. Horizon surrounded him on all sides. It was as if the place was in a constant state of sunrise. He didn't want to move.

Standing there in front of him, not ten feet away, was his Sarah. He could see her face. It was even more beautiful than he remembered. Her sharp blue eyes made the surrounding colors seem dull. Her mouth curled into a smile that could bring an army to its knees. Her light brown hair waved at him in a breeze he couldn't feel.

She didn't speak, only smiled. He couldn't speak either. It didn't matter. All those long nights, all those nightmares were worth one second of this view.

It was impossible to discern how long he was there with Sarah. It could have been a year. It could have been a second. But he was there. He saw her and felt the colors as clearly and vividly as he had ever felt anything. It was more than a dream. It was his life. He was vaguely conscious of what was happening, but he chose not to let his imagination run off. It was more than enough to just be there with her. He understood that. And with that understanding came a tidal wave of peace, peace like he'd never known. He thought he should cry, or laugh, or run to her. But he couldn't. All he could do was stand there and smile, embraced by color and warmth.

Slowly, Ryan began to sink. It wasn't like falling through water, more like gradually descending into quicksand. He didn't fight it at all. A part of him knew it was coming. Instead, he continued to smile at Sarah, his eyes never leaving hers as he sunk lower and lower into the ocean of color. Sarah's eyes stayed glued to his, her smile twisting up into a smirk as she watched him descend, as if she were amused by the whole thing.

For years Ryan had struggled to remember that smile. Her beautiful face had been so cruelly hidden in his dreams. But he would never forget it again. Whether he was descending into Hell, or wherever, it didn't matter. He had seen her again. And she was happy.

27

One month later

"Tommy," Old Man called. "Another shot of Tanqueray."

It was late afternoon, and the bar was empty, except for the bartender, Old Man, and his avid listener.

"And?" the young girl asked.

"And what?" Old Man said.

"That's it?" she said, frowning.

"That's it," Old Man answered. "What'd you think?"

She leaned back and crossed her legs. Her fingers tickled the rim of her vodka tonic. "I think you have an impressive imagination, Old Man."

Old Man took a sip of his dark beer. "You don't believe me," he stated. He put the glass back onto the coaster. Tommy the bartender slid a shot glass full of gin along the smooth bar. It came to rest beside Old Man's pint glass.

"I believe that you believe it," she said. "I think it's just a story you tell to justify your Quicksand Beach theory. But, hey, you succeeded in helping me kill an afternoon." She raised her glass. "So, thanks."

Old Man held her gaze a moment then looked at the shot glass before him, recalling a memory. "I guess you had to be there," he said.

She reached under the bar and pulled her purse from one of the hooks. She threw it over her shoulder. She fished out some cash and tossed a couple bills on the bar. "It was nice meeting you, Old Man," she said as she slid off her stool. "Hopefully, they'll give you an avenue or plaque, or something." She smiled. "It is catchy, I have to admit."

"Taking off so soon?" Old Man asked.

"I told you," she said. "I'm heading down the coast. Just a pit stop." She made her way to the door.

"Good luck with that," said Old Man, smirking.

Before the young girl could push on the handle, the door swung open, and a young man stepped to the side, allowing her to exit before he entered.

"Thanks," she said.

"You got it."

The young man made his way to the bar and told Tommy he was picking up an order to-go. He wore a white shirt and faded blue jeans.

"Ryan!" Old Man exclaimed. "We were just talkin' about you!"

Ryan scanned the empty space and frowned. "There's no one else here, Old Man. I'm starting to get worried about you."

Old Man smirked. "Smart ass."

Tommy told Ryan his food would only be a minute. Ryan picked up the check and pulled out his wallet.

"You know," Ryan said after tossing a bill onto the bar. "You don't *have* to sit at the end of the bar. It's a bit cliché."

"I like clichés," Old Man said. "Make the world go round."

"If you say so."

"Why don't you come join your old friend for a drink?"

Ryan's eyes fell on the untouched shot glass before Old Man. "Even if I did still drink," he said. "You wouldn't catch me anywhere near you and your damn Tanqueray."

Old Man laughed. Tommy brought out a white plastic bag from the kitchen and dropped it on the bar in front of Ryan. "I hear you and the Galloways took that space where the antique store used to be," Old Man said. "Something to do with furniture, right?"

Ryan grinned. "Yeah," he said. He turned to go. "We just had the sign put up. You should come take a look. I think you might like it."

"I'll do that," Old Man said. "Hey, spare a smoke?" he called before Ryan made it to the door.

"Fresh out," Ryan called over his shoulder. He pushed the door open and walked back into the real world.

Old Man looked at the shot, smiled, then threw it back.

Epilogue

Her breaths were measured. Her mind was free. And the water was cold.

But she wasn't racing anyone today. Her arms didn't rush through the water or explode through the surface.

Sophie glided, free and peaceful through a calm ocean as the sun peaked over the horizon. She took her time, savoring every breath and every stroke, satisfaction and contentment driving her forward just as much as her limbs. She pulled up and gazed toward the horizon. The sun's reflection created a deep orange river that cut through the endless blue. She breathed in deeply, treading water with ease. After a few measured breaths, she turned and made for home.

As she exited the water, she saw him, seated somewhere between the sand and the surf, waiting patiently with his arms over his knees. She could see his scar.

Sophie navigated the awkward surf with practiced ease, her new prosthetic feeling more natural every day. She closed the distance between them in a few strong strides. He rose to meet her.

"I have to admit," she said as she wrung her hair out. "Every morning I look at the shore I'm afraid I won't see you. I have this weird fear that you and that beat-up Jeep will be long gone."

Ryan took her in his arms. "I'll never leave this place," he said.

Before walking off the beach, Sophie turned back to the water. She lifted her head to the cloudless sky and inhaled deeply.

She could breathe again.

Acknowledgements

First, I have to thank my beautiful wife, Kay, for being incredibly supportive throughout the entire writing and editing process. It was an experience I will never forget, and I would have been lost without her. I also need to thank my mother. She taught me how to appreciate the sound of the surf, and how to see the beauty in the world. This book truly would not have been possible without her.

A big thank you as well to my friends and family who helped me along the way. My cousin and fellow author, John O'Neill, was the first person to read this story start to finish. His advice early on was extremely encouraging, and I'm grateful for his support. My cousin, Libby Montanye, and sister, Ashley Montanye, were also among the first to read early drafts of the novel, and their positive feedback helped push me toward the finish line. And, of course, a huge thank you to Emily Montanye for working with me through countless revisions to help create the perfect cover.

Finally, my sincerest thanks to you, the reader. It means so much to me that you took the time to read my words. I hope they allowed you to get lost for a little while, and I hope they made you feel something. Thank you so much.

Made in the USA
Middletown, DE
19 September 2021

48635831R00194